A long CRazy BuRn

A Long Crazy Burn

A DARBY HOLLAND CRIME NOVEL

JEFF JOHNSON

Arcade Publishing • New York

Arcade Publishing books may be purchased in bulk at special discounts for sales promotion, corporate gifts, fund-raising, or educational purposes. Special editions can also be created to specifications. For details, contact the Special Sales Department, Arcade Publishing, 307 West 36th Street, 11th Floor, New York, NY 10018 or arcade@skyhorsepublishing.com.

Arcade Publishing® is a registered trademark of Skyhorse Publishing, Inc.®, a Delaware corporation.

Visit our website at www.arcadepub.com.

10 9 8 7 6 5 4 3 2 1

Library of Congress Cataloging-in-Publication Data is available on file.

Cover design by Gigi Little
Cover photo credit Jeff Johnson and Morguefile
Leg art created by Sylvia Mann

Print ISBN: 978-1-62872-860-6
Ebook ISBN: 978-1-62872-861-3

Printed in the United States of America

A long CRazy BuRn

The phone rang just after three a.m.

Nothing good ever happens after three a.m. The screeching, static ending of a movie you couldn't stay awake through. Crappy Chinese takeout, eaten by the light from the open refrigerator while standing in the kitchen in your underwear. Sex maybe, but the sloppy, big-booze variety. Furnace fires. No one calls with the winning lottery numbers at three-oh-five a.m.

The ringing stopped, then started again. I was kicked back at my desk in the back room of the Lucky Supreme, nursing lukewarm scotch from a paper cup and tinkering with one of my tattoo machines. It was a shader, made by a guy up in Washington named Paco Rollins. I ran the stroke long and mushy, so it had rattled itself to shit again. I didn't enjoy dinking around with machines anymore, so I was still there mostly because I didn't want to drive home. My sketchbook was out and I was halfway through a tortoise with a hat of some kind, but I didn't want to work on that, either. Portland winter was in full swing, sleet mixed with snow on a thin crust of dirty ice. The steering wheel on my old BMW wagon would be so cold that the bones in my hands would ache just touching it, and after a twelve-hour shift they ached already. The car seat would freeze my ass on contact. I was partway through a seasonal mope and I knew it. Whoever was calling was only going to make it worse.

Ring.

It was still warm in the tattoo shop, even though I'd turned the little electric wall heaters off an hour before, when I put up the CLOSED sign in the window and turned off the front lights. It hadn't been a bad day for a Tuesday in February. I let my night-shift artist, Nigel, go home at midnight when it finally slowed down, so he could grab a few drinks with his new girlfriend before the bars closed. He had much going on in the way of skeeby on the side, and it was wise to give him time to pursue his activities away from the shop. My late-night drinking companion was once again the Lucky Supreme. It had been time for me to enter another period of tortuous woman-related activity for weeks, but I'd been putting it off, just like I was putting off the drive home. Everything had burnout written all over it. Maybe I'd decided, deep down inside, where thoughts grew up and then shuffled into hiding, that indecision was my only practical defense.

I studied the machine into the fourth ring. It was brass, and at some point I'd engraved WILL FIGHT EVIL FOR FOOD down the side in curling script. Every artist's motto, whether they know it or not. It still needed a new rear spring and I'd have to cut one, but that, too, would be a pain in the ass. I set it down on the desk and picked up my scotch at the fifth ring.

In the last two months, I'd spent too many evenings sitting in that chair worrying about things I couldn't do one damn thing about. Or wouldn't. A few months before, I'd had a bad run-in with the feds and a worse one with a rich psychotic scumbag that the very same feds had under their microscope. My landlord was having mental health issues, following a decline that had begun more than twenty years ago. Dmitri was a study of ruination in too many ways for anyone's comfort. As a person, he was a disgusting bummer of a human being. As a landlord, terrifying. The tenants fixed everything and said nothing. To even hint that there might have been a leak in the past, let alone the present, was to insult him, his sainted father, his entire family tree, and also by extension his ethnic heritage, which was unclear. Yesterday an insurance inspector had made a surprise visit and canceled my lame policy, citing the wall heaters, which were dangerously ancient. Now I needed an electrician to come in and upgrade everything so I could re-up the policy.

The ringing stopped. I looked at the phone and waited. It started again.

The back room was lined with shelves of art books. I stared at the collection directly across from me and then I squinted. A faint blue light was blinking over them, gently strobing in through the windows in the front of the shop and washing through the doorway to the back.

Portland's Old Town had seen a renovation boom in the last year, but it struck me as unlikely that anyone could be working that late on a cold Tuesday night except the most desperate whores, the B-string skag hawkers, and me. I sighed. *Ring.* The construction in the neighborhood had been a drag on business. The bar next door, the Rooster

Rocket, was down more than 30 percent, and that was a har-binger. I relied on bar totals as a forecasting tool. That and the weather, which was also shitty. The Rocket was owned by Gomez, the most enterprising Chicano in Old Town, and the business slump had hit him hard, mentally and spir-itually. Flaco, Gomez's brother or uncle or ancient cousin, had a taco operation in the old theater vestibule in front of the bar, and it was thriving. No one thought that was a good sign. And now some city crew had fired up something at three in the morning. My car was probably blocked in. I was just about to heave my boots off the desk and go check it out when I couldn't stand the ringing anymore.

"Lucky Supreme, how may I direct your call?"

The line was static, lashed with wind.

"Get out of there, white boy." It was little more than a gush of whisper. There was a click and the line went dead.

I took the phone away from my ear and looked up at the wall of books across from me. The blue light was still splashing over it, but it had been joined by dialing winks of red. Something huge was erupting on Sixth Street.

I walked through the shop to the front door and cau-tiously peered out the window, keeping well back in the darkness. The local police and I had a very specific arrange-ment, the very same one I'd recently cultivated with the feds—they didn't like me and I didn't like them, so we tried to stay away from each other. We were all very careful to stick to the program, too. So if they were out rounding up the nightlife as part of the new clean-up program, it would be in keeping with our arrangement for me to stay inside.

4

The block had been cordoned off at both ends. There were at least ten police cars I could see, plus three fire engines. And I was right in the middle of it. My car was parked down the street, past the north blockade. It was hard to tell from my vantage point if I was officially stranded, so I grimly decided to go fuck with them.

I unlocked both of the deadbolts on the reinforced door and stuck my head out. The reaction was instant.

"Someone's coming out!" a cop screamed.

"Get out of there!" a fireman yelled. He waved his arms to get my attention. "Move it!"

The words on the side of the engine closest to the fireman came into focus: BOMB SQUAD.

"Holy fuck," I whispered.

A young cop sprinted down the sidewalk toward me, skittering a little through the slush. It looked like he might be going for a tackle, so I raised my hands above my head and stepped out.

"Run, you fucking idiot!" He slid into me and almost yanked my arm out of the socket. The kid had a power lifter's build and was either fresh into his shift or adrenalized by terror. The door to the Lucky Supreme closed on the spring arm as the monster towed me at a flat-out run down the sidewalk to the corner, almost carrying me as I scrambled to keep up.

"Get in that fucking car." He was panting as he opened the back door to the chicken coop of the nearest cruiser. All the other officers that had been milling around when I looked out less than thirty seconds before were crouched behind the nearest fire engine, the big one that read BOMB SQUAD.

"Fuck you." I yanked my arm out of his meaty hand and pointed. "The bomb dudes are hiding behind a fucking fire truck, dumbass."

"Get down!" one of the firemen yelled.

I stiff-armed the big cop in the direction of the fire engine. He stumbled a little and his hand went to his side-arm, fumbling at one of the fashionable tasers they'd been pronging old ladies and hobos with for the last year. One of the firemen grabbed the back of the kid's jacket and pulled him down. I skirted the cop car and crouched at the edge of the group hiding behind the truck. The sleet was soaking my hair and the back of my T-shirt. My jeans were already plastered to my legs. I started to shiver.

"What the fuck is going on?" I asked everyone in general. There were at least twelve cops and as many firemen behind the fire engine.

"You were alone in there, right?" one of the firemen asked. He was the one who had pulled the cop off me.

"Yes, yes! Now, *what the fuck is going on*?"

He gave me a hard stare, then peeled back the sleeve of his big rubber jacket and checked his watch.

"We'll know in just about—"

That's when the bomb went off.

Agents Pressman and Dessel looked at me like the loving parents of a two-headed baby chicken. Mutually fond of my embarrassing, almost certainly brief existence, and proprietarily gloating at their proximity to the conclusion. Both of them would have given the last week of their lives to see me rotting in a prison cell for eternity, or at the very least reupholstering hot rods in Argentina. In our brief association, I'd destroyed a case they were building that would have made headline news. I'd gloated about it, too, and that was wrong. I know that now.

"You dudes get my Christmas card?"

Pressman was the older of the two, a homely guy with a pockmarked face and a beer gut he was ripening properly. He gave me a disgusted, girthy grunt. Dessel looked like a boy's underwear model on a coke binge. He beamed joyously, like he had indeed received the card and put it on his refrigerator next to the unicorn. They were both wearing shitty suits from a discount department store. It was their version of a uniform.

"Quite an explosion," Dessel said casually, almost like he was congratulating me. I'd just been ushered in via squad car, and the interview was officially off to a creepy start. It was an ominous sign that I'd skipped Police Central and been taken straight to the Federal Building. Even the cop who brought me in was spooked.

Dessel patted his pockets and came up with a bent generic cigarette. Pressman opened the window behind him. It was a no-smoking building.

I'd learned (from eavesdropping on the squad car radio) that the bomb had gone off in the Lucky Supreme's restroom. There was a low whump and the windows blew out, blowing glass and sheetrock out in a ring that spanned two city blocks. The roof of the building flapped up a few feet, rippling like a cotton sheet in the wind, and then came crashing down, warped but still there. Most miraculously of all, the toilet at the epicenter of the blast remained whole and sailed like a cannonball all the way through the bar next door, where it lodged in the far wall. White fire ripped through everything.

The little convenience store next to the Lucky went up like a gas refinery. All those plastic packages of greasy snacks, I guess. Thick black smoke gushed from the shattered windows of the bar. The Lucky Supreme had been alive with flames, a real ring-of-hell inferno.

I'd watched in mute horror as the fire department snapped into action, obviously ready in advance. As soon as the glass and plaster stopped falling, they were pumping several thousand gallons of water a minute into the roiling blaze. The heat almost dried my clothes from a block away. After ten minutes the fire had died down, but they kept spraying, really hosing the place down to ensure the most thorough possible destruction.

"Yeah, dudes," I told the feds. "It was like something out of a movie."

I'd been shuffled into the back of a cop car after that. Pressman and Dessel were waiting for me when we got to the Federal Building, a place I'd been spending way too much time in over the past few months. The two of them never seemed to sleep. So it was four a.m. and I was back in the interview room, but this time I had a gray blanket draped over me, I didn't have any cigarettes, and I was unemployed. My transformation into a street zero had been lightning-fast.

"So tell us," Dessel said with a tiny smile. "Everything. Especially the lies. Let's start with those wonderful lies you tell."

"Give me that fucking cigarette," I said quietly. Dessel handed it over and I put it in my mouth.

"Light," I prompted.

He leaned out and fired it with a dime-store lighter. I took a double deep drag and blew two lungs of generic smoke in his general direction.

"It started with lights on the street. I was working late fixing some broken equipment. When I went out to see what the hell was going on some cop dragged me down the block. Whole place was already cordoned off." I poked the cigarette at Dessel's smile. "They knew. Some fucker tipped those guys off."

"Interesting." Dessel leaned back in his chair. Pressman stared at me. That was his job. "So tell us more. I understand from the lead officer that there's been . . . oh, let's just say it was getting time for you to move your little circus. And we know it's possible you might want to. Plus, you sort of . . ." He sucked at his teeth. "You made some people really angry recently, and they might . . . oh, I don't know, maybe feel like blowing all your shit up . . . There's that. I'm just fishing here, trying to get a bead on the situation."

Agent Dessel was talking about Nicky Dong-ju, the crazy gangster I'd killed a few months ago and rolled into the river. He'd set me up in an incredibly complicated way to get his hands on some of the Lucky's old art, which had been used more than fifty years before in a smuggling operation run by a dead con man named Roland Norton. Nicky had been relentless, and in the end I had no choice. I would have nightmares for the rest of my life about the last minute of his life. They were still looking for him, and they suspected I was involved in his disappearance. It was the reason I'd spent so much time telling lies in the inter-rogation room.

"Think about this, Dessel." I took another drag and flicked some ash on the floor. "My insurance got canceled yesterday. What does that tell you?"

He shrugged, but I could tell it made him happy.

"Christ." I dropped the cigarette on the floor and ground it under my heel. "You two cretins think I know who planted that bomb? Believe me, if I did I'd be sitting in county facing murder one. Call me a cab."

"I love these little meetings," Dessel said thought-fully. He stroked his chin, at the soft little stubble there. Pressman grunted like he was on the toilet after a tour of the downtown burrito scene.

"Cab," I prompted.

"Pay phones are in the lobby. Let us know when you get a new cell phone." Dessel winked. "Don't leave town, but do leave that blanket. Can't have a bum in a welfare getup walking around Federal. Makes us look like regular cops."

I was glad my house wasn't on fire. It was an old yellow clapboard two-story pile with Tudor frills that had been divided into a duplex decades ago. I had the ground floor and the basement. The first thing I noticed when the cab pulled up was that the lights were on. All of them. I paid the driver and stood in the freezing rain and studied the place as the car pulled away. Someone had just blown up my life and now someone was in my house. I went over to the steps and rooted around in the semi-frozen dirt under the skeleton of the rhododendron until I came up with a hank of wire I'd hidden there a few months before. A fat braid of wire with a knob of concrete at one end and no conceivable previous felony on it. I pulled the muddy thing loose and hefted it. Half whipper, half sap. Normally I carried a metal ball bearing, but the whole explosion thing had caught me by surprise. The last one probably melted into the sooty remains of the jacket I should have been wearing.

I opened the door and Delia flew into me, her head smacking into my chest. I dropped the wire and held her as she sobbed. I could feel her heart hammering through her bony chest like a hummingbird's. We just stood like that for a minute.

11

Delia had worked for me for close to four years. She had a spare key to my place, so she could take care of my two cats when I was out of town or being detained by the police. Standing there with my arms wrapped around her, I realized for the first time that she'd lost it all, too. All of her art, her equipment, her job. Pretty much everything.

"I thought you might be dead, you fucktard," she sobbed. "I'd have to take care of your cats, like, forever."

"Nah." I rubbed her back. She also had a speech condition I thought of as robomouth. Her short hair smelled like lavender and cigarettes and puke. "I was just getting interrogated."

"Why didn't you call me?" She pushed me away and wrinkled her tiny pug nose. "You're all freezing wet and icky, dude."

"My phone was a casualty."

"Dipshit." She sniffed and smeared her makeup around.

Delia was one of the scrawniest little punk chicks imaginable, and her fashion sense ranged from the bizarre to the perfectly dreadful. It was five a.m. and she was wearing baggy black rubber pants, an imitation snake skin belt with a Texas rodeo buckle the size of a coffee saucer, and some kind of shirt that looked like it was made out of pantyhose. The bra underneath was more of a half-corset, with eyes where her tits would be if she had any. Dangling from her right earlobe was an earring she'd made out of the tooth of a hipster dork who got his ass kicked in front of the Rooster Rocket.

"We got any beer?" I asked. She wiped her eyes again.

"Go change. You smell like a trash fire. We have vodka."

"Bitchin'."

I went into my bedroom to change while Delia busied herself in the kitchen. My two cats looked up at me from the bed, insulted by the commotion. Chops was an ugly little guy, so he projected bad vibes with ease. His sidekick Buttons was huge, red, and glorious, but close to vegetables on the intelligence totem pole, so for him projecting anything was a fleeting affair. I stripped my shirt off and dropped it in the hamper. It did smell like fire. The pants did, too. I smelled like a burning building, and it was deep in my pores. I wanted to take a shower and wash the ashes of my life off my skin and out of my hair, but I wanted the vodka more, so I pulled on a pair of cords and went barefoot into the kitchen. Delia handed me a double on the rocks and we carried our drinks into the small dining room and sat down at the table. She fired up two smokes and passed me one.

"So what the fuck?" It came out of her with a tiny pause between each word, and it wasn't a question.

"I was sitting around when Monique called. I'm sure it was her, even though she tried to disguise her voice. She's the only person who calls me white boy." Monique was a local hooker we'd adopted. "Anyway, I looked out and the street was blocked off. Went out and the cops corralled me." I stared at my drink, remembering. "About a minute later the place blew. I watched them hose it down for as long as it took for them to get the call to bring me in to see Dessel and Pressman. Radio chatter said the bomb was in our bathroom."

Delia shook her head and took a sip of vodka. Her hand was shaking.

"We're in shock," she stated. "We need medication. I'm in shock, Darby. I feel like I'm about to have a heart attack. You're sitting there like a mental patient. You're blank."

"I know." I squinted at her. "We have any drugs?"

She shook her head. "I hurled my emergency Valiums an hour ago. Biji said she could bring by some Xanax."

"Fuck."

She poured us more vodka.

"So Pressman and Dessel are still wicked pissed at me," I went on. "But it says something that the first people who grilled me were those two guys. Interstate crime. They might already know something."

"Jesus, Darby. It's personal with those two." She studied my face and her expression went from worried to sour. "You got all smart-mouth again, didn't you?" Her nerves were shot, I could tell, her movements jangly and wrong.

"I did."

"Biji called me a few hours ago and told me it was on the news when she got home. I drove down there, but they wouldn't let me anywhere near the Lucky. They wouldn't even tell me if you were in there." Her lower lip quivered and her eyes watered up again. She took a quick drink and sniffed. "And then I came here and you were gone. I let myself in and did your dishes." She shook her head and looked up at the ceiling. "What the fuck are we gonna do?"

"I don't know yet," I said, "but we'll figure it out. We always do."

Delia sniffed and looked up at me. She smiled a little.

"So I guess this means I don't work for you anymore."

14

"Way to look on the bright side. But don't even think about putting my dick on your menu."

Delia barked out a laugh and curled her legs under her.

"Like I'd even think about it after seeing your underwear."

"Least I wear some."

I went into the kitchen and got the bourbon and brought it back, then splashed a little into our glasses. It was time for mixed drinks.

"Darby," Delia said after she'd taken a few meditative sips, "you better find out who did this. You know the feds have been trying to bring you up on something after you blew their last big case. This could be their golden opportunity to hang you."

"I know." It was true. "I'll start tomorrow. I mean today, I guess. After I get some sleep."

"I'll call Big Mike and Nigel. They're both going out of their minds. Why don't you go rinse off the soot." Big Mike and Nigel were my two other former employees. Neither of them would have had anything to do with it. Nigel would have killed someone the moment he caught wind of a bomb and then demanded some kind of reward for it. Big Mike usually needed a hug after he hurt anyone or anything. There were also Earl and Ted, but they were new, as in two weeks new. I ruled them out as suspects immediately because both of them hadn't been in for a few days and the bomb had been planted in the last twelve hours, plus they were both salon tattooer hipster pussies. We'd never see either of them again after this. I sighed as Delia took out her phone.

"Thanks."

She looked up from dialing and cocked her head. "I'm glad you're alive, Darby Holland. It's a daily fucking miracle."

I grinned, even though I felt empty. Delia was right. I was in shock, and somehow, for me, it had taken the form of nothingness.

When I finally got out of the shower and into some pajama pants and a T-shirt, Delia was asleep on the couch. I got a spare blanket out of the cabinet and covered her up. The sun was coming up. I was bone-tired when I crashed down on the bed and pulled the quilt up to my neck, but as soon as my head touched the pillow the explosion went through my head on a continuous loop, replaying over and over again, punctuated by flashes of Dessel, smiling and laughing, and Nicky Dong-Ju, coming at me with dead eyes and a hole in his face where his nose should be. Slowly, the booze caught up with the ten-second movie reel and blurred it into flashes of light and echoes. After about an hour of that, I heard the soft patter of bare feet on the kitchen floor and then the bed rocked a little. Delia climbed in under the quilt behind me and wrapped an arm tight over my chest.

"Cold," she murmured.

I could feel her tooth earring pressed into the back of my neck. She snuggled around a little, burrowing for warmth, and then her breathing became soft and regular. It was that sound that finally lulled me to sleep.

I found Clarissa standing on the corner of Burnside and Broadway, smoking a long menthol cigarette under the awning of a strip club called Mozie's. Clarissa was tall and black, and for all I knew she might have actually been a man under the insane wig made out of silver Christmas tree tinsel and the low-cut black dress that hugged her extra-jumbo boob job. With her heels on she was around six foot three. Big enough for the doorman at Mozie's to leave her alone if she wanted to blow any of the horndogs going in and out of the place for a fifty. I ducked in next to her and lit up a smoke of my own.

"Darby Holland," she purred. "The deposed tattoo king of Old Town. Wazzup, little white fool? Been what, twelve hours since the Lucky lost its rabbit foot. You can't have got the 'me' kinda lonesome that fast."

I shrugged. "Same old same old. I'm looking for Monique."

Clarissa squinted down at me. Her large brown eyes were ringed with blue. She shook her silver mane.

"What she got I don't? Always knew you had a thing for that bubble-butt piece of trash." She blew some smoke in my direction. Her breath smelled like she'd been chewing on mothballs and urinal cakes.

"Got some money for her." I took a drag off my cigarette to filter the air as Clarissa barked a sharp laugh into my face.

"Fuckin' lame. Like I give up a sister. You want to lie to me, you need to get creative. Shit, I thought you used to be an artist."

"I'll tell you what I'm thinking." I took another drag and stared out at the wide street. "I'm thinking two things. Whether I should take you into Mozie's and buy you a beer and maybe slip you some cash, or if I should put this cigarette out in your eye and steal your wig. How's that for creative?"

Clarissa stared at me.

"Think fast," I prompted. "My feet are getting cold."

"Guess I'll take me a Heineken." She flicked her smoke into the gutter.

The inside of Mozie's was dark. The doorman glanced our way and refocused on whoever he was texting on his phone. A rubbery naked chick was crawling around the stage on the other side of the room, flexing her butt cheeks and doing Juarez yoga for an audience of three. It was still early. Clarissa and I took a seat at the bar, well away from the action, and I ordered two Heinekens. When I tossed a twenty on the bar I slipped a fifty over to Clarissa, who neatly made it disappear.

"So," I prompted. "Monique."

"Yeah." Clarissa took a pull off of her bottle and then absently swirled it around. Her hands were long and bony, with big, mannish knuckles.

"Ain't seen that crazy bitch in a few days, which is rare. Cheeks runs 'em seven days a week. Don't matter if a ho got polio, she be out slingin'."

"Cheeks is her pimp?"

Clarissa snorted, but there was a little fear in it. "Big nigger faggot is what he is. Some girls go to him because he's gay and they think he won't be fuckin' 'em all the time. Thinkin' he might be sensitive. Shit. That man is a lunatic psycho. He carves an X into a bitch's ass so they know who they belong to. Monique has one." She looked at me. "You seen Monique's ass?"

"My old toilet has. Keep going."

Clarissa shrugged. "Cheeks is convict trash. Hit the streets hard three years ago and picked up a string. Keeps 'em cooped up out on the interstate at the Sands, right across from that tiki bar. He herds 'em in around three a.m., maybe a little early on a shitty night. You maybe find Monique there, though like I say, I ain't seen her since your place blew up." She gave me a flat look.

"Good," I said. "Anything else?"

She downed the rest of her beer, signaling that my time was almost up.

"I don't know if I should tell you shit, Holland. I heard you a good man with bad edge on him, but it pisses me off, with that beatin' on me mouth you got. Just so we clear, I tell you one more thing, an' then I bounce, as in you don't know me. Cheeks's a big time psycho, but he's a crazy man with a crazy plan. You lookin' for a girl he got hid up or dead, don't be lookin' right in front of him."

I drank the last of my beer.

"He better not know I'm coming." I stood up and patted Clarissa's beefy shoulder. "He does and I'll be seeing you. No talking at all next time."

I'd parked five blocks up, close to the big bookstore in the opposite direction of the Lucky. It was still raining and the gray sky was running fast toward night. I missed my coat. After our midafternoon breakfast of Delia's special nuclear pork chop tacos, I'd gone through the coats of yesteryear and settled on an old gas station jacket with a missing name tag, but it didn't quite cut it. The engine was still warm when I got back in, so I cranked the heater and went from wet and cold to wet and lukewarm before I set about phase two of my crappy plan.

The Sands Motel looked like a place that might have had character about forty years ago. It was a two-story cinderblock dump, but most of the big neon sign with a palm tree and VACANCY still had juice. I sat in my car in the parking lot of the tiki bar across the street and watched the place for a while. The sleet was finally turning into a light snow, but none of it was sticking. Something about looking at a neon palm tree through snowflakes struck me as bad luck, so I eventually stubbed out my cigarette and braved the tiki bar for a drink.

The inside was no busier than Mozie's had been. A few hipsters were drinking in a booth, and a couple was sitting at the bar with their faces about six inches apart. None of them looked like a giant gay pimp named Cheeks.

Theme bars can be irritating, but the place was as old as the neon across the street. I sat down at the far end of the bar from the first-date couple and nodded at the bartender, a chunky girl with big hair, big eyes, and big tits propped up in a mega band under her tight black T-shirt.

"Whatcha havin'?"

"Jameson rocks."

She shoveled some ice into a tumbler and gave me a heavy pour and set it in front of me.

"Slow night," I said, looking around.

"Snow on a Wednesday," she replied. "People just stay home. I'm from Minnesota. Ninety-year-old ladies with bald tires tear through shit like this."

"I hear ya." I raised my glass and took a sip. "What's good to eat here?"

She put a menu in front of me. "I like the steak. Get it with the onions. Grady is bored back there, but I know he's got some slow cooking for me for later."

I slid the menu back. "Medium rare it is. Fries."

She poked the touch screen and I swiveled a little on the barstool for a casual view of the door and the Sands parking lot. No new cars had pulled up and the snow was still coming down. It was beginning to stick a little, so I could look for tire tracks every few minutes. I turned back to my drink and my new cell phone rang. It was probably Delia, so I fished it out of my jacket pocket. I'd picked up the phone at a 7-Eleven earlier and she'd been the only person I'd called. I'd memorized her number a long time ago, because you only get one call when shit goes sideways and I doubt the police will look it up for you.

"Darby," I said.

"Duh, I called *you*, dummy," Delia said. "How the fuck did you ever graduate from high school?"

"That whole high school thing is a sham," I said. Delia had gone to Cal Arts, a closely guarded secret I made fun of at every opportunity.

"Where you drinking?"

"No place you need to be."

"Whatever."

"So, couple things I've been thinking about."

"Really? Got your little tinfoil thinking cap on?" I could hear the clink of ice in a glass in her background.

"We'll see. I'm still hunting for Monique. Didn't stop by the shop."

She didn't say anything.

"Prying into the world of our pet hooker has been fascinating. *This American Life* kind of deal. Heartwarming snapshot of the streetwalker experience."

"Darby," she said firmly. "Where are you?"

"Some tiki bar, waiting for a steak. I have an appointment to meet Monique's pimp in an hour or so. I might not get back for a while. Feel like watching the cats for me?"

"I'm at your place right now, dumbass. Drinking the rest of the booze and eating leftovers. Pick up beer and get me some gas station nachos, extra cheese squirts."

The waitress was bringing my steak. "Can do. The cats will try to get out if they can, but if they do they'll blame you personally for the snow."

"The little piggies are lying on my lap right now. We're watching *The Two Towers* on my computer. You really need to get a TV, Darby. It's kind of like having a colon or a belly button, if you see what I mean. People generally have one."

I thought about that. I thought about Delia in my place, watching my cats and cooking. About her curled over my back last night. But mostly what flashed through my mind was an image of her on the last day the Lucky was alive, tattooing some biker with a big head, ribbing him about shoe polish, laughing and vibrant. Happy. There was something forced in the lightness now.

"I'll see ya later," I said. "We need anything else?"

"Maybe get me a hot dog, too, everything on it. Just load it up. Especially jalapeños."

"OK."

"OK."

We listened to each other breathe.

"Be careful," she said finally.

"Not tonight." I hung up.

I finished off the steak and fries and another Jameson's as slow and quiet as I could, but a few hours later it started to look too much like I was stalking someone. I tipped out the now-suspicious Betsy the bartender well, mostly because it was a slow night and I felt bad for her. Then I went out and sat in my snow-covered car and watched the neon palm tree across the street through a little hole I rubbed out in the windshield before I got in. Classic surveillance.

Just around three a.m., my new witching hour, two cabs pulled up. Eight loud women piled out and went up to room 117 on the second floor. No Monique. In spite of what I'd said to Clarissa, I'd recognize Monique's cartoon bubble butt anywhere. It was true that she was crazy, and

I couldn't imagine her getting along with monster ladies like Clarissa, but I'd let her use the bathroom at the Lucky to wash her hair and brush her teeth and probably shoot up for two years. I knew her voice from those years of her screaming at me and listening to her cry. Monique cried softly, with a little voice that reminded me of roosting pigeons. She yelled impossibly vile things, just like most of the women I'd known, only louder. She had a butt out of comic books.

Half an hour after the stable came in, a low-slung Lincoln with gold spinners rumbled into the Sands parking lot. The suspension heaved and two enormous black men draped in thousands of dollars of wool got out. One of them was fat. The other one was just plain big. The fat one was carrying a box he'd had in his lap. The just plain big one had a bottle of something in a paper bag. They went up to room 119 and the lights flicked on behind the curtains. The fat guy came back out, went next door and collected money, went back.

I gave them a few courtesy minutes to warm the place up and settle in and then I got out of the car. The snow was still falling, but it was small stuff, almost like flecks of styrofoam. I ducked down in the collar of my jacket and stuck my hands into the pockets, then went up to meet Cheeks. I could hear music through the door, a floaty disco with a strong backbeat. I uncurled one of my hands and knocked on the door. The music dialed down and big feet tromped in my direction. The peephole went dark, the chain came off with a loud rasp, and the door opened wide. I was briefly stunned mute by the gaudy interior of the place, just visible around the frame of the scowling fat guy. Old lamps, velvet paintings, leopard rugs, beaded wall hangings. They'd redecorated the motel room completely.

"I help you?" the fat man rumbled. His voice was mixture of cigar smoke and rock grinder.

"Here to see Cheeks."

He looked me up and down and then peered out into the snowy parking lot. "You pig?"

"Just a dude."

He stood aside. "C'mon then."

Cheeks was sitting on the floor in front of a turntable, looking at an album cover. He was probably six foot four and a hard 250. I'm five eight, but solid. In his eyes, I was half his size. To me, he was just plain big. He looked up at me and smiled, revealing a grill of gold teeth.

"Motherfuckin' Darby Holland," Cheeks said brightly, even warmly. "I thought I saw you sittin' in your piece of shit Nazi wagon across the street."

I kept my hands in my pockets. Cheeks showed me the album cover he was holding.

"Sylvester. Original. Now that nigga knew his shit." He gestured at the records stacked around the turntable. "CD is for pussies. I'm old-school vinyl. This fuckin' record here might get me five bills on eBay, but I ain't sellin'." He casually took a huge gun out from under a scarf sitting beside him and pointed it at my face.

"What the fuck you sellin', boy?"

The fat guy chuckled.

"Nothing," I replied. "I'm buying." I slowly took my hands out of my pockets and held them up, palms

25

out. Cheeks's massive hand tensed. "I'm looking for Monique."

Cheeks cocked his head, playful. "Really. And for that little drunk-ass crackhead you disturb my evening. While I'm getting' me some Sylvester. I been looking for this wax for three fuckin' years. Then it snows an' my bitches run up a cab fee, an' then you knock on my door."

The gun never wavered. His eyes narrowed.

"Know how I know you, tattoo man? You let my bitches into the bathroom at your old place. Always watching' 'em, 'cause you know, it's what I do."

"You probably have to," I said, sympathetic.

He squinted. "I thought you might be gettin' a free tap on some ass, an' shit, I'd a put chunks o' your brain in that john. Bitches squat behind a dumpster they need to shit. Fuckin' pee in their pants. I own every hole on they bodies, ain't no one gets in free."

Cheeks got up, the gun still on my face. "But you never tapped that." He laughed and his eyes grew wide, the size of chicken eggs. "Maybe 'fraid of what might happen to your precious little white pecker, 'fraid you might get a crab off some bitch's ass." He laughed and the fat guy did, too. "'Cause they got em! Red Lobster buffet up in them G-strings."

Cheeks took a step forward and touched the barrel of the gun to my forehead.

"Thing I can't figure out," he said softly, "is why you ain't afraid of me." The humorous period of the conversation was over.

I shrugged.

"Just stupid, I guess. My friend Delia thinks I'm having a mental episode. Shock."

He whipped the butt of the gun into the side of my head, and as I went down his knee crashed into my face. The fat guy kicked me in the ribs at the same time. The gun hit me again on the top of my head and a foot went into my stomach. I was blind when someone stomped on my hand. Then something heavy put a dent in the back of my skull and I was out.

Consciousness returned at a glacial pace. I found myself contorted in a cold, rancid-smelling darkness. My left eye wouldn't open, but when I turned my head I found a ribbon of blurry light with my right eye. My ears were ringing like I had my head in a giant bell someone was repeatedly ramming a car into, and I was shivering in seismic jerks and shudders. Even through all of that, I was able to size up where I was.

I was in a dumpster.

I pushed a bag of trash off my chest and tried to sit up. Pain exploded through my chest and stomach and I vomited something coppery and lukewarm down my chest. My right hand was just a numb thing dangling from my wrist, so I pushed at the heavy lid with my left, praying it hadn't been locked down. It groaned open and I flopped out over the side into two inches of snow.

When the shivering forced me to think about getting up, I spent a lost period of time dragging myself up the side of the dumpster. With one eye, I looked around. I was in the NW industrial area outside of a warehouse. It had a sign on it, but I couldn't read what it said. The sky was black and starless, but the snow had stopped falling. A wild tremor ran through me and I almost went down. If I did, I knew I would never get up again.

My coat was gone, and so was one of my boots. Everything was gone. My pockets were empty. I looked down at my numb foot and the sock was covered in blood. When I tilted my head down a few drops of blood rained out of my nose and pattered into the new snow around it.

"Gfug," I gargled. That was when I discovered my jaw had been dislocated.

I thought about screaming, just howling like a mad animal, but my ribs were too sore to get a breath. The vague memory of being beaten on by two black guys in a motel room swam to the surface and I felt a sudden spike of fear. My head lolled to either side, but I didn't see any cars.

I'd been left for dead.

I took as deep a breath as I could and blew out a white plume and coughed. Then I staggered along the side of the warehouse. When I reached the corner, I stood swaying and shivering in a light wind and studied the street sign. I knew some people who lived around here. Jane Shannon. A crazy old bartender who worked the stick at the Mallory. She had a big red neon heart in her living room window. Off to my right I could make out a row of old houses. One of them had a reddish blob. I started limping toward it. The world was spinning and I couldn't breathe, so I paused at every pole and sign along the way to steady myself and breathe. When I finally got to her front steps, an eternity of staggering later, I knew I'd never be able to climb even one of them. I summoned the last of my strength, every ounce of anything I had left, and collapsed on the wooden steps and started pounding on them with my left hand.

I'll never know how long it was before hazy yellow light touched my eyelids. A woman screamed. My left arm was still pounding away, like some broken robot appendage. I couldn't feel it and I couldn't make it stop. Something impossibly hot touched my cheek and I tried to open one of my eyes.

"Darby?"

I suddenly remembered who I was.

"No cops," I lisped. And then the blackness swallowed me again.

Somehow that tough old broad dragged my dead weight up her stairs onto the rug in her front room and covered me with a dusty flap of it. When I came to, she was wiping my eyes with a wet dishtowel or a sponge. It hurt like fire. I tried to slap her hand away, but my arms didn't seem to be working.

"You need a fucking hospital," Jane sobbed. "Jesus fucking Christ."

"No," I managed. "Cops." My jaw had slipped back together, but I couldn't close my mouth.

"Fuck, Darby," she said. "What if you die or go into a coma? Then what the fuck am I supposed to do?"

"Sit up," I whined. Jane Shannon was wearing a bloody pink bathrobe. Her gray and brown hair was a mess, her eyes wild. She reached down to take my right hand and drew back.

"Fucking Christ," she said again, sobbing.

"Booze," I tried to say, though it came out as "pooze." "Thigarette."

I held my left hand out and she pulled me into a sitting position. I would have screamed if I could have, but I could only gasp a few times as she propped me up against her ancient green sofa. I closed my eye again.

A minute later she was back and tapping my cheek. She'd tossed a blanket over me. I opened my eye and almost started crying. She was holding out a shot glass full of something brown and a lit smoke.

I reached out with my right hand and noticed that my pinkie was jutting out at an odd angle and that the whole hand was crusted in dried blood. I took the cigarette between my thumb and forefinger and tried to get it into my mouth. I think I rammed it into my forehead and my bad eye a few times before Jane guided it to my swollen lips.

"Good," I said as I exhaled. I took the shot glass into my shaking left hand and dumped it into my mouth. A line of fire traced its way all the way down into my groin. I took another drag.

"Thousand bucks," I murmured. "Cash. For one more drink. Advil."

"What happened to you?" she asked. "Where's your car?"

I was about to answer when I passed out again.

The next few days were a blur. Someone making me drink lukewarm tap water. A brief, bright pain in my right hand.

Pain everywhere. The gong of a concussion ringing in my ears, flashes of light and long periods of darkness. I was incredibly thirsty most of the time, and I couldn't breathe through my nose. My swollen, cracked lips could barely contain my massive tongue, and the back of my throat felt like someone had branded it. When I was finally lucid enough to moan something like a real word, Jane was there. She'd been sleeping in a chair next to the sofa I'd been levered onto. I was warm, covered with a gore-spattered comforter. My entire body felt like it had been stomped on, which it had.

"Water," I rasped.

Jane padded off in the direction of the kitchen and returned with a pint glass. She'd reset the pinkie finger on my right hand and wrapped it in an old shirt with a tongue depressor sticking out of it. I propped myself up on my elbow and took the glass in my left hand. It felt as heavy as an anvil. I drained it and my mouth watered like I was drinking the tears of angels. It was the best thing anyone had ever given me.

"Thanks," I managed. "Thank you."

"You're incredibly fucked up, Darby," Jane said in a flat, angry voice. "I set your pinkie. Stitched up the side of your head. You peed out some blood on my couch a few times. Whoever beat on you carved an X into one of your ass cheeks. I stitched that up, too."

She sighed and fired up a Pall Mall, then held it out for me to take a drag. I looked at the lipstick around the base and cracked my mouth open. The second best gift of my life.

"You've been out for three days. That first night you stopped breathing. I poured some water on you and slapped your bad eye. It worked, so don't bitch about it. I didn't know what else to do. Cops are looking for you. Your face is all over the papers, not that they'd recognize it now." She laughed a little and then coughed to cover a sob. "Had my boy come over and get you up on the sofa. Wasn't too happy about that. Why in the world did you come to my place?"

I thought about it for a minute. Both of my eyes were open, but my right eyelid felt like it was fighting a strip of Scotch tape. I made a motion with my head and she held the cigarette out again. I took a deep pull and leaned back.

"Fuckers tossed me in a dumpster a few blocks from here. Sorry." I was breathing a little better, but the ribs on my right side felt like a horse had stepped on me.

Jane blew out a plume of smoke and squinted though it at me.

"What you feel like doin'?" She asked the question in a casual way, but I could tell she was tired and scared.

"I dunno," I said honestly, "but it's gonna be way fuck-ing stupid."

Jane rose to her feet and retied her bathrobe. My dried blood was still all over it, like a giant rust stain. She'd washed it more than once, I could tell, but it was never going to be pink again.

"I got to get to work now that you're awake," she said. "I'll get you some more water and some Advil before I go. No more pissing the bed."

"Deal. I'd love you forever for a couple of those smokes."

She took four out of her pack and put them on the coffee table.

"Just light 'em on the stove."

I stopped. I was out of words.

"You just be calm," Jane said gently. "Try not to go back to sleep."

"I owe you."

She smiled sadly. "You owe me big time, Darby Holland. Way super fuckin' big time."

I lay there for the better part of an hour, smoking and thinking. Mostly thinking that I had to take a leak and I didn't want to get up and see myself in a bathroom mirror when I did. I also didn't want to see what my pee looked like. I didn't want to throw up the pint of water in my stomach if my head started spinning, because I doubted I could clean it up, and I was already pushing my welcome.

I thought about Jane, too. All the late nights I'd spent at her bar and then given her a ride home. The time I'd come over for Thanksgiving dinner with a random pack of misfits almost a decade ago. I hadn't seen much of her over the past few years, just like hundreds of other people I knew in Portland. I sort of felt bad about that now, all things considered.

I thought about Monique and the Lucky, how it looked like I'd been right about some kind of connection there, how it had been her on the phone, and how Cheeks knew about it. Those thoughts took about a quarter of a cigarette. For the rest of it, I thought about how I was going to get whatever information I needed out of Cheeks before I beat him to death.

Jane appeared in the doorway, dressed in black for a shift behind the bar.

"Old Crow on the kitchen counter, if you can make it that far. Pack of smokes in there, too. Don't overdo it. Sardines and crackers in the cabinet. Advil is in the bathroom. By the toilet."

"Sardines. Yummy. Have a good night. I promise to be a good boy." I stubbed the butt out in the ashtray on the coffee table she'd pushed up next to me. "Don't tell anyone I'm here."

She cocked her hip.

"I'm not an idiot. Moron."

I tried to smile and my lips felt like they were going to crack and burst like microwaved hot dogs. The cigarette had made me light-headed. I felt like I had the worst hangover of my life and I'd just eaten half a jar of mayonnaise.

"I'll get you some money," I said, trying not to move. "Soon as I'm up. A couple thousand. Swear to fucking Christ."

Jane frowned.

"Considering my nursing skills, you might want to pay me in Monopoly money. But the couch, Darby. You ruined my couch and my carpet and my robe."

"Yeah. Shitty. And I owe you a thousand bucks for that drink, too. I remember that."

She smiled.

"I'll see you tonight when I get home. Maybe we can watch one of my old movies." It was then that I realized something both fortunate and sad. Jane was lonely.

"I fucking love old movies."

As she walked past, she reached out to pat my head and drew her hand back. A half cough came out of her again. The door clicked behind her. A bad indicator about what I was going to find in that mirror when I took that leak.

Still, a drink sounded good. Especially some of that tap water and about eight Advil. Old Crow was a cheap, sweet whiskey, in my advanced opinion, but beggars didn't even get to pick their city sometimes, much less what they planned on paying an imaginary thousand bucks for. I smoked another cigarette. I smelled like piss, vomit, shit, and rotting trash. I'd destroyed the sofa. Jane was right. I did owe her a thousand bucks for that drink that was waiting about fifty small steps away. I also owed her another double handful of bills for stitching up my foul body. It was time to pee.

Getting up took several painful tries. Eventually, I got my knees underneath me when I fell off the couch. The carpet looked like someone had dumped a bucket of rust on it. My blood, all dried up. It was a fake Ikea Persian, but still, it was too bad. I got my legs underneath me and stood there. I still couldn't see too well out of my right eye, but the spinning had turned into something like waves. There was some sensory distortion, but I could see and I could limp.

Jane had dressed me at some point over the past two days in green sweatpants and a green hoodie. The socks were thick and white, spotted with red on the swollen foot I'd walked on with no boot. My right ass cheek hurt almost as bad as my eye, and the sweatpants were sticking to it. Bummer.

The ribs hurt especially badly on the right side, but my stomach seemed almost OK. I worked out a lot, mostly out of paranoia, and that was one of those instances where a few hundred sit-ups a day paid off. So I went in search of the drink before the mirror.

I limped into the dining room and headed for the bright light of the kitchen. It took some time. My legs felt like they were made out of wet clay. My back made several alarming crunching sounds and my neck felt like a toothpick holding up a pumpkin. My vision had tremors in both eyes, very high speed, like a J. J. Abrams movie, very vomit-inducing. But the Old Crow was on the counter as promised, and next to it was a full pack of Pall Malls. I tucked the bottle up against my sore ribs with my right arm, spun the cap off, and poured some into the waiting tumbler with the hand that worked, about four fingers. I'd need it before I went into the bathroom.

The first sip went right into the sink. I rinsed my mouth out with some tap water and tried again. The next one burned all the way through me. I shook a cigarette out of the pack and fired it up on the gas stove. The taste of bourbon in my mouth and being upright with a smoke dangling in my good hand cemented the fact that I was alive. I took another sip of cheap booze and gagged on it, then another fast mouthful and the glass was empty. I puffed on the cigarette and leaned on the counter, feeling my heartbeat. I did that until the smoke burned down to my knuckles. I put it out in the sink and dropped it into the pop-top trash can that reminded me of a dumpster. It was time.

Whiskey sometimes made the hideous into the forgettably nasty, transformed the bland into the desirable, the beautiful into pure fantasy. Evidently, I'd need the rest of the bottle to climb up to the bottom rung. I looked like a leper fresh from a high-speed car wreck. My face was a swollen mask of blue and yellow. My nose, already flattened several times, was a little flatter. It was a good thing there was no cartilage left in it to break. My eyes looked like oysters, the right one with sauce in it. A long cut, stitched up with black thread, ran out of my matted hair and down my right cheek. Jane was right. I'd seen better stitching jobs on animals. Much better. She'd probably been half drunk just to deal with such a grisly mess. I sighed.

I turned the shower on and stripped. There were more stitches on my blackened right ribs, but just two. Not so bad. The sweatpants peeled off my ass with a tug and I used a hand mirror to look at the damage.

An X had indeed been carved into my right butt cheek. Jane had sewn it up with all the care she had put into my face. I put the mirror on the counter before I dropped it. My hands were shaking that much.

I stood under the hot water until it started to go cold. The entire time, while I scrubbed my aching body and tried to rinse all the filth off me, I was thinking about one thing.

I spent two and a half more weeks at Jane's. The morning after my first shower, she brought me the most unlikely breakfast for dinner when she got home from work: a huge chunk of blue cheese, four hard-boiled eggs, and something that might have been lasagna a week before. I really wished I had my wallet with my bank and credit cards, even though the newspapers she'd left lying around showed that a man-hunt was under way. Even ordering a pizza would have put me in lockdown. I wondered how much of a pizza I could ram down before the feds collected their new Unabomber. Probably half of it. I thought about that pizza a lot.

Jane seemed to enjoy having a half-crippled fugitive on her couch. Someone to talk to when she got home, bitch at in the morning. We played a lot of chess. I did a great deal of thinking, and when I drifted into the dark space between thoughts and zeroed out, she'd bring me a tumbler of that crap whiskey and wait until my eyes focused again. She had a collection of old black-and-white movies we spent many a late night watching. She knew all of the words.

I wanted to talk to the guys from the Lucky. A drink at the Rooster Rocket, Gomez laughing at one of his rated-G-for-gangster jokes. Flaco's Tacos, my source of vital nutri-ents, street gossip, the way it smelled on a cold winter day.

Nigel's sinister company, his moving commitment to redefining the word "shady." Big Mike's childish but endearing women problems. Delia was watching my place, I knew, but I missed my cats. I missed her like coal miners miss birds. She'd be worried sick. I missed every part of my old life. But I missed the Lucky Supreme most of all. Every time I thought about it, something like a frozen migraine touched me inside and squeezed so hard I couldn't breathe.

After ten days I could do three push-ups. After twelve I could do it again. After two weeks I still looked like hammered shit, but the ringing in my ears was more of a continuous buzz, and my pupils were almost the same size most of the time.

Jane's ex-husband or an old boyfriend had left some clothes in the basement, along with a few boxes of assorted crap, including a set of golf clubs. I ran a load of the clothes through her washer and dryer to get the mold out of them. Everything was too big, but it was better than walking out in my underwear with one boot.

White golf shoes, checkered pants, a green shirt with a big collar, and a sweater vest Mr. Rogers might have liked. A tan trench coat over that. I looked like a beat-up alcoholic circus clown. The last thing I took out of the basement was a golf club, one with metal at the end. The one it looked like you used it to hit something really fucking hard. I used a few twist ties from the trash bag box to fix it into the inside of the coat.

It was close to midnight and Jane was at work, shaking martinis at the Mallory. She kept a jar of change on the kitchen counter. I had a final shot of her whiskey and then fished out ten quarters. It was all I'd need, one way or the other.

I went out through the back door and took a deep breath of the night air. My ribs were still incredibly sore, but the sharp, pulsating pain had given way to a dull ache, punctuated by random stabs. I'd taken the strange cast Jane had made for my right hand off earlier. The knuckles in my pinkie still hurt like hell, and the rest of the fingers were a little stiff, but I could make a satisfying fist, as long as I didn't hit anything bigger than a roll of toilet paper with it.

The snow was gone and it had rained earlier. The world smelled good and clean after almost three stuffy weeks of old lady and the chemical reek of my own fear. I adjusted the golf club in my baggy jacket and went down the stairs into the dead winter weeds.

The nearest stop for bus number 20 was about ten blocks away. I took it easy, moving slow and old. The few people that were out looked away when I passed them on the sidewalk. When I got to the bus shelter on Burnside, I lit up one of Jane's smokes and waited. The bus rolled up in less than ten minutes.

The driver didn't give me a second glance as I climbed aboard and dropped the quarters in the terminal. He tore off a transfer pass and handed it over while he looked in the side mirror for an opening to pull back into traffic. As soon as I crossed the yellow line, he bullied his way in. I sat down in the first seat and adjusted the golf club.

Portland is a beautiful city at night, full of wet lights and shining surfaces. The streets were alive with activity, even though a misting rain had begun while I was waiting.

No one had an umbrella. We passed the big bookstore and then rolled past Old Town and 6th Street. I closed my eyes then, until the bus started up the Burnside Bridge.

The river was its glossy, oily usual, a vast, dark conduit sluggishly pumping through the heart of the city. I caught a reflection of my face in the suddenly black window and tried to refocus on the distance, but my pupils weren't working right and it just made it seem like I was staring at my own blurry ghost. A really beat-up pair of them. I pulled the cord to get off at the next stop.

"First stop east side," the driver called. I got out into the mist and the bus rumbled off. Across the street by some small used car place was another shelter, for the number 6 that would take me all the way out to the tiki bar and the Sands. I walked over and sat down in the bus stall. Some asshole had left the paper wrappers and sauce packets from the Taco Bell across the street all over the ground, even though there was a trash can just to the right of the shelter. I reached into my oversized coat and fingered the haft of the golf club. I could feel a bad mood coming on.

The bus finally came and I flashed my transfer at the driver and sat down. It was empty, except for one middle-aged bald guy on the nod in the back row. I watched the east side roll past. I felt hungry after the smell of the food wrappers. I'd probably lost fifteen pounds in the last three weeks. I closed my right eye because it was starting to throb and all the pretty lights came into some kind of focus. I'd almost had all of it taken away, and the list of people trying to take it could fill up a phone book. Dessel and Pressman had even taken out ad space.

A fuzzy neon palm tree came into view some time later. I pulled the next-stop cord and the bus slowed to a stop. Normally I thank the driver, but I was rude and just got off.

My car was gone from the parking lot of the tiki bar. Either it had been impounded or Cheeks had taken it to a chop shop. It didn't matter, since I didn't have the keys anyway. I lit up the very last smoke and studied the Sands. It was a shitty night, but the Town Car with the gold spinners was in the parking lot. My new ride.

I walked across the street with my head down. Just another guy out in the rain, with a limp and exceptionally poor taste in clothes. When I got to the edge of the motel, I leaned up against the wall and looked up with both eyes. The lights in 119 had been on when I got off the bus, but after a minute or so I hit on what I was looking for. A shape moved behind the blinds, and in the distance, over the sound of the street and the rain, I heard the shitty stylings of disco.

I walked around the side of the building, into the darkness by the dumpsters, and pried the golf club out of my coat. The sight of the stinking metal boxes, overflowing with moist trash, took away any last trace of fear. In a flash, I knew I had somehow gone totally and instantly insane. My chest felt like it was on fire and a rhythmic clicking was all around me. I realized it was my teeth, biting the cold air like a windup toy.

I clenched my jaw shut and slid the golf club up my right sleeve and held the meaty end in my hand. The oversized coat covered it. My heart was hammering at my aching ribs as I drifted around the corner and quietly walked up the stairs. When I got to 119, I didn't bother to knock. I let the golf club slip out of my sleeve and caught the handle. It was nice and warm. I was betting that the door was unlocked, that two huge, heavily armed pimps, with a string of whores about to stop in dropping cash off in the next few minutes, would leave it unlocked so they didn't have to get up every five minutes.

I twisted the doorknob and pushed.

The door opened. So I stepped inside and closed it behind me.

Cheeks was sitting on the floor by the stereo, a record cover in his giant hands. The fat guy was sitting on the edge of the bed clipping his toenails. Both of them looked up at me with blank expressions, then their faces changed simultaneously. The fat guy looked at the big, gold-plated revolver resting on the nightstand and then back at me, with the face of a man who had just woken from a distorted dream and was trying to figure out if it was good or bad. Cheeks beamed like a kid who had just robbed his first candy store. He reached out and turned the music down a few notches.

"Muthafucka," he said, laughing as he got to his feet. "Seems you be the dumbest thing since Clamato."

"Easily true," I confessed. "Now, back to Monique. I'd still like to talk to her."

Cheeks shook his head and chuckled. The fat guy did, too.

"Shit. I don't like me no white meat, so I didn't fuck on you last time. Bony ass an' all. But this time you gonna get some party, white boy."

"Muthafucka's gonna be pregnant we done," the fat guy sang.

Cheeks flexed his huge hands.

"Time to fuck you up, boy," he purred.

"I'm already fucked up."

Cheeks came at me and I brought the golf club I'd been hiding alongside my leg up in a whistling arc. It bounced off his cheekbone and I sidestepped his falling body and gave him another good crack on the top of his head. The fat guy lunged for the gun and I spun and rapped him across the back of the hand. He whipped the broken hand to his mouth and I cracked him in his upturned elbow.

When I raised the club again he leaned to one side, so I scooped up the gun and kicked him in the face. He was still sitting on the bed and I had the perfect angle, so I did it again. The fat guy flopped back on the bed after the second kick, and I rapped him hard once across the kneecap to slow him down for the rest of his life. No response.

Behind me, Cheeks sputtered and managed to roll over onto his back. He coughed and blood burped out of his mouth onto his face. The disco record was still droning on.

"Fug," he said.

Then I started hitting.

"That"—to the forehead—"is for"—ribs—"the fucking X. And that"—face—"is for the dumpster. And this"—Cheeks moaned—"is because you made me fucking kill you!"

He tried to raise his hands, but I beat them down with the golf club and got him a few more times in the face. Nose. Chin. Eyebrow. Then I was just hitting, over and over again. I stopped when my arm felt like it was going to fall out of the socket.

I stood there panting for over a minute, maybe longer, with a gun in one hand and a dripping golf club in the other. The disco record was still spinning. I raised the gun and pointed it at the turntable. When I pulled the trigger, nothing happened. I looked at the side of the gun and realized it must have a safety.

"Fucking shit," I wheezed. So I put the golf club to the stereo a few times. Then I had to sit down on the bed next to the unconscious fat guy. Cheeks was still breathing on the floor a few feet away, but he was winding down. The fat guy next to me was snoring, though it sounded weird because I'd broken his nose. I tried to catch my breath and let go of the golf club. I couldn't do either one. My hand had cramped into a ball on the handle of the club. After a minute I heaved and some air finally went into some closed compartment inside me.

There was a pack of Camels on the top of the cheap dresser across from the bed. I looked at the gun again and then cracked the fat guy across his broken nose to see what happened. He gargled a little and kept on breathing. I sighed again, as deep as I could. All the excitement had closed my bad eye again, but the double image problem had gone with it.

I got up, stuck the gun in my coat pocket for the moment since everyone was sleeping, and crossed to the cigarettes. I plucked one out of the nearly full pack and pocketed it, then picked up the Zippo that had been next to it and fired up.

The room was a mess. As I smoked, an unsavory calm came over me. I thanked a god I didn't believe in that I hadn't been able to shoot anything. The cops would have been all over me if I had. I had just enough time between my fifth drag on the cigarette and three a.m., when the stable cabbed in, to get to phase two of the plan I had worked out for the last few weeks.

The money. And some car keys.

Cheeks had a roll of eighteen hundred dollars in his right front pocket. The fat guy had eighty-four bucks. I pocketed it all, and the keys to the Lincoln, and then I tossed the place. I found my keys and my blood-crusted wallet in a drawer in the dresser with some other junk. There had to be a stash of dough in there somewhere. I found it about five minutes later. Somewhere around twelve thousand, stuffed into a paper bag that was itself stuffed into a hat that was crammed into the back of the closet. Cheeks had been doing OK, I guess, but pimps didn't keep bank accounts. Scumbags of his order seldom do, a fact I'd exploited before.

I set the bag on the dresser and looked around. The place was totally trashed. Cheeks was still breathing, but it didn't sound good. The fat guy was snoring through his broken nose. I went into the bathroom and dug a coffee cup out of the trashcan, scooped up some water out of the scummy toilet, and carried it back out. I poured it into the fat guy's face and backed up and pointed the gun at him. He sputtered and moaned and his eyes opened.

"They say breakfast is the most important meal of the day," I said. "Although the nutritional value of toilet water?" I shrugged. "I dunno. So, Monique."

The fat guy reached up and pawed at his nose, then looked at the watery blood on his hand.

"You fuckin' broke my face."

"Yep. I'm fixing to blow your crotch open with this big-ass gun next. Tell you what there, chubby. I'm pissed at you guys."

"Yeah. Fuck."

"Try to sit up. You tell me what I want to know, this might work out with you still breathing."

The fat guy struggled into a sitting position. I'd really done a number on his face. He spit a tooth out and glared at me.

"You gonna shoot me? You're gonna shoot me. I know it."

"Likely so," I said. "But you do have a chance. Now, I'm not saying you have a really good chance. We're talking Vegas odds. I won't lie to you."

"Fuck you, then." He coughed and touched his nose. "Aw man, this motherfuckin' stings. You really pour toilet water on me?"

"Sure did." The gun was getting heavy and I was getting dangerously tired. I sat down on a chair I hadn't broken and rested the gun on my knee with the barrel pointed right between his legs.

"You left me for dead in a dumpster, you fucking idiot. Toilet water is like holy water in this situation." I tapped the gun on my knee. "So like I said, I won't lie to you." I sighed. My ribs hurt like hell and my good eye was hazy. "What the fuck is your name? I can't keep calling you chubby."

"Clarence."

"OK, Clarence. I'm Darby Holland. You already know that, because you took all the money out of my wallet. Since I took it all back with interest, I figure we're even there. But the whole dumpster thing, the beating, the X one of you motherfuckers carved in my ass, well, let's even that up, too. Cheeks over there, he's not going to make it. Can't talk to him now. What we have there is a vegetable. But Clarence, I get the feeling you might be able to tell me what I need to know."

Clarence's face was swelling up pretty bad. He looked at the gun, then at my face.

"Shit. OK. Shit. Let me get this straight." He was trembling now. "Can I get a smoke? Maybe a drink? We got some."

"Sounds good to me. I need a break."

Clarence rose to his feet and slowly limped over to the nightstand, where there was a bottle of something brown and a pack of Newports. His knee was crackling like a bag of pretzels, but he didn't seem to notice. Maybe I hadn't hit that part of him hard enough.

"Don't do anything foolish, Clarence," I cautioned. "I'm not what you'd call a marksman, but this is a small room."

He shook his head and grunted.

"And don't get any of your bloody toilet snot on that shit. I want some."

Clarence carefully unscrewed the cap on the bottle and dumped about five fingers into a glass I hadn't broken. Then he drained it and shuddered.

"Sit that bottle and those smokes on the dresser and sit the fuck down."

He picked everything up and set them down next to the bag of money. When he saw the cash bag, he wheezed and his shoulders slumped.

"Yep," I said. "So fuckin' sad."

He crashed down on the corner of the bed and lit up a Newport with a match.

"I told Cheeks you wasn't dead," he said around the smoke.

"Get talking, Clarence." I tapped the gun on my knee a few times. "Got about five seconds to start."

"It's like this." He took another drag. "Cheeks was gettin', I dunno, I guess he was gettin' fucked with. The bitches was gettin' picked up an' sweated by the cops. You know the story. Old Town changin' into some new fuckin' thang. No room for a pimp to grow, right? As a businessman." He took another drag.

"But Cheeks, he a smart fuckin' niggah. Least he was. Figured he'd upgrade with the times, start hisself a real house. Espresso an' bitches. Upscale. Like a pussy factory Starbucks. Shit." He shook his head.

"I don't know what the fuck happened. Met up with his old cellie, white junkie piece o' shit name Ralston. Him the one blew your shit up. Ralston knew some big motherfuckas, don't know how, but they's the ones hired him." He sucked down a last drag. I tapped the gun on my knee.

"Ralston got scared while he was makin' that bomb. Things lookin' shitty. He come to Cheeks an' they talk an' Cheeks do the pimp thing, become his representative. Start talkin' to the big boys. An' then yo' ass shows up."

I clicked my teeth together and a spasm ran down Clarence's leg.

"Yeah, see, Cheeks did that carve. Swear on my soul."

I got up and plucked out a menthol, keeping the gun on Clarence's crotch. I stuck it behind my ear and then spun the lid on the bottle with my free hand and dumped some into my mouth.

"That X thing, Clarence, don't talk about that." I took another sip. It was hard holding the gun on him. "Makes me feel homicidal. Just so you know."

"OK."

"So, Monique."

"Cheeks got Ralston up in this motel on 82nd. The Bismarck. He sent Monique to stay with him and do some trollin', get some new streets down. Fuckin' all I know, I swear. I got no idea who hired his ass." He raised his hands.

I thought about it for a moment.

"OK, Clarence, here's what happens now. Cheeks there"—I gestured with the gun—"well, he's gonna pass into the next world soon. I got a little carried away. I'm taking his car and that bag of cash. You, I guess you live. But if this Ralston knows I'm on my way, I'll do some really bad shit to you. Understand?"

He nodded.

"That dumpster? Might be a good place for big boy here. But I noticed two closer ones on the side of the building."

Clarence nodded again. He still had his hands up. I got up to leave.

"You just sit there for a little bit. I'm gonna go now, but I might just hide outside the door and listen to hear if your fat ass starts moving around. Then you get every bullet in this gun. I might just go. But you won't fucking know."

"I gotta take a shit," Clarence said. "Like to get the toilet water off my broke-ass face, too."

"Cool. You do that. I'll just sit right here. You come out with anything bigger than a toothbrush . . ."

"Believe me man, ain't no way."

"Get on, then." I waved the gun at the bathroom door.

Clarence rose unsteadily to his feet and walked slowly. He could feel his knee now.

"Close the door," I said. "I don't want to hear whatever falls out of you hit the water."

He closed the door behind him. I snatched the cigarettes and the bag of money, tucked the bloody golf club up my sleeve, slipped out and clicked the door shut behind me, then made my way quickly across the landing and down the blurry stairs. I stuffed the gun into my pocket on the way down.

Cheeks's Continental started on the first try. I rolled it out of the parking lot on purr and gunned it once I was on the interstate, squinting, just able to see enough to drive. The snow had stopped and it was turning to slush. My hands were shaking and my right eye was still closed. As I drove I dug the smokes out of my pocket, ripped the top off the pack with my teeth, and dumped them on the seat next to me. At the first stoplight, I managed to get one into my mouth and hit it with Cheeks's engraved Zippo.

I had a pimp's car, his gun, and his entire cash wad. Two weeks of planning, and right then it looked like Delia was right about me. I was stupid. Because I didn't know what to do next. That was my entire plan.

6

I pulled into an all night drive-thru burrito stand and got four *al pastor*, wet with red sauce, with two sides of beans and rice. The burritos were crappy, but I made it through two of them sitting in the Continental with the heater running. Then I drained a bottle of lime soda and tossed all the wreckage on the passenger floor. I wouldn't be in the car for long, so there was no point in worrying about the trash.

It was four a.m. and I was sickly tired. The black sky was misting something that almost qualified as sleet again. I needed drugs, booze, and sleep, but I was shit out of luck on all three counts. I couldn't go into an all-night pharmacy for aspirin looking like Frankenstein, the bars were closed, and Jane's was out. I just couldn't bear the thought of going back there. The trench coat I was wearing was flecked with blood. My clown shoes were red. I'd noticed all the blood at the burrito drive-thru. None of it was mine, but it was too much. I owed Jane money, not another night on her ruined couch, this time fresh from a murder.

I wheeled around northeast Portland, keeping to the side streets. Cheeks's car smelled like cigars, potent cologne, and now burritos and onion. Not a great mix. The night was wet and quiet. I fired up a chain of menthols and just rumbled around, half-blind and plan-free.

I knew where Monique was. She was chilling with the guy who'd blown up my life. If I tried to drive out there in this ridiculous pimpmobile, I'd be in handcuffs in less than ten minutes. Driving around in a tricked-out pimp ride, dressed in blood-spattered clown clothes with a poorly stitched together head, a big gold-plated gun, and a bent and bloody golf club next to a paper bag full of cash and two crappy burritos was a sign that the crazy I'd felt come over me at the Sands was still too close to the surface.

I wanted to go home, but Dessel and Pressman would have someone on my place. It occurred to me that I didn't fit my profile picture anymore. And I was driving a different car. I had my keys again, so I might be able to sneak over the back fence and slip through the back door. Delia might be there. I wanted to see her. My nose tingled and my good eye watered up. My cats. I missed the little shit-heads. I wanted to smell their fur, that mix of dust and sweet. I took the big car on the scenic route, hitting every side street. It took about five cigarettes to get to 29th. When I passed by on the corner, I saw Delia's restored old red Falcon in the driveway. There was an unmarked Chevy on the corner; two guys were lounging inside, like they'd been there for hours.

I pulled around the corner and found a pool of dark-ness between the streetlights, up a few blocks. I cut the engine and pocketed the gun, stuffed the money bag in the other coat pocket, got out with the golf club, and locked the door. The street was only randomly dotted with parked cars, and a few feet behind the Continental was a sewer grate, one of the big, wide ones made for the yearly slurry of fall leaves. I looked around as best I could until I was sure that the night was free of witnesses, took the gun out, and tossed it. It skittered into the sewer mouth and I heard a satisfying plunk as it hit the water below the street. I tossed the golf club in behind it and was forced to kick it around a few times to make it go down, but it finally did.

Then I walked quickly for a few blocks, away from the car, my head down, just another guy on a shitty night, face down. When I was far enough away to relax, I stopped and took a deep breath, then lifted my face to the black sky. The cold felt good on my pulsing face. I blinked and let the icy water run into my itchy eyes. All the stitching itched ferociously, but the freezing rain on my face was so sweet that for a minute I forgot about everything and stood there like a meaty flower in a storm. Little by little, drop by drop, the crazy started washing away.

When my face and hands were finally numb, I hobbled like an old man down the sidewalk on the next street over. When I got to the house behind mine, I silently limped down the side and into the backyard. I could see through the chain-link fence that my bedroom light was on.

Getting over the fence took everything I had left, and I tore the crotch of my clown pants. I had to lie panting in the mud and dead grass for a few minutes when I was finally over it. If there was a cop inside with Delia, I was fucked. I might have been able to run about as fast as I'd normally be able to crawl.

The back door led to the laundry room I shared with my upstairs neighbors. In an inspired moment a few months back, I'd snapped my house key off in the ignition of some guy's car, so my hippie neighbors had left their key in a strawberry pot on the back porch and we'd all been too lazy to make a copy yet. I fished around for it and my fingers closed around metal.

From there it was easy. I unlocked the back door, dropped the key back in the pot, and locked it behind me. The dirty wooden stairwell to one side past the washer and dryer led up to the neighbor's landing and their back door. My back door was directly across from me. My left pupil was still a pinhole and I couldn't see anything.

I fumbled around for my keys. Since I couldn't see well enough to make them out, I tried them all and one of them finally turned the dead bolt. I opened the door as silently as I could. The kitchen lights were on. Delia was standing in the center of the room, stunned, wearing a Cramps T-shirt, big wool socks, and holding a huge knife. The knife dropped out of her hand and we stared at each other for a few heartbeats.

She crashed into me and squeezed my ribs. I gasped and she let up and looked at my face.

"I fucking thought you were dead!" she screamed. "Again!"

"I'm sorry," I whispered back. "I'm really, really fucking sorry."

Her eyes were puffy with sleep. She'd scrubbed all of her makeup off and her skin looked like living paper. When she started crying, staring at my face, something in my chest snapped like a bowstring.

"I had so much shit I wanted to say if I ever saw you again." She leaned into me and slipped her hands into my wet jacket. "I can't remember any of it." She sobbed a few times and then turned her watery eyes back up into my face. "You look incredibly awful, Darby. Who sewed up the side of your face? A monkey? The cops are out there! What the hell are you even doing here?"

"Nice old lady sewed me up," I rasped. My ribs really hurt after the fence and Delia's squeezing. "Might have had shaky hands. I came over the back fence. Tore my new pants."

"Jesus." She pushed me back and studied me closely, frowning. "Your right eye. You're lucky it's still in there. What the hell did you do?"

"We got any booze?"

Delia looked my face over again and sighed heavily.

"Vodka. I killed all the brown stuff. You want rocks?"

"Too cold."

She poured us a few shots and lit a couple of cigarettes on the stove. I took the shot in one hand and the cigarette in the other. When she saw my right hand her eyes widened and she quickly looked away, her face twisting. I tossed the shot back and took a drag.

"Darby." She downed her shot. "You're sort of covered in blood."

"Not mine. At least most of it. I think."

She stared at me, waiting, tapping one foot. I squirmed a little.

"See," I said. "I just had to kill this dude . . ."

Delia crossed her arms, cigarette dangling from her lips.

"Went looking for Monique. Her pimp and some fat guy beat the shit out of me and left me for dead in a dumpster. Carved an X in my ass cheek, too. So when I went back to talk to them . . ." I shrugged and winced. "I feel like I might pass out, sweetie."

I tried to blink a few times and a wave of vertigo washed over me. I staggered and dropped my smoke.

"Bed," I croaked.

Delia guided me into the bathroom and I fell into the tub. I woke up after she'd stripped me bare. Warm water washed over me and I started shivering. She put some burning thing on the stitches on my face and I came fully to, grabbed her hands.

"Easy," she cooed softly. "Easy."

I gasped when she ran something searing over my ribs. Climbing over the fence had been a bad idea. But I was getting really good at bad ideas. My right eye had closed entirely and I couldn't see her very well.

Delia lathered my hair while the hot shower water pounded on me, then rinsed it with a small basin from the kitchen. I watched rivers of pink swirl down the drain before the water was finally clear. Then she put in the stopper and the tub began to fill. She dumped in some bubble bath and a yellow plastic ducky I'd never seen before.

"Soak," she whispered.

"What?"

"Darby, I'm getting the stitches out of you. Tonight. These fucking things are sewing thread. As in infected."

"Aw."

"Yep. Soak. I'll be right back."

When she returned, I was drifting in and out. She stuffed a few pills into my mouth and made me drink a pint of water.

"There's pimp money in my clown coat," I began.

"I found it," she said. "Along with some car keys. Where's the car?"

"I dunno. Around out there somewhere. I think I should go to bed now. After one cigarette. Give pills time to work."

I blinked again to get some focus. She was poised over me with toenail clippers in one hand and tweezers in the other.

"I hate looking at you right now," I said.

Delia made a spinning motion with the clippers, I turned onto my side and almost went under. The arc of my hip stuck neatly out of the bubble bath.

"Darby," she breathed out, inspecting my butt cheek, "you killed the guy who did this, right?"

"Golf club. Just now."

"Good."

I heard a clip and felt a little pain, then pulling.

"Jesus," she whispered. "My first really good look at your ass."

"I'm told it's bony."

"It is."

"Like yours is any better."

More yanking. Delia *tsk*ed.

"You're a fucking idiot, Darby. Cops outside, you're all fucked up, you just killed a guy with a golf club, and now I'm removing stitches from your ass and you have the presence of mind to criticize mine."

Yank.

"I stole his car, too."

"Splendid."

59

Yank.

"And all his money."

"That's a good boy," she said.

Yank.

When she was done, I settled back and held up two fingers for a smoke. I itched all over, but the oils and the warm water were sinking in. Delia wiped her hands and lit up two smokes, then placed one between my lips.

"You know," I started.

"Yes, yes. Women can be so cruel. Here's a really good example. I'm gonna take your blood-spattered clown outfit and bag it. It's going into the basement for later incineration or burial. So your attempt at a lame-ass new fashion trend is over. Try that on for mean."

"Cunt."

She rubbed some burning stuff on my face.

"Then you're going to eat whatever I make. It won't be good, but you look like a dog from some shit hole in India. I can see your ribs."

"I've been on a diet."

"Get your ridiculous ass up while I burn some food for you to stuff into that thing you wear as a face. You're lucky my dinner was almost ready. But first—" She held up the clippers. "Your face."

"Oh no."

I closed my eyes. With each clip she made a soft little noise, like she could feel it, too. When she was done she lathered up her hands and gently washed my face, massaging it until the crust was gone, and it felt so good that I never wanted to open my eyes again.

When she was done, she went into the kitchen without a word and started cracking eggs and banging around pans. Some men have a little trouble with nudity. I mean their own. I was never one of them. Being naked generally meant something good was going to happen. But being naked in front of Delia gave me pause. Then again, she had just pried some rotting stitches out of my ass and described me as a starving Indian dog. So there was that. I opened my eyes and stared at the ceiling until I felt brave again. Then I got out and quickly padded through the kitchen naked, into the bedroom.

"Pants, jackass," she called over her shoulder. I closed the door and sat down on the edge of my bed. My bed, with its familiar comforter, the newly dusted antique headboard I'd gotten at a garage sale and partially restored myself. My old, flat pillow. My brain felt like it had been turned off, utterly numb, like a foot that had fallen asleep. After a few minutes the smell of sizzling pork and enchiladas wafted in, mingling with the comforting smell of furniture polish. I got a pair of soft, worn jeans out of the dresser and slowly pulled them up over my butt. They didn't fit that well anymore, so I let them sag around my waist like a rap kid.

When I went out into the kitchen, she had a small restaurant operation going on. I paused to sniff and Delia elbowed me out of the way.

"Dining room table, droopy drawers. You have time for one more smoke."

I drifted out and sat down. The bottle of vodka was there, but I'd left my glass by the bathtub and I didn't have the energy to go back and get it. I took a pull off the bottle and then lit a smoke from the pack on the table. I looked around.

"Ever notice," I said, gesturing with my cigarette, "how a place always looks different when you get home? This table looks bigger." The pills were talking.

"Yeah, well, that eye helps. Here we go."

She came out of the kitchen and set a plate down in front of me. Steam curled off a small mountain of scrambled eggs, two leftover green enchiladas that were crispy at the edges, and some sliced tomato. She plunked a bottle of hot sauce down with a fork and napkin and I smiled at her. I dumped some on the eggs and laid into them. They were perfectly light and buttery. After a few bites I carved off a big chunk of enchilada and stuffed the entire thing into my mouth. Delia smiled, watching me eat.

"Roasted squash and goat cheese. I made them the other night and I still have half the pan. Chew, Darby."

"Mmm." It was all I could say.

As soon as I was halfway through with the plate, she padded back into the kitchen and came back with a pan full of breakfast sausages that had been cooking. She shoveled six of them out and then went back into the kitchen and came back with two glasses of orange juice. She picked up one of the little sausages and nibbled it, thoughtful.

"I love these little things," she murmured. I glanced up at her and then back down, quickly. Delia was crying, with the sound turned off.

I speared one and gave it a few rapid chews, nodding. Pretty soon the plate was empty and my stomach was groaning. I guzzled the orange juice and stared at her for a long minute.

"Sleep," I finally managed. She held out her hand.

"C'mon, then."

She guided me into the bedroom and I fell face-first onto the bed on top of the comforter. I was dimly aware of her trying to pull my jeans off and finally giving up. She covered me with a heavy flannel quilt I kept in the closet, turned out the light, then went out and closed the door behind her. Somewhere millions of miles away, I could hear the sound of her doing dishes and singing something, an old Germs tune. What seemed like hours later I surfaced from a deep sleep and found her curled against my back, holding one warm hand over my chest, her face nuzzled against my neck. Then dreamless sleep.

My interview strategy had been marginal so far. That was the first thing I thought of when I woke up. Also, I'd been a little foggy since the beating. Whatever kind of concussion I'd sustained didn't make a shit bit of difference, though. I was just too stupid to have a pack of cops hunting me to begin with, especially federal ones with a vendetta. Maybe I should have shot for something easier to manage in life, I thought. Like a career as a guy living out of a shopping cart.

Delia was snoring next to me. It was six o'clock at night. I turned a little and thought about a cigarette. I smelled good, I realized. Like soap and shampoo. Not so bad. I'd made a little money that week already. Also nice. Two fat big cats were between us, looking like they'd just fallen out of orbit and impacted on the bed. Also good.

So what to do? I felt like going and talking to this Ralston guy. But he was just the anus of the worm. I needed to find the head if I was going to get anywhere. Life can be a funny thing. Also short. I'd always had simple goals. Do art, make a living, get some pussy, maybe shack up someday and have a kid. A few beers along the way, maybe a trip to Spain, or at least Tijuana. Possibly take up painting again. Watch the first season of *True Blood*, which meant taking a bold step toward a TV purchase.

But it didn't seem to be working out for the most part. I listened to Delia's snoring for a minute and didn't have a single thought at all. When my brain finally kicked back into gear, it was because my new scars were itching. As soon as I got up, the snoring stopped. Instantly.

"What are you doing?" Delia asked in a muzzy voice.

"Need a smoke."

"Stay away from the windows." She curled her skinny arms around Chops and pulled him in like he was a doll. The big old traitor purred once and pushed himself into her flat chest. She sighed into his neck and started snoring again.

I was still wearing the pants I'd fallen asleep in. I got socks and a Ramones hoodie out of the dresser and a pair of steel-toed work boots I hadn't worn for years out of the closet. I missed my old boots. In the top middle drawer was a broken watch, a handful of old coins, some old photos, and four one-inch stainless steel ball bearings. I took out two and closed the drawer without making a sound.

It was already dark outside. I sat down at the dining room table and put the socks on, then the boots and the hoodie. Coffee sounded good, but if I made some it would wake up Delia, and then she'd insist on coming with me. I dug an old peacoat out of the closet and pulled it on, too. Then I cautiously peered out the front window through the blinds.

I didn't see any poorly disguised cop cars on the corner, but after the newspaper campaign I didn't want any of the neighbors to see me, either. The back fence again. I went back to the dining room table and picked up the keys to

Cheeks's ride and the remainder of the fat guy's smokes. Delia had put all the pimp cash into a clean paper bag and put it in the dining room bookcase, so I pulled it out and dug out a few hundred in assorted denominations and pocketed them as well, then put the bag back. I opened the back door very quietly and crept out through the laundry room into my backyard.

No spotlights hit me. The night air was cold and smelled like rain and grass. I let my eyes adjust to the darkness. My right eye was a little dim, but it seemed to be getting better. It was hard to tell. At least it was open again. I flexed my right hand and it didn't make any crunching sounds. I took a deep breath and nothing popped in my guts.

The fence was a little easier the second time. I went up to the corner and got into Cheeks's car. The steering wheel had a few flecks of dried blood on it, but it smelled like the lemon-shaped thing dangling from the rearview. I tore it off and tossed it out the window, then lit up a smoke and hit the gas.

Glisan to 39th, then over to Sandy, then a straight shot up to 82nd.

People were just getting off work and the streets were packed. For some reason it always makes me a little angry when I have to stop behind some snowboard dickhead's SUV sporting a GREEN OREGON or I VOTE SOLAR bumper sticker. It happened twice. It's true I was in a stolen Continental and I'd killed the owner, so I didn't dwell on it, but I was a little grumpy when I hit 82nd, a big, nasty slick of shit I normally avoided. I was thinking about Ralston, bombs, my face and my ass, the stupid car, the cops, and I don't know. I just felt wrong.

I trolled down 82nd from the deep end, just another fucked-up guy in a tricked-out ride, surfing for poon, one of hundreds. But I could feel the fuse burning in me. My right thumb was twapping away on the steering wheel. I took a deep breath and tried to settle down. When I lit another cigarette, I felt my heart beating in my swollen face. I thought about Delia and the cats, sleeping in the warm bed, and then I wondered if the cops were back in front of my house eating donuts and drinking coffee.

I spotted Monique and the Bismarck motel at the same time. Both had seen better days. I pulled into the parking lot of a bar about a block away, on the far side of a pickup. Monique would recognize Cheeks's ride and I didn't want to freak her out.

The Bismarck was a crappy one-story place with a lit-up vacancy sign. Monique was standing out front talking on her cell phone. A passing car full of kids honked at her and she flipped them off, so she wasn't working. I went around the back of the bar and cut across several parking lots and dumpster zones to the courtyard of the motel. There were a few plastic benches littered around between the doors to the rooms, some of them with bags of trash on them.

"Ambience," I said to myself.

I sat down on one of the benches and pulled up the collar of my coat, then lit a smoke. I was looking for a stringy white junkie in his forties. Unfortunately, that probably described half the people on 82nd, and at least half the residents of a shitbox like the Bismarck. So I did what I could. I smoked and I waited.

After about half an hour, a bald tweaker and a woman who looked like she was pregnant went into room 11. Not my guy. A little while after that a scabby-faced guy in a leather coat and pajama bottoms raced out of one of the rooms to the vending machines, got a Coke, and raced back. Not my guy. I was getting really cold after an hour and running low on the fat guy's cigarettes when a tall, lanky white guy wearing cowboy boots and sporting a greasy pompadour appeared, coming off the street down by the office. He was carrying a six-pack of Dr Pepper in one hand and a 40 of Old Colt in the other. Monique's dinner, as she liked to call it. He went into room 17, two doors down from where I was sitting.

Ralston had probably just scored. I waited through another cigarette. I didn't feel like fighting with him. I just wanted to beat the shit out of him and then talk to him. Then maybe beat on him a little more. Giving him enough time to shoot up and slow down was a good idea.

When I was done with the smoke I took the pair of socks out of my pocket and stuffed one inside the other, doubling them up. Then I dropped in the two ball bearings I taken out of my dresser. With one quick twist it spun neatly around my hand. My pinkie was still in pretty bad shape. Then I got up and went to the door. I rapped on it with my knuckles, the ones not wrapped in my favorite socks.

"Pizza," I called.

No answer. I rapped again.

"Pizza." Louder this time.

"Fuck off." Weak and distant, even sleepy.

"Got pizza. Half off."

"I said fuck off!"

I thought for a second.

"Clarence is going to butcher you."

Silence.

"Got a little information. You got some money, I mean." I let that dangle. The door opened and there was Ralston, gun in hand.

"Maybe you should come inside," he suggested quietly. "We could take a walk, but—" He gestured with the gun.

I cracked him across the back of the hand and the gun went down. Before he could swing I put my boot into his knee and then I was on him, pounding the shit out of him with my good left hand. It took about fifteen seconds for him to go limp. I kicked the door closed and turned back as he spat a little blood up onto his already bloody face and started to wail, so I kicked him one last time in the stomach. He stopped.

His gun was a flat black thing with a magazine, rather than a rolling device. I looked it over for some kind of safety and there it was. I clicked it around and pointed at his head.

"See, dude," I began, "I don't like guns. You had one and now you're all fucked up and I have it." I prodded him with one boot. "You listening?"

"Fuck you," he whined.

"Good! So here's the deal, slim. Your gun has this little clicky thing on it. I really want to talk to you about a couple things, but I'll be honest with you. I'm angry. Fury management issues. So let's play a game before we get to the question and answer part of the evening. I can't see all that well right now. Any idea why?"

He looked up at me. "Your eye is all fucked up."

"Good answer. And like I say, I don't know shit about guns. But the clicky thing, I'm betting it's the safety. Maybe it isn't. But I got it pointed at your head and I'm going to pull the trigger. Just can't make out the writing and I clicked it back and forth. So you have a fifty-fifty chance. How's that sound?"

"Fuckin' shitty," he whimpered, eyes wide.

"Fuckin' shitty is right. But when you blew up my tattoo shop, well, I'd rate my odds at about almost zero. So I'm being really fucking nice here."

Ralston's jaw dropped.

"You," he gasped.

"Me," I replied.

"Don't!" He sobbed. "Don't! I'll talk. Just don't."

I looked at the gun. I thought about it. Urine spread across Ralston's pants around the zipper and his right thigh and he covered his face.

"Shit, dude." I lowered the gun a little. "Why don't you get up and sit down in that chair. I was only kidding about the shooting you in the head thing. Plenty of crap I can blow off first."

"I think you broke my leg."

"No I didn't, you big fucking baby. But if I start stomping on your knees with these boots and shit . . . I'm getting sick of threatening you. Get the fuck up. Right now."

He peeled his hands away from his eyes and stared at me. "OK, just, shit. I'm a little shaky here."

"I'm sure. Now get in that chair."

"So." I sniffed the gun and looked at it. It smelled bad, like potato chips mixed with pencil shavings, and I still couldn't make out any of the code on it. Witnessing the act of someone smelling a gun had a bad effect on some people. A shudder went through Ralston and he made a toy dog whimper. I pointed it back at him.

"So," I began again. "You blew up my tattoo shop. I know you did. Who hired you?"

Ralston sagged in the chair he'd made it into. "Shit, I don't even know where to start."

"Start at the beginning."

"OK, OK. It was this dude named Cheddar Box. That's like a nickname. This kind of cracker out of the commissary in Deerburn. Fuckin' guy lived on 'em."

"Cheddar Box."

"Yeah." Ralston rubbed his oily scalp and his hand came away bloody, but not bad. His hand looked like it was swelling after the smack I'd given it with the sap. He looked at the whole mess and licked his lips.

"Dude," I prompted. "Still here. Cheddar Box."

He let out a big breath. "Yeah. Real name's Chet or something. Puerto Rican or Mexican or some shit. Anyway, I knew him when I was inside. He was in the pile. Dudes

72

lifted anything they could. Cheddar's a big fuckin' mother-fucker. They took all the weights out at some point, but this dude, he just lifted people. Pumped. Like a fuckin' Mexican Conan, but, I dunno, he sort of had class, if you see what I mean."

I made a spinning motion with the barrel of the gun.

"Yeah, so anyway. He gets out. I don't see him for a few years. Then I get out." He rubbed the top of his head again. "So, like, about twenty years ago I was in the army. I fucked with bombs. Not as stupid as I look. Anyway, one day Cheddar comes up to me in this little burger place down on 11th, you know the one?"

I rotated the gun again. He nodded.

"Yeah, so he's wearing this nice suit. Nice ride, too. Some big new Escalade type of thing. Told me he'd seen me through the window and wanted to chat."

"Bullshit," I said. Ralston let out a poof of breath.

"Same thing I thought. Cheddar knew where I was. Him talkin' to me? Right then? Shit, that night, I mean, shit. Didn't even have enough for a fuckin' toothpick after the fries I was eating. Ketchup can go a long way if you see what I'm saying, so yeah. I listened." He looked at the gun. "He'll probably kill me if I tell you the rest."

"I definitely will if you don't." I sniffed the gun again for effect.

"Figures. So Cheddar offers me some big dough to blow up that building. Sorry, dude, but I needed the money. Bad. So yeah, I took it. Got some C4 off these guys I know. Built a timer an' all that. See, that took me about a week, an' man, I started to get scared. I was living in the Jack

London downtown and Cheddar was coming by every day to sort of check on my progress." He scratched his chin with his clean hand.

"I kinda sorta got the feeling that Cheddar was gonna do something bad to me when I was done, like cut my head off. Tidy up the trail, that kind of thing. So I went to see Cheeks." Ralston shook his head.

"See, that's when shit really got all fucked up. Cheeks was my cellie for a couple years. That fuckin' nigger is scary and way fuckin' smart, too. Cheddar Box, well, he's not scared of a piece of shit like me, but Cheeks? Different story there.

"So Cheeks, he does what he does. Great big fucking faggot becomes my representative." He squinted at me. "See, same dudes that wanted you out of Old Town to build them yuppie loft spaces, they were hittin' Cheeks's string hard. Cop action down there is fierce on his end. They're cleaning those streets. Spotters calling every time a girl gets picked up." He shrugged. "Hard for a pimp to make a buck."

"Ralston, you're a fuckin' retard. But keep going."

"Yeah, so Cheeks represents. Next day when Cheddar comes around, Cheeks is waiting with me. Just like an old friend, lazin' around, watching TV. Cheddar, he wasn't happy."

Ralston stalled out. I knew why. He knew about the dumpster.

"Can I get a smoke?" he asked politely.

"Go for it. Do anything stupid and it's showtime."

"Sure, sure. You want one?"

"Got my own."

He got up and limped over to the dresser, shook a menthol out of the pack there, and fired it up with a match. After a couple of massive drags he sat down again and let the cigarette smolder between his yellow fingers. His eyes were hard then, like marbles.

"So Cheeks, he's going to upgrade. Start himself a real, like, bordello. That's like a whorehouse. Top string, fuckin' martinis and the whole nine yards. See, he's going with the flow. They want to upgrade the hood, he wants it, too. So there. Cheddar's workin' for some Russian dude named Turganov. Oleg Turganov. A real estate guy. I never met him, but Cheeks did, bunch of times. They had plans."

"Hmm."

I considered. Ralston puffed away.

"So Cheeks set you up out here? With Monique?"

"Yeah. Fuckin' bitch is crazy. Gives good head."

"Ah. I see. So we're almost done here, Ralston. Last question." I curled my fingers tight around the gun. "The last question is the hardest. If you don't answer, I have to shoot you, but it's the big one. Where is the fuckin' money you got to blow up my shop?"

Ralston took his fifty-fifty odds and came out of the chair as quick as a snake. I pulled the trigger and nothing happened. His big foot, all dressed up in a snakeskin cowboy boot, hit me right in the sternum.

I flopped back in the chair I'd been sitting in and he was on me, wrestling for his gun with both hands. My wrist was bending, so I snapped out and bit off his ear. I wrapped my legs up around his chest and scissored off his scream, then started pounding on his head. He let go of the gun and I used the butt of it to finish.

When Ralston stopped gripping me, I gave him a few more choice thumps and rolled him off me. He didn't make a sound. He was still breathing, but it was whistling in a bad sort of way.

"Well, fuck," I said. "Number two."

Every shitty motel has a big TV bolted to the wall. Every shit-ass with a pile of cash unscrewed the back of it and stored their crap inside. It took me about a minute to fish out a stack of bills, everything the bleeding junkie on the stained carpet had earned from taking so much from me. About twenty thousand, in hundreds. I turned him over and fished through his pockets. A hundred and eighty-three bucks. I took that, too.

The whole wad barely fit in my coat pockets. Twenty thousand in hundreds is roughly the dimension of a standard brick. I looked at the bloody gun I'd tossed onto the dresser and decided to take it. Ralston wouldn't need a gun for a few days, and I really had to look it over and find out how to make bullets come out of one of the damn things. I stuck it into the back pocket on my pants, hoping I wouldn't butt-dial and shoot myself in the ass.

Ralston didn't look like he'd be getting up anytime soon, if ever. Still, he'd been a little tougher than he looked. I pulled his boots off and he groaned. His feet smelled like a ripe, unlikely sort of foreign cheese.

"Well," I said. "Nice chatting."

He bubbled a little. Outside, the night air was below freezing. It still smelled like the boots I was carrying. I walked through the trash-littered courtyard of the Bismarck, tossed the boots over a fence into a weedy lot, and then I realized I'd left something. I'd left the cigarettes Ralston had been smoking. I only had one left.

When I came out of the dark lot behind the buildings, I looked back at the motel. Monique was still on her cell phone. It looked like she was crying.

I got into Cheeks's car and lit up the last smoke. Then I set it in the ashtray and rooted around in the burrito garbage I'd tossed on the passenger side floor the night before. I took two thousand bucks and stuffed it into a greasy paper bag, got out, and walked in her direction.

Monique didn't see me coming. I looked into the office. No one at the desk. I casually wandered over and stood next to her. She was yelling at someone, barking into the phone between sobs.

"The fuck, muthafucka, fuck you!"

That was how she spoke.

"Niggah-ahhh!"

That's how she cried.

I couldn't stand it anymore, so I bumped her with my elbow. She whirled on me, her face the very definition of fury. Then she drew back and snapped her phone closed.

"Darby?" She was suddenly out of wind. It was just a whisper over the wet tires on the street in front of us.

"Got a smoke?" I asked.

Her nostrils flared. "Fuck I don't, muthafucka!" Her wet eyes began to gush. "Fuckin' Cheeks's dead. Think that fat ass biggie C shot his ass." She sobbed, and for a second it looked like she was going to throw her cell phone. But she didn't. Instead she looked my face over.

"Thanks for the call," I said.

"Didn't do much good, looks like. You fuckin' deaf?"

"Nah. Well, a little."

"You—" She paused. She was pretty drunk, I realized. "What in the fuck you doin' in my face, white boy?"

"Hard to say."

"Yeah?" She had a little foam around the edges of her mouth.

"Yeah. Don't go back to the hotel room. I had to ask Ralston some questions and it didn't go too well."

She gave me her big stare. "He dead in there?"

I shrugged. "Maybe."

She hissed. "Damn fool. Cheeks set me up out here to keep an eye on his stupid ass. Nasty man had a stick on him. Fucked on me like some kinda pig thing." She glared at me, like it was my fault.

"Well," I said. "There you go."

"Yeah. Now Cheeks's dead, Ralston all laid up, and here your stupid ass is, throwin' change into a can for me to dig out. What the fuck I supposed to do now?'

"Go back where you came from," I suggested. "Or wherever. The feds are all over this. One of them has a brain."

We looked at each other. I handed her the burrito bag and she looked in, then looked at me.

"So you can run."

"Shit," she said quietly. "Right when I had this city by the balls, too."

"Yeah. Where you goin'?"

"Like I tell you, crazy burn." She stuffed the money in her big hooker purse and struck off into the rain. I watched her go, and it occurred to me that I would have something in common with that furious woman forever. We both had an X.

I walked back to Cheeks's car and thought about rain and bombs and how streets smell when they're wet. That was the last I ever saw of Monique. I never even knew her real name.

On the drive home, I tried to think about what I was going to tell Delia if she was still there. I had someone else's gun again. Someone else's money. A pissed-off whore was on her way to the bus station and our bomber was short a few teeth and possibly crippled or dead. I had a great big heel-shaped bruise forming in the middle of my chest and I was still driving a dead pimp's car. The night was young.

Portland glowed at night. It glowed because everything was wet. In the winter daylight everything was softly lit through the fat clouds, but at night, at night it shone with a countless number of colors, all made slightly more beautiful when blurred. The light from the streetlamps and signs and headlights make multi-hued streaks on every surface. Oily pavement, windows, cars . . . some things can be striking without even trying.

It was one of those evenings. As I wheeled on to Glisan, half-mesmerized by the city around me, I had to rein in my impulse to joyride. It was time to dump a few things. I pulled into a side street and motored around looking for a storm drain, one of the big ones. In a wet place like the Pacific NW, they weren't hard to find. Locating one without a streetlight over it was a different matter. I'd been lucky the night before. City planners set things up in a certain way, but even with a bad eye, I found one after a few minutes. I pulled up next to it and hurled the gun through the car window into the gutter mouth. It had a chunk of Ralston scalp clinging to the little accuracy fin at the tip of the barrel. A good thing to ditch, though I never did figure out how to fire it. Then I moved on. A few blocks further, I dug the socks with the ball bearings out of my other pocket. I rolled the window down and shook the balls out as I drove. About ten blocks later I chucked the socks into the gutter. I felt a little lighter with the gun down the drain. I realized I didn't even have a pocketknife at that point.

Of course, that's when the universe shits on you. I parked Cheeks's car eight blocks away from my place and walked through the light rain to the house behind mine. I felt like the fence was going to be easier this time as I came up on the place. Delia might even have made smoothies.

The window rolled down on a Prius parked on the street and Agent Dessel's head popped out. He gave me his boyish grin.

"Hey Darby," he called. "Hop in back. Let's go for a spin, shall we?"

"I'm thinking about a number between one and, oh, say, life," Dessel said pleasantly.

I was sitting in the back of the car. Agent Pressman snorted from the driver's seat. Dessel was turned around with his arm over the seat, smiling. He looked like a really big ten-year-old boy who had just gotten his first crack pipe.

"I'm thinking zero," I said. "I did your job for you. Found out who bombed my place."

Dessel gave Pressman a playful cuff on the shoulder.

"Did you hear that?" Dessel had a truly annoying laugh. "Darby Holland said he was thinking! I mean, shit, like as in stuff was going on in his head. Which sort of looks a little beaten up, by the way. But damn, wow. Thoughts. This is like watching alligator eggs hatch."

Pressman was driving slow and aimless. I guess they wanted to torment me a little before we all went downtown.

"So tell me, genius, what did you find out? Just out of curiosity."

"Guy who hired the bomber is named Turganov. He's a Russian real-estate guy."

Agent Dessel smacked the back of his seat.

"That's the sound of one hand clapping. I know you were wondering."

I thought about punching him. They hadn't handcuffed me. They hadn't even bothered to search me yet, which was good, considering all the cash I had stuffed in my pocket. But still, Dessel needed a nose job.

"I think I know what you're thinking," Dessel declared. "I bet you want to punch me. Damn, I'm good." He whacked the seat again.

"You still smoke?" I asked.

"Oh yeah. Sure." He lit up a generic and passed it back to me, still bubbling with joy. I took a big drag and blew it at him. He blinked and his smile got even bigger. Which was an amazing thing, sort of like watching someone stick their legs behind their head. A circus trick.

"Darby, I can call you Darby, right? Instead of Mr. Holland?" He went on without waiting for me to say no. "You're just about one stop down from most of the animals in the primate section of the zoo."

I took another drag.

"See"—Dessel cradled his chin—"I like the zoo. All those weird creatures locked up and on display. Exotic things from all over the world in little boxes. But I really like the primates. Know the difference between a monkey and an ape?"

I took another drag. "Monkey has a tail."

Agent Dessel laughed for almost a minute.

"Yeah!" He snorted. "My favorite joke, a time like this."

Agent Pressman turned another corner and crept along, in no hurry to get anywhere.

"So, I was getting to something," Dessel said. He cocked his head. "Know what it is? Man reads a *National*

Geographic, smart man like you, picks up my favorite joke, it's like we're the Smothers Brothers or Cheech and Chong. Like we've been doing this for years. If we're going to take our act on the road, you have to, like, intuit."

"You already knew this Turganov guy did it."

"Bingo!" Dessel shrieked. "Shit, I wish I had a trophy."

I rolled my window down and pitched the butt out into the street. Dessel lit up two more and handed me one. I took it.

"Best I can do, trophywise. Someone gave away the Pulitzer already this year. Bummer." He took a drag and blew it at me. "So, detective. Your face. The disappearing act. This whole Turganov-bombing thing. Just fill me in."

I shrugged. But now I knew two things. One, Ralston had really fessed up, and two, that Dessel was going to let me off. I might spend a few days in county, but he had something building. He had a conviction. And he wanted what I knew. So it was my turn to smile.

"Fuck you." My lips hurt. "Boy."

Dessel nodded, like I'd just complimented his clip-on tie.

"Yepper." He took about a one-inch drag off his ciga-rette. "I feel you, my primate. I wish I had a pinecone or something for you to play with. Just to see what you'd do with it. So I'm going to give you one. Because I, well, I'm the zookeeper. I think you know that now."

"You really love this." I gestured with my cigarette. "Driving around giving people weird talks about zoos and monkeys and listening to yourself."

Dessel's eyes glittered. "It's true, I do."

"Everybody has a hobby." I took another drag. Dessel did, too. His eyes were all over my face.

"Bob," Dessel said. "Pull over."

Agent Pressman hit up a slot in front of a church. Dessel guffawed.

"Yeah," he began, "I guess now that we're good friends, we get to play Ping-Pong and stuff like that. I'll call the baby dogs off. So that's over. You get to go and have the other side of your face worked on. Smile. That's how you want it."

"I wiped out on my skateboard. It was snowing."

"Wow. Weird. Anyway, be seeing you. Get out."

I got out and looked at the nearest street sign as the Prius pulled away. I was about thirty blocks from my house. I flipped them off, but who could say if they saw me. If they did, that little shit Dessel was probably laughing.

It was nice that they hadn't bothered to search me. But thirty blocks through the rain that had shifted from a freezing mist to full-blown frigid pissing made me start to think about Dessel's voice, and Pressman's chuckle. The shit about monkeys. I had a record with those two guys, and it was an ugly one. But they also had a record with me. Pressman was an idiot, but Dessel liked to dance. He liked to fish. He liked using guys like me as chum, the bloody crap you dump off the back of a charter boat to attract sharks. He had his patterns and I had mine. When he said we were getting to know each other, he was right.

I walked with my hands tucked into the pockets of the peacoat, my good hand wrapped around the brick of money. My hood was up and the rain was getting worse, but the drops beaded off the coat and I had a boot on each foot. It wasn't a bad night for a walk, but a hat of some kind might have been nice.

Delia's car was still parked out front when I got back. All the lights were on and the door opened as I came up the steps. There was Delia, all ninety pounds projecting a scowl. She crossed her arms.

"I thought it was cops again," she said. "What happened?"

"Went for a walk."

I sat down on one of the chairs on the porch and started unlacing my boots. She looked my face over when I glanced up at her.

"No new gashes or giant bruises. Maybe we can take the training wheels off your big-boy bicycle now. But before we get carried away, what the hell are you doing walking right up the front steps, and I mean seriously, did you forget about the police? That little problem?"

"Yeah, that. Well . . ." I tucked my wet boots under the chair. "Had a little happy time with Dessel and Pressman. Hunt's over. Except for my car. I still have to hunt that down."

"So you went downtown without a lawyer?" Delia tapped a finger on her arm.

"Nah. We just rode around in a car for a few minutes. They snagged me a block over."

"Let's towel off your messed-up head before you get pneumonia."

I followed her in. The house smelled like enchiladas were in the oven. I went to the dining room table and emptied my pockets. Delia's eyes widened at the brick of bills, so I answered her question before she asked.

"So, the bomber dude. This is what he got paid. At least what he had left. I gave a little to Monique."

"Is he, oh, I don't know, breathing?"

I took my coat off and hung it over the back of a chair.

"Last I saw he was."

"I made some dinner. Just cause I had to be here in case your stupid ass didn't make it back. I hate that canned sauce. Just a few anchos and some long Californias in water, a blender, little garlic and some soy sauce. It might even be good."

"It smells good."

I went into the bathroom and dried my hair off, then went into the bedroom and changed out of my wet clothes. Delia was in the kitchen clanking around, singing a personalized version of the Butthole Surfers' CIA song. So I knew she wanted me to talk about the money, Agent Dessel, pretty much all of it.

"Wash your hands," she called. "Dinner."

I went back into the bathroom and scrubbed up. When I looked at myself in the mirror, I realized the walk through the cold rain had done me some good. The swelling was down. The long freeze had made the scar more inflamed pink than angry red, and the blackness around my right eye had taken on a bluish quality.

Delia was setting out some plates. Three gigantic enchiladas with unknown contents and a pile of salad for me, one smaller enchilada for her with a little splash of spinach. I'm not a big man, but I eat big and I had some serious making up to do. She plunked a bottle of Tapatío in front of me when I sat down.

"Try to talk between swallows," she cautioned. "I don't want you spraying little chunks my way." She eyed the pile of money she'd swept over to the edge of the table.

I sliced off a big chunk of enchilada and shoveled it up. Zucchini, onion, chicken. The sauce was a dark, rich brown, vaguely sweet and smoky.

"Gmmf," I managed.

"Chew, Darby," she said as I dug in. "Considering your new look, it's amazing you even have teeth."

I swallowed.

"Never had a cavity," I replied. I took another bite, gave it a few chomps, swallowed. "Don't believe in 'em. Last time I went to the dentist I had to get a wisdom tooth taken out, though."

Delia picked at her salad.

"Why doesn't that surprise me?"

"Yeah. Guy said I had deep roots. He was really impressed." I started in on enchilada number two.

"So, this icky pile of money, Dessel, all that?"

"Mmn." I shrugged and swallowed. "Yeah. So I found the dude. Beat the fuck out of him, took all his money and his gal. Standard stuff."

"It's nice at least one of us found a new job."

"Just temp work." I kept eating. She kept picking. When I realized she not only was not going to say anything more, but that she was probably getting mad, I put my fork down. All that was left was a ribbon of sauce and a single spinach leaf.

"So here's what went down. I beat some info out of the bomber dude. Ralston, last name whatever. He had a sort of cool-looking gun, by the way. It's in the sewer now. Anyway, he tells me some fuckin' whack job named Cheddar Box hired him to do the deal. This Cheddar guy works for a real estate developer named Oleg Turganov." I looked at her plate. "You going to eat that?"

She pushed her plate over. I ground off a corner of enchilada and chewed a few times. Delia did her finger-tapping bit.

"So." I swallowed. "Came home, I was about to go over the back fence when that wicked little fucker Dessel busted me. Creepy little bastard gave me this lecture about monkeys. All very weird. But it turns out they already knew who bombed the shop. I mean, not the bomber, just who hired him."

Delia reached out and plucked a single leaf of spinach off her plate and popped it in her mouth. She munched on it meditatively while she watched me eat. When I was done she smiled.

"So, Darby, ever wonder how you can fart without peeing?"

"All the time."

"Good. Know how a girl does it?"

"No idea."

"Yeah." She shook a couple of cigarettes out of a fresh pack and passed me one. "It's because you never asked."

I fired up the smoke and leaned back.

"I get it. You're saying I should have asked Dessel a few more questions."

"Just a thought."

"Funny. He talked about thinking, too. Then he talked about the zoo, and now you're talking about chicksplosions and pee. What the fuck? I mean seriously."

She picked up the empty plates and stomped into the kitchen. I heard the water run for a minute and then the clatter of the plates hitting the rack. She came out wiping her hands on a new dish towel.

"So I'm out of here," she said. "My dildo is getting jealous."

She was referring to Hank, her current boyfriend and the singer in a punk band called Empire of Shit.

"Might call Nigel and Big Mike," she continued, "but of course you'll need to, oh, you know, get a phone. Their numbers are on the fridge. So's mine."

"Right. Phone."

"Going to need to do some thinking."

"Right. Fart pee monkey action."

Delia pulled her jacket on and gave me a long stare.

"The boys are going to want to know about stuff like their employment future. I was kind of wondering about the same thing. I mean, you have your little side gig, but the rest of us . . ."

I gave her back my own hard stare. It probably looked pretty good with the new scar and whatnot.

"I do have a plan," I said. "I just need to figure out exactly what it is. You need some dough? It's bloody and kinda sticky, but—"

Delia left.

I was a little tired after beating and robbing Ralston, walking thirty blocks through the rain after an interrogation, and then eating four enchiladas, but I couldn't sleep. Instead, I took a long shower and when I got out, I wiped the mist off the cabinet mirror and looked at the new heel-shaped bruise forming on my sternum. Just when the rest of them were turning yellow or blue, I'd gotten a nice new purple one.

The phone thing was at crisis level. Again. I didn't have a landline, so I might as well have been in the hinterlands of Nepal. If I wanted to operate, I needed a few new things and I needed to get rid of some other new things. So I put on some clean clothes and headed back to the dead pimp's car I'd left eight blocks away. It was the best I could do in the way of getting my shit together.

There was a Circle K twenty blocks down with disposable cells. Keeping track of the devices was getting to be a problem. It struck me as a good idea to paint my name on the new one in toenail polish. I was entering an idea frame of mind.

Cheeks's car was where I'd left it. I got in and started the engine. The rich mélange of cologne, hooker-grade perfume, burritos, and cigars was a little overpowering. It was my last night in the thing. I'd ditch it after I wiped it down and then get my car out of whatever impound lot it had been renting space in. I had a few customers who could chop the pimp ride up and have it spread all over the West Coast in about a day, but their numbers had been lost in the explosion. Too bad.

I pulled into the Circle K and went in. I'd bought cigarettes and beer there for years, but the pasty woman behind the counter, Nancy by her name tag, didn't even recognize me. I plucked a phone and a card out of the rack and slipped them through the slot in her cage so she could scan them.

"Pack of smokes, too," I said. "The yellow ones." I had a nasty wad of Cheeks's slightly moist and bloody money in my pocket. I peeled out a hundred dollar bill and plunked it into the tray. She picked it up with her fingernails and looked at it. Then she looked at me.

"I hate this fucking job."

"Yeah," I replied. "Still, it's still better than, oh . . ." I thought for a second and shrugged.

She stuffed my change through the slot and got to work on her hands with a handy wipe. I gathered up all my new crap and went out to the pimpmobile. The bright lights of the place had done something to my right pupil, and having the eyes of a deluxe menu clerk at a dump of a convenience store skitter over my face and then complain about my money somehow made me a tiny bit concerned about my dating future. My new look and the quality of my cash didn't even impress Nancy. I wished I could kill Cheeks one more time.

It was raining again, but just little wintry droplets. I dug the phone out of its plastic package, slotted the card, and then got back out and filled up the garbage can with the new trash and the burrito mess from the night before. The clerk watched me through the window with a dead expression, utterly bored. It made me feel a little better. I might be a beat-on looking guy, but at least I enjoyed my new profession. Having a demoralizing job gave you the face of the zombie in that window, watching me ferry crap through the rain. My job had given me a new face entirely.

I drove the pimpmobile around the wet streets, smoking and pondering my new face. It didn't seem like anyone was following me, which was good, but it was hard to tell with the whole right eye issue. I wanted to call Nigel and Big Mike, but I didn't at the same time. The other two guys had probably left forever. I couldn't even remember their names. But Nigel and Big Mike, they would be waiting.

It was time, however, to ditch the car. I drove up to 39th and Belmont and got a big bottle of Windex and a two-dollar T-shirt at Walgreens. I drove the car around the corner into the parking lot of a church with tow warnings all over the lot and used Windex and the shirt to wipe out all of my prints. I'd left some blood behind, so I considered torching the thing when I was done, but it seemed excessive. I nuked the driver's seat with the Windex and kicked the door closed.

Walking around at night with a bottle of Windex in one hand and a wet shirt in the other is never a good cover. I wondered where I would be without sewer grates. At the next one, I chucked the bottle and stuffed the shirt in behind it. At the next block down, I held up the keys to Cheeks's car. There were six of them on the ring. I wondered what the other five were to for a moment before I under-handed the wad of metal into the sewer. Another mystery unsolved, but a little more shit down the drain.

It's weird, the things you think about at that time of night, especially if you can't see too well. I thought about paper. I thought a little about bugs. My mind drifted over some abstract notions about the merits of certain kinds of pies. The list of shit I had to do never seemed to shrink. I ducked a little further into my coat and stared out at the dark, blurry world and tried to direct my rambling brain in some direction. I needed to get my car. I had to call my former employees. I needed to start up a new shop. I had to stash all my greasy new cash and get rid of those bloody golf clothes.

But mostly I really needed to fuck up the Russian dude.

When I woke up, I took a shower, then smeared triple antibiotic ointment on my face and my ass. There was a good song in there somewhere. Johnny Cash was gone, but Empire of Shit might be in the market for new material.

After I got dressed, I went into the dining room and looked at the pull-up bar I'd installed a few years ago in the doorway to my little home office. I used to do a hundred a day. I gripped it and got through twenty before my right hand started to hurt and my ribs stiffened up. Still, I felt better. Sometimes it was all about trying to convince myself that it wasn't this year that I stopped bouncing back, that it wasn't this time I discovered the cigarettes had ruined my lungs and the booze had ripped my guts up beyond repair, that it wasn't this week that I would slow in my long running with the wolves and suddenly become food. Sometimes.

I ate the cold leftovers of Delia's enchiladas in the cold, quiet house and considered. The first order of business was to get my car. Second, call Nigel and Big Mike. Third, visit my landlord Dmitri. That was going to be a bummer, but it had to be done. Then I had to book an appointment to see the Russian dude. I'd learned in the last few months that if you really wanted to fuck with the wealthy and powerful, you generally had to check in with their secretary first, just to make sure they had the time.

When I finished washing the dishes, I stared out the kitchen window for a minute before I plucked the note Delia had left on the fridge with everyone's cell phone numbers and sat down at the table. Nigel was first.

"'Sup," he answered.

"It's me. Darby."

There was a pause. In the background I could hear the clink of glasses and a droning sound, like a vacuum cleaner. He was probably at his favorite bar.

"Oh hey, dude." Just like I'd talked to him yesterday. Nigel was one of the most purely sinister men I'd ever met. It was nine a.m. and he was probably wearing a tailored Italian suit and drinking something foreign and awful out of a strange-looking glass.

"So," he continued. "Big bomb. You disappeared. The cops. Also, my job." He yawned.

"Right. Got beat up. Spent some time healing at a resort spa. The cop thing looks OK for now, but that's strictly temporary. I'm getting to work on a new setup for the Lucky in the next few days or so. Got a few things to tidy up first."

"Right on," he said. "Right on."

We listened to each other's background noise. He spoke first.

"Good to hear from you, boss. Delia says your face got fucked up. You just let me know about that. And let's get back to work."

More silence.

"I got you," I said eventually. "Thanks, bro."

"Anytime."

Next up was Big Mike. He picked up on the first ring.

"This better be you!" he barked.

"It's me."

Pause. "Darby?"

"Yeah. Who were you expecting?"

"Karen didn't come home last night. So, uh, what's up? Delia told me you got all mangled and shit. And the cops, man . . ." He trailed off. "Should you be calling me?"

"Don't worry. The mangling is going away, and so are the cops. Both may be temporary situations."

"Oh."

"Yep."

Big Mike had constant problems with women. He gravitated toward abusive, needy types, and had the same awful experiences with them time and again. It was the subject of many of our discussions. I was in no mood to be his therapist at the moment, but it was oddly reassuring that nothing had changed for him.

"So, Karen," I prompted.

"Yeah. Big fight. She threw a beer on me and I freaked out. Then she was dancing with this other dude, way too close and grindy. Long story. Plus she made me buy new curtains, and I'm currently unemployed."

"Shitty."

"Yeah. So, um, good to hear from you, boss. I was afraid you were dead or something. We all were. I'm kind of wondering when we get back to work. I mean, no pressure, I got some money saved up, but shit. You know, the future and all that."

"No worries." I tried to sound convincing. "We'll be back up and running soon. I got a few plans in action."

Big Mike blew out a sigh of relief. "That's really good news. I don't think this whole thing with Karen, I mean my being home all the time, I just dunno."

"I understand."

"Oh!" I heard a rustling as he sat up from wherever he was reclining. "I sort of did something. I went down to the Lucky a week or two ago and I broke in, you know, past the police tape. I went under it."

"OK."

"Yeah. I was looking for my shit. People had been in there stealing everything. I got one of your machines and most of the flash. Been drying everything out at my place here. Shit's kind of moldy and water-damaged, but we may be able to use some of it."

It was my turn to sigh. One tattoo machine and some warped, damaged, moldy art that was on the bad side to begin with. The best possible material to start a new business with.

"How's the place look?" I asked.

Big Mike cleared his throat. He was the sort of man who got emotional.

"Pretty much fucked. I mean, the walls are still there. Mostly. The mini mart is completely toast. Gomez's place, well, lot of water damage. Broken glass everywhere. The Lucky is . . . Ah, shit." He stopped talking.

"Well, I'll have good news soon, dude," I said quickly. "Just try not to think about it. We needed to remodel anyway."

Big Mike coughed.

"So, like where we goin', man?"

"I'm exploring a few options." I felt like shit lying to him, but sometimes lying was the right thing to do. "This is one of those times when, I dunno, we have a chance to upgrade. Stay in step with the bigger game. Some business guys were telling me about it yesterday. We were golfing, if you can believe it."

"Hm. Sounds good to me. Fucking slow season anyway."

"Yeah."

"Yeah."

"So you want me to do anything? I mean, you know . . ."

"I might," I replied. "Let's see how everything shakes out in the next few days."

"OK." He coughed again. "Darby, I was sure worried about you. Even Nigel went looking. Delia almost lost her mind, man. This is your new number?"

"You got it."

"Cool. Call me if you're going to lose your phone again. If you see what I mean."

My right eye pulsed. "I see what you mean, bro. I'll get back to you in a day or so."

"Your car is in an impound lot out by Holgate. Take about eight bills to get it out. Is this your new number?" Delia was chewing something, probably gum. She didn't eat very much.

"Just until I lose the phone. How'd you find my car?"

"Well, they have these things called tow truck companies. They in turn have these people who work on these tricky fucking things called computers. It's all very complicated."

I laughed, but not so she could hear me. It made my face hurt.

"So you call Nigel and Mikey?"

"Just now," I replied.

"Good. Since I don't have a job right now, I might be able to find the time to give you a lift out there."

"You know, that'd be great."

"You eat the rest of those enchiladas?"

"I did."

"Good. Skinny whipped-on dog. How's your butt feel?"

"Same as my face. Funny you should ask. I was thinking about a song your pet dildo might want to write along those lines."

"Those creative juices. I left this mega jar of hippie vitamins in your bathroom, plus a bottle of Percodans. Take two of the big vitamins a day, one right now and one before you go to sleep. And go easy on the pills. They go good with booze right up to this barfy point, which sort of sneaks up on you. I'll come get you in an hour or so. I have to find my bra."

"Ha ha."

"Up yours." She hung up.

14

Delia pulled up in her restored fire-engine-red Ford Falcon an hour later. The custom exhaust made it sound like a helicopter was landing. I was on my porch in one of the wooden chairs, smoking, wearing my damp peacoat, a wad of the worst of the nasty money in my pocket. I'd vengefully pulled all the most ruined, wet, bloody, snot-crusted, toilet-water-stained, hooker-crotch bills out of my new collection. A tow truck lot was the most ethically satisfying place to cash them in.

It wasn't raining, but the sky was dark and heavy and a steady wind was blowing. I went down the stairs and climbed into Delia's car. It was warm inside and smelled like vintage car heater, hair spray, bubble gum, and whatever perfume concoction she'd dumped all over herself that morning. Angel food cake mixed with cookies.

"Seatbelt," she said. "Got enough messy shit going on with your face without making it worse."

I gave her the once-over and she stared back, her face set in a pre-pout. She was wearing a lime-green sweater that hugged her birdlike frame like a second skin, a rabbit fur vest, and weirdly rubbery gray leather pants that terminated in her favorite gratified combat boots. Almost conservative.

"No fashion tips, golf boy." She hit the gas.

"Did I say anything?" I fumbled with the seat belt.

"No, but I know that look, even with your new face."

"You might actually be the worst telepath ever born, Delia. I was actually thinking about your perfume. It reminds me of dog shampoo and semen."

"Special blend. Goes with the vest."

"Fabu."

We drove in silence for a while, Delia smacking her gum, me staring out the window with one eye closed.

"So how'd it go with Nigel and Mikey?" she asked casually.

"Good, I guess. They both want to know when the Lucky is going to be back up. They want to help."

"Ah." She fished a cigarette out of the pack on the dash and passed it to me to light for her. "That's good. Everybody is ready to be pointed at something."

I lit the smoke with Cheeks's Zippo, took a drag, and passed it over.

"Yeah. Just have to figure out where to shoot."

"This Russian guy you were talking about seems like a good target. Unless you think that's exactly what Pressman and Dessel want you to do."

"My instincts tell me that they still want to hang me for something, plus Dessel actually told me as much, so . . ."

"You have done your share of fucking up."

"Yeah." I looked out of my left eye at the passing city.

"So," she continued, "I have an idea."

That didn't surprise me.

"Good thing someone does. Let's hear it."

Delia took a drag and paused to collect her thoughts. It took the little genius monkey about a minute.

"Have you been down to look at the Lucky?"

"Nope. Big Mike said he snuck in there and got some of our stuff out."

"Huh. Well, I've been down there a few times. The building is pretty wrecked, but it's mostly just the roof and all the furniture. So here's my idea." She paused for dramatic effect.

"Go ahead," I prompted.

"I say you buy the place."

I let the idea tumble around in my head like a marble in a kaleidoscope, turning it this way and that, looking at random outcomes. Delia continued.

"Bargain price. A half-gutted shithole. But think, Darby. We have all those contractors in our customer pool. We can trade for part of the work. All the backup equipment you have in your storage space? The shit you've been hoarding? You also have all those clever yuppies you tattoo, with jobs like mortgage broker and real estate agent. One plus one equals three here, man. Do the math."

Our landlord Dmitri had been steadily losing his mind for years. It was entirely possible that he might be receptive to the idea of selling me a building that had just been blown up, even though he probably thought I was the one who'd done it. In that light, it was also possible that he might try to shoot or stab me on sight. Dmitri owned two buildings in Old Town, one "mitri's izza," the other the shell that had once housed a Korean convenience store, the Lucky Supreme Tattoo, and the Rooster Rocket. He also owned a dilapidated four-story tenement down the street, where he ran a pizza operation with toppings like rat droppings and roach eggs. The city had been pressuring him to move on for two years. Dmitri was the fragile sort of trust fund kid who had aged disgracefully into a depressed, bored weirdo, and then he'd rolled with it all the way through to morbid freakazoid. I'd been trying not to think about him, and now that I was, I caught a whiff of some kind of pattern resolving in the ether of possibility.

It was possible that Dmitri had put the place up for sale and the prospective buyer had decided to lower the price.

It was conceivable that the constant pressure the city had been putting on him to renovate or move had driven him into a nutty decision to partner up with people he never should have met.

It didn't strike me as unthinkable that Dmitri might have placed me in a situation where my options were death, prison, or the new scars I had. Then again, I had to consider that the batty fucking lunatic was just as lost as ever and didn't have a clue.

"You still in there?" Delia asked.

I took a cigarette out of the pack in my coat and fired it up.

"Yeah. I was just thinking about how nice it was going to be to see Dmitri again."

Delia cackled and almost choked on the wad of gum in her mouth.

"And you tell me I'm a crappy telepath," she managed.

"Yeah, yeah. I know you're big on swallowing, but keep it down over there."

She snorted. Delia could make a powerful snort for a woman with such a small nose. I was often struck by her similarity to a nuclear device—not too big as far as bombs go, but next-level potent.

"I actually don't have any idea what to say," I confessed. "That's either the best idea ever, or the absolute worst. It isn't anywhere in between."

"Don't think too hard. Your bad eye might pop out if you squeeze your brain. Plus, I've already done most of your thinking for you. If you're going to go fuck with Dmitri and this Russian guy, might as well get something out of it other than stitches."

"Hey," I protested, "I got two guns so far, a car, a shit-load of cash . . . I was even up four burritos at one point."

"Uh-huh. You already lost the car and the guns and you have new cop problems and the face transplant I keep harping on."

We pulled up in front of the impound lot. I could see my car. It looked dirty and lonesome, even older.

"There's just no winning with you, is there?" I yanked at my seatbelt. The attendant in the little booth by the gate watched us with the same expression as the gal at the convenience store. I realized in a flash that it was probably the exact same expression as the photo on his driver's license.

Delia gave me an exasperated sigh.

"'Course not. I'll wait until you drive out, just in case you need help dealing with the retard in that little booth."

I nodded and got out. The guy in the booth stared as I approached. He didn't say anything when I stopped in front of the window, just glowered at me, prepared for the rudeness he was accustomed to. I smiled. He looked wary.

"Hey," I began. "That maroon BMW wagon over there is mine."

He sat forward and picked up his metal clipboard, looked out at my car and then back at me.

"License and proof of insurance?" He was hostile, but in a controlled way. I pulled out my crusty wallet and peeled out my license and my insurance card and passed them through the security slot. He scowled down at them and punched some numbers into his computer, then pushed the tray back, all without touching them.

"Seven hundred and ninety-seven dollars," he reported. He squinted at me, prepared for an explosion. Instead I nodded and pulled an even grand out of my pocket. I peeled off eight truly disgusting bills and slapped the bills in the tray, scooped out my card and ID, and pushed the tray back toward him. He looked at the money.

"Jesus," he whined. "What in the fuck. That ain't money. I need exact change anyway."

"Keep it," I said. "You got anything for me to sign?"

"No," he replied. "And I mean no, as in I can't take this money. You tampered with it. That's illegal." He folded his arms. I pointed up at his security camera.

"It's illegal for you not to take the money, dumbass. Open the gate and we won't have a problem."

He gave me his hardest look and I had to smile. He hit the gate buzzer and the chain-link fence rolled open. I winked at him and walked across the muddy lot to my car.

I gave the inside a quick once-over after the cold engine finally turned over. Whoever had stolen all my CDs had muddy feet, but that was about it. I drove out the gate and flipped the guy off as I passed. He shyly returned the gesture. I pulled to a stop next to Delia and rolled my window down. She cranked hers down as well.

"I bet those fuckwads stole your Doobie Brothers CDs, didn't they?" She was grinning.

"Cleaned me out. Even the bad ones. Three Dog Night, too. My fuckin' Creedence. Least they had taste."

"Lame."

"I think I'm going to get drunk tonight. What are you doing?"

"Empire of Shit is rocking the Equinox. I told the dildo I'd be there." They'd been going out for two months by then, a record for Delia.

"OK. I'll call you tomorrow."

"Don't lose my number."

I tapped the good side of my head with my good hand.

"I memorized it. Like, really."

Her smile went from grin to sweet. "And here I was wondering if you had brain damage. A whole phone number."

"Later."

She smacked her gum, once.

Getting drunk in Portland is as easy as falling down a staircase. There were more strip clubs per capita than any other city in the world, but the day I had to pay to see a naked woman was the day I blew my brains out, so those were never on the menu. That left a wide spectrum of old man dives, theme taverns, and garden-variety hell pits. The trick, of course, was to pick the place that matched your mood, and that was an art in and of itself, but the city was very accommodating in that way. There was something for every occasion.

I stopped on the way home at one of my favorite Mexican drive-thru operations, a place called Beanco, built into the shell of a retired Kentucky Fried Chicken. Portland was filled with those kinds of operations. There was actually a Taco Bell right next to it, with a long line of sorry people on their cell phones, waiting in their cars for their usual, oblivious. I zipped through the no-wait at Beanco and got a jumbo al pastor burrito, four rellenos, and a double side of refried beans with lard and four pickled jalapeños, then drove home and parked my car for the night. There was no reason to drive later, considering the variety of bars close to home and my ever-decaying popularity with the police.

When I opened the door, the cats rampaged in without so much as a hello and went straight to their food bowl. I sat down at the dining room table and unwrapped all the Beanco goodies. When the cats were done, they came out and watched as I made my way through all of it, even the rellenos I'd been planning to save for later, plus all four jalapeños. I knew from experience that they wouldn't eat Mexican food, but they liked watching me do it. When I was done, I threw all the wrappers away and wiped off the table with one of Delia's new dishrags, then lay down on the couch, too full for the moment to move. It was early yet for Operation Drunk as Possible, and I was tired anyway. I closed my eyes and almost immediately I was out, way down deep in a dreamless place.

When I woke up I was hungry again. I dug my new cell phone out and looked at the time. It was a little after eight and I'd missed two calls from Delia. I'd slept for six hours. I got up and stretched, and I wished I'd taken my boots off. After I brushed my teeth and gently washed my face, smeared some ointment around, I studied myself in the bathroom mirror, my eyes tracing the details of my new scar. My purpose became as clear and strong as a hurricane wind. I needed to have fun. I needed to get laid. I need to wash a ton of bad, clingy crap out of my mind, to howl and maybe even dance. I need to feel free, even for just one night. I needed a goddamned break and I was taking one. Not tequila, not vodka, certainly not wine or anything with an umbrella. It was whiskey night. Even the weather was in line.

The Fart Club, as it was affectionately known, was the skanky greasehole second home of union skinheads, creepy chicks with a big dick in their thought bubble, and trolling art-school hipsters brave or stupid enough to make a run at the place. The owner was a washed-out skinhead drunk and possibly one of the shittiest humans ever to walk the earth, so it was the perfect match for my mood—a soup of bristle and horny chaos, garnished with madness and the type of gaiety born from desperation. Plus I knew all the bartenders, since I'm the steady sort as far as moods go.

The bartender that night was a pear-shaped little monster with bad teeth named Daisy. We never got along too well because I'd beaten up a guy who I didn't know was her boyfriend a few years back and she sold shitty diarrhea coke to the hipsters, which I considered low and mentioned one too many times. A steady stream of generous tips had helped ease the tension to the point where she almost smiled sometimes, which was a step up from the way she treated most everyone else. The place was only half full as I took a seat at the bar and nodded at her. She didn't even recognize me.

"Whatcha want," she snapped.

"The usual. Jameson's rocks and a beer back."

She squinted at me and nodded. When she plunked the drinks down in front of me she gave me her brown and yellow half grin. I slid a relatively clean ten across the counter.

"You change your hair or something?" She actually seemed concerned. Maybe we were turning a corner.

"Nah. Just a little monkeying around with my head in general. Why? Do you think I need a haircut?"

She shrugged and slid the ten back.

"On the house."

It really was a first, so I slid the bill back.

"Buy yourself a diamond."

She flashed me the full grin and pocketed the bill. Daisy didn't let me pay for another drink all night, which is how I got so impossibly wasted at a time when I should have been holding my shit together a little better than I did. Blowing off steam is one thing, but the booze animal wriggled out of my grasp once again, and true to form, the unusual happened.

I was into my third round in less than an hour and the bar was packed when I noticed the woman sitting next to me. She was pretty, in a sunburned, ski-bum-chick kind of way, with short brown hair and high, wind-blasted cheekbones. I used to be pretty good at picking up women in bars, or even being picked up by them, but that was before the modifications Cheeks made. I was suddenly terrified to have an attractive woman sitting next to me. My mouth went dry, and my hands got cold and clammy. She glanced over at me and my right pupil pulsed.

"Cool scar," she said immediately. "You get that on the mountain?"

"Nope. Golf."

She laughed, a high, clean sound, and like a miracle the tension left me. I took a sip of Jameson's.

"I love golf," she said. "It's too bad I'm terrible at every part of it."

"Me too. I have a good swing, but that's about it."

"I like to board." She fiddled with her drink, something brown. With her free hand she touched one of her cheekbones. "Hence the sunburn. Looks like we both have sports-related injuries, although I think you win."

"Yeah, I do. But yours looks pretty good."

She smiled at that, but there was no way to tell if she blushed. She did do the equivalent with her eyelashes.

"Why, thank you."

"So, uh." I'd never been this awkward. "My name's Darby."

"Suzanne," she replied. She stuck her hand out. Her fingers were incredibly long and chapped, the nails short and plain. We shook and she almost broke the tender bones in my right hand.

"Pinkie," I gasped.

"Oh. Sorry."

I took another sip of Jameson's. She downed her shot and waved at Daisy, who ignored her.

"This place is packed," she commented. "Getting loud, too. Nice to meet you, Darby."

"There's a little wine place next door," I offered. "They have beer, too."

She smiled ruefully down into her empty glass and at that instant Daisy appeared with a bottle of Cuervo and refilled it.

"This one's on Darby," she said. She glanced at my half-full tumbler and topped it off with some Jameson's. It was the beer backs that were doing me in. Daisy helpfully plunked a fresh one down in front of me.

"Guess we'll stay for a while," Suzanne said.

"Looks like it," I replied. I took a slug of whiskey, a real mouthful, and the level in my glass didn't change. Daisy was pouring with mystic power.

"Three days on Mt. Hood," Suzanne said, cradling her shot glass in her long hand. "The shots up there were hell of

expensive, but I have to say, conditions were sooooo good."
She glanced at me. "You board?"

I shook my head. "Nah. I ski, though. I fell down so many times learning how I didn't want to go through the whole thing again."

"Skateboard?" She seemed genuinely curious.

"Like a motherfucker," I said proudly. "I even collect 'em."

"You should be able to pick it up with a decent teacher, and hey, it might even spare you another golf injury."

I had to laugh. She laughed at my laughing.

"So what else do you collect?" she asked. I shrugged.

"Fossils, meteorites, cats, books, figurines. Antiques. Art crap."

She put one hand under her jaw with her elbow on the bar, angling herself at me. Her brown eyes played over my scar.

"I wonder," she said pensively, her voice almost lost in the crowd, "what a man who collects stuff like that does for a living."

"I'm sort of on hiatus. But usually I'm an artist."

I didn't like her looking at my scar. She could sense it, maybe read it in the rest of my face.

"Stand up," she said.

I slid off my barstool. Suzanne got off hers, and I understood the pensive smile when I had suggested we go next door to the wine place. I'm five eight and I used to be a hard one-eighty. I was getting it back. Suzanne was around six foot five, maybe taller, and lean as a whip. I looked up into her beautiful face and even with one and a half eyes I could see the same fear and doubt I was feeling.

"Wow," I said. "You know, I've always had this thing."

"What thing." It wasn't a question. She folded her arms. They were corded with muscles and tendons and veins.

"This thing for outdoorsy athletic women," I went on truthfully. "I'm sorry if I just squirted saliva on you. I swear it was involuntary. Like a sneeze."

Her face lit up. "Still feel like hitting that other place? The quiet one? Talk about meteorites and fossils?"

I held my arm out and she took it. And that was how I met Suzanne.

I woke up around five a.m. with the kind of hangover that isn't easy to describe. For a few minutes I didn't know where I was, but since I couldn't really move, it gave me time to piece it together. Jumbled images of the night before skittered through my aching head, like brief flashes caught in the headlights of a speeding vehicle on a bumpy road at midnight. Talking to a tall, tall woman I really liked. Lots of unfortunately varied booze. Gnarly, passionate sex. I looked over next to me and there was Suzanne, asleep on her stomach and naked, snoring, with a condom I had evidently left unceremoniously draped over one rock-hard ass cheek. I think I let out a small whimper then, maybe a low sort of moan. Then I peeled a second condom off my stomach and got up. My neck felt like my head had been twisted around a few times, my lower back was numb in some places and sparking electrical current in others, my crotch felt bruised, and my right eye was swollen shut again.

In the bathroom, I used her toothbrush after I flushed the condoms and considered a shower for a solid five minutes, leaning over the sink and waiting to see if I puked. I couldn't remember how, but we'd torn the shower curtain off. First big idea of the day, shot down. So I looked at the drain in the sink for a few more minutes.

When I was done with that, I went off in search of my clothes. I found a sock in her living room and one of my boots nearby. The other boot was all the way back under the shower curtain, but no sock. My shirt was by the bed, my pants next to hers in the kitchen.

No underwear, mine or hers, was ever found.

I put on the remains of my clothes, tracked my peacoat down to its hiding place behind the couch, then found a pen and an envelope in the kitchen, which I used to write the lamest, most incoherent, poorly-thought-out love letter in the history of humanity.

"Dear Suzanne (sp?),

I super dig you. Don't know my phone number. Used your toothbrush. That's why it's wet. So come over to my place."

I wrote down my address. The writing was more than a little shaky, bordering on scribble. I included my name as an afterthought, and then the dim realization that an intelligent woman might actually read the papers and thus be aware of my recent spat with the police swam to the surface, so I crossed out my last name.

"Shit," I said. But I left the note.

The rainy walk home brought the situation into greater focus. I paused under a big tree and lit the first cigarette of the day and savored a few drags, staring in meditation into the predawn darkness. The rain felt good on my face and my scalp. The cold wind was fine on my knuckles. I was slowly coming back to life, which I had a bad feeling was going to come in handy in the immediate future. I kept walking, my thoughts skittering with dyslexic hangover dementia.

I'd finally met a woman I really liked, at the lowest point in my adult life. And I did like her. Everything about her. She had nothing in common with the usual string of needy players and flat-out horndogs taking a break from the naked parade machine, the thirtysomethings who wanted a baby without the love, the hard professionals who wanted a taste of madness to wash away all the stale. She was into rock climbing and snowboarding and travel in general. She liked to cook, as I did. She worked as a law librarian and a freelance travel writer. I'd always had an embarrassing fondness for nerdy chicks with an outdoorsy flair, but I hadn't had a serious relationship in more than five years, and that had been an awful torture session with a severe woman who flew helicopters for the forest service and had an all-woman feminist speed metal band called the Captains of Industry. The thought of her made my skin crawl. Delia had almost killed her toward the end, and had finally decided to give me the silent treatment until I either broke it off or allowed her to run the woman over.

It was true that Suzanne was a foot taller than me, but damn did she have nice legs. I pictured her in a black dress, lean and powerful, walking into a restaurant to meet me for dinner, and my mouth watered. It would make me feel good to be with her in public. I knew most of the men she had ever been with had some sort of masculinity issue with being seen trotting around with a woman like that, but I felt just the opposite. Deep down, I would have loved to be seen with her on my arm. It appealed to my impossible vanity, for one thing. To be measured as something equal to such a rare creature, to be her companion. Also, a woman like that was tough as nails. She would keep up, just like she had last night. For the first time in my life, the shoe might actually be on the other foot. I might have trouble keeping up with her. Still, to dream of all those lonesome dreams of corny romance I'd all but given up on . . . to see the rhododendron valleys of Nepal, to skirt the edge of the Sahara desert at dawn, to play some kind of idiot flute on the Great Wall of China, that kind of thing. She would like that. It sure as hell beat my current sense of romance, which was pretty much getting drunk in a crappy bar and washing my dick in the sink in the morning. I shook my head. Suzanne was dreamy.

I, on the other hand, was unemployed, in trouble with the police, recently disfigured, and about to mount an assault on a Russian real estate developer who had a body-guard named Cheddar Box. I'd also been robbing people lately, though a case could be made that they all deserved it. I didn't get the feeling she would buy it. The timing was almost comically bad, and I would have laughed if it had been Nigel or Big Mike. But it was me.

I considered beating the shit out of a mailbox. I considered a few other things. But mostly I walked through the rain and thought about the fact that one of my boots had no sock in it. Delia would have been overjoyed at the flaw in the foundation of my early morning reflection.

When I got home, the cats raced out and vanished into the darkness beside the house, unconcerned by the rain.

I turned all the lights on and cranked up the heater, then stripped in the dining room and limped naked into the bathroom. While the shower was heating up, I looked at myself in the bathroom mirror. Everything was healing. If I could just keep from adding to the damage for a few more days I'd be back into something approaching a leaner version of my top form, which would at least be one good thing to bring to the table in regard to Suzanne. I needed some seriously fatty food for breakfast, like five link sausages with a stick of butter as a starter. Two of Delia's hippie vitamins on top would be good.

By the time I got out of the shower my hangover had diminished from train wreck to lawnmower accident. I considered working out, but I'd worked out enough with Suzanne to last me for a few days. It was almost six and the cafe around the corner would be open. I dressed in black wool pants, a black V-neck sweater over a fresh T-shirt, and thick socks, and laced my wet boots back on. I studied my wallet for a moment before I pocketed it. I needed a new one, which was sad in a sentimental way. The pile of bills on the counter beside it looked like the kind of thing I couldn't believe I had to touch for the very first time since I'd been handling them, but I did. Smokes, Cheeks's Zippo—which I realized linked me to him and had to be disposed of—and one of my two remaining metal balls. I was ready to once again sally forth and do questionable things.

I paused on the step out front and turned up my collar. A cold, windy sleet was in progress. I always wondered where the cats went on a morning like this. Maybe under the porch, and then maybe to some hideout I had no idea about, filled with bird skeletons and milk bottle caps, the kinds of things cats might collect. I had a sudden urge to find their hiding place and draw the things I found there. My right hand was still stiff, but beyond cigarettes, beyond booze, beyond even pussy or the word, art would always be my worst addiction. I needed to draw to stay alive. It was just that simple.

I stood there and thought about my sketchbook, the one that was lost in the explosion. There were others, somewhere in the warm house behind me. They were full of sketches of the little figurines and broken microscopes I collected, the mummified foreign beetles, roses, unusual leaves, and pencil renderings of old Salvation Army photographs. It smelled, I remembered from so long ago, like soap and tobacco. I let my mind wander over all the things I wanted to draw, but somehow I kept going back to Cheddar Box. There were too many obstacles in between me and fooling around with a pencil, and Cheddar Box was first on the list. On impulse, I went back inside and into my little library/home office, but I didn't take down a sketchbook or pause to look at any of my strange little marvels or glorious old broken things. I took the phone book out and carried it to the dining room table and sat down.

And there he was. In the real estate section, a quarter-page ad. Turganov Investments. I had Dessel's card, and since the asshole never slept, I thought about calling him on my new cell phone and bragging about my phone book skills, but I didn't. It would be far better if everyone thought I'd given up.

Cheddar Box really was one seriously big motherfucker. Unfortunately, there was a brain in his huge head. I was lounging under the awning of the building across the street from Turganov Investments, studying the place and waiting for the inspiration for my next move, when the Mexican Conan stepped under the awning next to me. It was seven a.m.

"Got a gun?" he asked. His voice was low and rich, a deep, cigar-shaped vibration. He didn't bother to stare me down, just joined me in watching the building across the street.

"Nah."

"Smart." Then he did look down at me and I looked up at him. He flexed his hands. My neck hurt.

"Yeah," I continued, "I brought a bomb instead."

Cheddar Box had a nice smile. Not a Dessel high beam or a Delia snarker, just pleasant.

"Mr. Holland," he purred, "I think you're lying to me."

I shrugged. "Maybe." I was. I'd just gotten there. All I had was my ball bearing and the cup of coffee I'd gotten on the drive over. I was holding the metal ball in the same hand as my cigarette.

"I was expecting you sooner." He rolled his head and some massive thing in his shoulder or neck popped. He was wearing a gray Bill Blass suit.

"My girlfriend is a little taller than you," I said. "I dig the suit, but the shoes, man. Heels, if you get me."

He let out a deep breath. "How about one of those smokes? I quit. Wrecks my cardio, but a morning like this . . ."

I didn't want him to see my metal ball, but he was almost three hundred pounds and less than a foot away, and on top of that he seemed oddly depressed. I stuck my cigarette into my mouth, slipped the ball back into my pocket and brought my hand out with my pack, shook one loose for him. Cheddar Box plucked it out with fingers that reminded me of burned tree roots and lit it with a tiny silver lighter. Then he turned back to the rain.

"I don't like this job," he said. "I'm not a morning person, for one thing. Little fucking dickheads like you comparing me to your girlfriend. My boss"—he stabbed the cigarette at the building across from us—"he's a Russian, and I don't want to be a racist, but I can't stand those fucking guys."

"Sucky." I took a sip of coffee. We looked at the rain.

"Yeah," he said finally. "Ever eaten that shit they call *lángos*?"

"Can't say I have."

"It's some kind of lumpy fried bread with salt all over it. It might be Hungarian, but I don't fucking know." He took a big drag and blew it out. "Sausage. So much sausage. And I swear, that vodka thing? Fuckin' true. Morning, noon, night, and everything in between. It's just unbelievable."

"I got a guy used to work for me. Ate hot dogs every day for lunch. And nothing on 'em. Just a blank dog."

"Jesus."

"Yep."

We smoked.

"So," Cheddar Box continued. His cigarette was already down to his giant knuckles. "So standing here, me just rappin' with you, that's the good part of both our days."

"Figured as much. I'm still shaking a hangover."

"Yeah. So now we go see Oleg. You probably won't like this. Don't make any wisecracks. I can appreciate a sense of humor, but only when I'm standing around smoking a butt I just bummed off a retard. You ready to go?" He reached out and pinched my arm, once, a grip that almost fully encircled my bicep.

"Ouch."

"Sorry." It was his turn to shrug. "Don't try to run or I'll shoot you."

A few months ago I'd been in the office of a guy in San Francisco. He'd been a rich man, but his office was a shithole in a crappy warehouse. This was very different. The lobby of Turganov Investments was what I'd call Bank Modern, or even Trumpy. The entire lobby was carpeted in gray. There was an unmanned desk in one corner, surrounded by a range of insect chairs from a Scandinavian witch farm. A big, fake plant, possibly a weensy palm, was right in the middle of the place. There was a black security bubble on the ceiling, the kind you often found in grocery stores.

"Why in the hell are rich people always so damned tacky?" I asked.

Cheddar Box sighed in shared disgust. "No idea. But I constantly wonder the same thing. I mean, is it so hard to read *Architectural Digest*? One issue?" We stopped in front of the elevator and he stabbed the up button.

"Maybe it's hard to find the time. Counting up all that change. The nickels alone . . ."

"The smartass thing," he warned. "Though I can see your point." The elevator doors opened and we stepped in. He hit the button for the top floor and the doors closed. We listened to the soft muzak. Billy Joel.

"I kind of like *Décor*," I went on. "The paintings in the background, et cetera. Sunny pictures."

Cheddar Box harrumphed. "I sort of like that one, too. It strikes me that you might be the kind of man who likes a good cooking show." He glanced down at me appraisingly and then back at his warped reflection. "You Martha or Julia?"

I had to consider. "Julia, I guess. Tough call."

"Damn right. My book, Julia gets the sauce and the protein, Martha gets the sweet stuff." The bell chimed.

"I like how you put that," I said.

"Yeah," he said quietly. He craned his head at me again. "The bomb. I almost forgot."

"Oh. That's me," I replied. I felt bad saying it. He shook his head sadly and faced forward.

"No detonations. And no more talking until he asks you something. Otherwise I got to flush you."

The doors opened right onto Turganov's sprawling office, a sterile replica of what the CEO of General Motors' might have been, imagined by a dude who had never been in one of those offices. I certainly hadn't, but Oleg evidently hadn't made the Christmas card list, either. The same short gray utility carpet was everywhere, held down by a centrally located expensive desk that had a presidential feel in a discount, third-world kind of way. There were a few chairs that looked like they'd been ripped out of a Walmart super sale, and to top it off, it smelled like someone had blown up a bottle of very shitty cologne, and then burned a string of fat cigars through rotten teeth.

"Shut it," Cheddar Box intoned, very low. He sank down in one of the chairs to our left.

Oleg Turganov was on the phone, pacing around behind the Dictator of New Jersey's desk. He didn't bother to look at us. Oleg was dressed in an unusual suit made out of a slightly shiny cloth, like cotton mixed with rayon. He wasn't fat, but he was close. His gray and black hair was thick and slicked back with something like bacon grease. His florid, jowly face was the mug of a guy with the humble origins of a talentless but dedicated street fighter. I sat down next to Cheddar Box.

"Might be a while," he said.

"I got time," I whispered. "I'm in between jobs right now."

"The mouth," Cheddar Box reminded me. He reached into the interior of his suit jacket and came out with a folded copy of *The New Yorker*. I audibly sighed with relief.

The Russian droned on for about twenty more minutes. I sat there watching him for the first few minutes. Then I looked over at *The New Yorker*. Cheddar Box angled it a little toward me and in that fashion we read an article about seals and caught up on someone's opinion of Norman Mailer. I was just beginning to consider trying to walk out by way of a visit to the restroom when Oleg finally hung up.

"Who ze fuck is dis?" he snapped at Cheddar Box. His little eyes were raw with hangover and red with malice.

The big man next to me folded his paper and tucked it back in his coat.

"Guy owned some tattoo shop down on sixth. Beat the fuck out of a guy named Ralston, if I'm right. Put him in the hospital. Seems like Cheeks might have met him as well. No gun, no wire the door scanner picked up. He's got some metal in his pockets. Mouthy, too, but . . ." He let that hang.

"Cheeks!" Oleg smiled. "I heard of this man." The smile flashed off. "Vat do you want?"

I looked at Cheddar Box, who almost winced in anticipation.

"This dude sounds just like Chekhov from *Star Trek*," I said. "I always wondered if that guy had it down."

"The mouth," Cheddar Box said seriously. This close, I could see the tiniest hint of a smile, just around the edges of his eyes.

"Right." I crossed my legs and slumped casually. "So I wanted to drop by and chat. Just a few little things. I know you have the cops in your pocket, fire department, shit like that, but the feds are a different story. Those guys have you on their radar. One of them is this creepy little bastard named Dessel. He told me this bizarre story the other day about apes and monkeys."

"Apes and monkeys," Oleg repeated slowly, mystified.

"Yeah. They don't like me, but I get the impression that they aren't all that happy with you, either. They seem to think you hired the guy who bombed my shop, so I thought I'd pop by and give you a heads-up."

Oleg stared at me with a flat, dead expression for a full thirty seconds. I stifled a yawn.

"Vy tell me dis?"

I shrugged. "Because I'm about to do a whole bunch of shit, and it's important for you to know just how fucked the situation is."

Oleg looked at Cheddar Box and tossed his head at the elevator doors. He turned back to his desk and picked up his phone.

"Time's up," Cheddar Box said. We both got up and walked to the doors. I pressed the down button and then turned back.

"Be seeing ya," I called. Turganov didn't even glance our way.

"Mouth," Cheddar Box said. The doors opened and we stepped in. He pressed L and the doors closed.

"So, these feds," he began. "They the smart kind, or the Princeton variety?"

"One of them is a very clever little motherfucker."

"Shit." Cheddar Box didn't like that. "I'm still on parole."

"Bummer."

The elevator doors opened. Cheddar Box made no move.

"You go on," he said. "No way I'm going out there now."

I nodded. "Some mornings are better than others." I wasn't looking forward to this, either. I patted his wide back.

"Later," I said.

"Yep."

The doors closed and I walked through the quiet, empty lobby and out into the rainy seven a.m. darkness. The white Prius was parked in front, just as the Mexican Conan predicted. The passenger window zipped down and Dessel gave me his monster grin, the real showstopper.

"Darby! We've been looking everywhere for you. I wanted to see if you had time to toss a frisbee later, but this rain. Not really flip-flop weather. Why don't you hop in and we can do a little sightseeing instead."

Dessel liked to lean over the seat like a really big puppy and look at me. Agent Pressman stuck with his drive and grunt routine. The car was littered with fast food wrappers and the ashtray was overflowing. Sloth was a essential element of their disguise.

"So what," Dessel began. He made an exasperated little noise. "So what's up? I mean, what the fuck were you doing in there?"

"Mostly talking about cooking. Martha Stewart and Julia Child."

"Cool. I like that one guy, the peppy one." He snapped his fingers at Agent Pressman.

"Bourdain." Pressman offered. Dessel shook his head.

"No. I'm talking chefs here, not mouth jockeys. That one guy . . ."

"Bobby Flay."

"That's the one!" Dessel's laugh was so high-pitched it made my tonsils hurt. "BBQ. Fuckin' master class. So what else?"

"I had some quality time with this dude who evidently really likes a certain kind of cracker. It might actually be referred to as a snack chip. I'm in the dark on that one."

"Tough distinction," Dessel admitted. "Please, go on."

"You guys aren't going to drop me off twenty blocks from my car, are you? The cold makes my feet hurt."

"Dunno," Dessel replied. He slapped the back of the seat and Pressman did his grunt. "Sort of depends. I can hold you for twenty-four hours, so maybe we'll drop you off in Idaho this time. I bet you like a good potato. So keep going."

"I told the Russian we were quits. I just want to move on. He was very receptive."

"I see." Dessel's fingers played along the back of the seat. "I'm wondering so many things right now, Darby. Like why you didn't just call him and leave a message, for starters."

"I like to make an appearance."

"I see." Dessel nodded. "I obviously like doing the same thing. Timing is everything. Why so early in the morning?"

"No appointment. Figured a rich dude might be the type to get an early start. Probably how they get rich in the first place."

Dessel tapped his temple. "Impressive."

I shrugged. Pressman grunted.

"So paint me a picture." Dessel said. "You used to be an artist. We can use this car as the nice warm canvas you're used to and you can use words as your . . ." He snapped his fingers.

"Pigments," Pressman said.

"Bingo!"

"To start with, I totally ratted you fuckin' guys out. It's partly because I don't like you, but also because I don't want any confusion down the road. If you two godforsaken morons ever get this scumbag, some crazy fucker might blow up my house. I have two cats to consider."

"Cats," Dessel said. He was grinning again.

"They're rude, but it gets so you like 'em. I don't know why. It also struck me, and let me just take a page from your book, but it struck me that you two boys are like baboons. Big snouts. So if you go truffle hunting in this guy's patch of dirt, I want to make damn sure he knows I'm not even close to involved."

"Baboons," Dessel said, considering. "Truffles. I have to remember that."

"Yeah, nice of you to pick me up right in front of his place while his bodyguard is watching. Almost like a miracle of bad timing on your part. Speaking of timing." I looked at the watch I wasn't wearing.

Dessel drummed his fingers some more. "I can't say any of this makes me happy, Darby."

"Sorry to say I don't give a shit."

Dessel's boyish face grew hard. It was expression I never suspected he could pull off.

"Bob," he said softly. "Let's pull over."

Agent Pressman pulled up to the curb. He'd been driving aimlessly, but we were still at least ten blocks from my car.

"Get out," Dessel said, every bit of chummy gone. "We can save our road trip to Idaho for another day. Like maybe tomorrow."

My car had a 108-dollar parking ticket on it. It didn't surprise me. I threw the ticket in the gutter, fired up the engine, and turned the heater on high. After the inside warmed up, I lit a cigarette and fiddled with the radio. Nothing but commercials.

The next stop was going to be depressing, but it had to be done. Dmitri. He used his lame pizza shop as an office and he often got there early. It was also probable that he had taken to sleeping on the floor behind the register. But it also meant I would be in close proximity to the ruins of the Lucky Supreme, and I didn't want to see it just yet. I pulled onto 6th Street a few blocks down and parked. If Dessel and Pressman had stealthily followed me, they'd done a really good job.

The partially burned out neon sign reading "mitri's izza" pretty well summed up Dmitri in every way. He was old-school fucked up. Not only would the sign never be fixed, but to Dmitri it was a symbol, a testament. He believed that change was bad, that entropy was his personal curse, and above all that fixing anything encouraged the cosmic forces at work around him to break two things in return. The windows were wet with rain on one side and slicked with an accumulation of airborne orange grease on the other. I peeked in through the glass of the front door. Dmitri was sitting at a random table, doing nothing. He was wearing lime-green pants and a bulging parka of some kind. His eyes were closed. Either he was deep in boozy meditation or he was unconscious.

The door was locked so I kicked it, hard. My hands were too cold to knock. Dmitri stirred and frowned and pointed at the street. He didn't recognize me. I kicked the door again, harder this time, three solid whacks. Dmitri scowled and wobbled to his feet. He'd been a morning drinker for years, but some days he was better than others. It was evidently a vodka morning rather than white wine.

His rheumy eyes seemed to focus, and his scowl transformed into almost comical shock.

"Open this fuckin' door!" I yelled.

Dmitri walked slowly to the filthy glass and then just stood there, staring at me.

"I didn't do it!" I yelled.

"I know," he replied, so quietly I was reading his lips.

"Then open the door!"

He cranked the deadbolt and I pushed in.

Mitri's izza smelled like he'd been sleeping there for weeks, maybe since the explosion. Dmitri himself looked worse than I'd ever seen him. His dump-rejected wardrobe was spattered with mustard and beer and the crotch of his lime pants was darkened with either urine or something he'd spilled in his lap. His bizarre raft of gray hair was matted and shining like he'd rubbed his head with French fries. Even though he was a nutjob, he'd always maintained a certain edge in the past. The filthy, withered thing in front of me was a broken-down old man who'd lost his ghost.

"It stinks in here," I said.

"Your face looks good," Dmitri countered.

"So, the police." Dmitri walked back to the table where he'd been sitting. "They've been looking for you." He sank down into the chair and stared out the filthy window at the rain.

"I talked to the feds earlier, so I'm clear with the minor-level pigs for the time being." I sat down across from him. The table was sticky, so I folded my arms.

Dmitri shrugged and hunched into his parka. The place was dark, and so cold I could see my breath. I lit up a cigarette.

"They're coming," Dmitri said in a slurred voice. His eyes slowly closed. "I'm only waiting now."

"Yes, yes," I snapped impatiently. "I know. I have a few fucking questions for you, so wake the fuck up."

Dmitri squirmed deeper into his parka.

"So how'd you know I wasn't the bomber?"

"How do you know I wasn't?"

I couldn't tell him that I'd already beaten most of the information I need out of Ralston and put an ambitious pimp on the golf course, so I smoked.

"Same reason." I blew his way. "Why the hell would either of us do it?"

Dmitri made a tutting sound, pleased.

"So," I continued. "You know about the Russian."

Dmitri's eyes opened, but he didn't point them at me. He was looking at something ten miles and ten years away.

"Oh yes," he whispered.

"Well, isn't that fucking great." I slapped my left hand down on the table. "You goddamn piece of shit! Look at my face! This is what it cost me to find out!"

Dmitri scowled at me. "I think it looks good. You look like Pierce Brosnan's criminal brother. The young one. But you need a haircut."

"Fuck you."

He shrugged.

"Dmitri, you better start talking. You're not my landlord anymore, remember? I always hated that word, by the way. 'Landlord' pisses me off just to say it." I pointed at him. "So you, you're just a piece of shit to me. How's that for a new title."

Dmitri shrugged again.

"And," I added, "your new contract has an 'I beat the fuck out of you' clause. Optional."

"The police, they . . ." he trailed off.

"I'm so not in the mood for your bullshit," I said, my voice rising again. "You start talking right now or I wreck this place and smash your skull flat. Spit it out."

He roused himself enough to steeple his fingers beneath his chin.

"Choices, choices," he said softly. "Everyone keeps giving me the same ones, too." He took a deep breath and blew some smelly air my way as a preamble. "You know that Old Town is changing, Darby. Lots of money involved. My father bought these two buildings long, long ago. And now I'm going to lose them both. A man will come. A man with a briefcase. He will have papers in it. This will happen soon."

Not this week, I thought.

"I feel bad for you, old man. Looks like you're finally going to retire. You have to understand a few things now. Are you paying attention?"

Dmitri made a tiny dismissive wave, his only response.

"The way I see it, Dmitri, is that you owe me. And I mean big time. As in hugely. I've put up with your bull-shit for way too long. For years, I fixed all the discount second-rate crap in that fucked-up building at my own expense. And then some shitwad Russian decides to move you out because you're a crazy roach farm type of guy. The perfect target. You're a fuckup, dude. And you dragged me down with you."

I paused and lit a new cigarette off the butt of the first one. My face scar was pulsing. Dmitri stared at me, blank.

"So, fucktard, when that man with the briefcase shows up, you do two things. You know what they are?"

Dmitri closed his eyes.

"Here's what they are," I continued. "You sign those fucking papers, but with a provision. I'll give you the details later, but you aren't doing this alone. I'm going with you."

His eyes were still closed, so I reached out and slapped him as hard as I could. He tumbled out of the chair and landed on his back. Wild terror spasmed across his face and he cowered as I tossed the table aside and stood over him. I stared into his wide eyes and slowly ran my index finger down the new scar on my face.

"You fuck up what I'm about to do, you get one of these, but I'm not really known for restraint. Get me? Understand?"

Dmitri nodded, once. It was hard for him since he was on his back and it seemed like his mad hair was weighing him down.

"Well then, we're all good," I said pleasantly. "You have a nice day. Go visit a barber and Nordstrom's. Aruba awaits."

Then I went down to the street to visit the Lucky Supreme.

People tend to trust a tattoo artist. We have a unique cultural bus pass, a strange ticket to the odd and often dark places inside of people, and I was potent in that already powerful way. Everyone knew I wasn't going to rat them out. Not because of ethics, and certainly not because of honor. People understood, deep down, on a visceral level, that I wasn't even close to fitting in. Whatever logic had guided me all the way to the fringes of everything, that was behind my improbable occupation and towered in the heart of my worldview in general, made me trustworthy in the same way a foreigner was trustworthy. I didn't give half a shit what anyone was up to and they could tell. And on the off chance I did, no one would believe me.

From that position, I'd been privy to a wide variety of things best not known. Stories of love gone off the rails, the unhinged ways of businesses great and small, the obscene hiding places, the complicated lies and desperate half-truths, the secrets the perpetrators themselves had long since rinsed from their minds with rivers of booze. Twenty years of that shit was hard-packed in my head and I'd never really needed to know any of it, not until now. The exotic burden of my station in life had been a naked knife I gingerly carried and accidentally cut myself with from time to time. It was all about to take on a different value. I was going to hold it by the handle and start disemboweling everything left in my way.

That was the first real thought I had when the tidal wave of rage receded. The Lucky, my Lucky Supreme, was the most tragic thing I'd ever seen. I stood there alone in the rain and gaped at it for I don't know how long. The windows had been swept into piles behind the tattered police tape that cordoned off the sidewalk. The door was gone completely. I could see into the darkness inside, and it was the strangest thing. A thousand memories scrabbled like phantoms through the wreckage. Every twisted chair had a laughing specter in it. All the wet, scorched trash still looked like art, a terrible joke made by Banksy on peyote. The pitted walls were pregnant with a magic that had cost something high in the currency of the human soul, and that magic was trickling away into the gutters right before my eyes. I could see Delia in there, laughing, and I knew that this was where she finally found herself after a lifetime of looking. This was where Nigel felt safe for the first time in his mysterious life, in a place paradoxically filled with danger, where he had built his first psychic nest. It was where Big Mike whiled away the minutes and seconds of his miserable existence and found momentary peace in the distraction of chaos. And it was where I had been something as simple as myself.

Any doubt, any second-guessing, any discord between logic and passion inside of me vanished as I surveyed the ruination. I was halfway there and I'd done it all alone so far, and that was about to change. I'd killed a pimp who had beaten me half to death and left me for dead in a dumpster, then I'd stolen a ton of disgusting cash, pissed off some feds who already had every reason to want me in a cage, beaten a junkie bomber to within an inch of his life and robbed him, too, and I'd baited the Russian who hired him in an effort to stall him for a few days, in the hope that while he waited for the heat to die down I could steal the fire. It was a start. From there, I had to work more thoughtfully. But I was going to have to rise, once again, into a role I avoided whenever possible. It was time to become a gutter king and risk more lives than my own.

The Rooster Rocket, which we shared our north wall with, looked salvageable. The windows were gone, but they'd been boarded up with sturdy plywood, as had the rectangular hole where the door had been. Gomez wouldn't have gone to that much trouble unless most of the booze was still in the bottles. I'd have to call him soon, as in top of the to-do list.

The Korean mini mart on the other side of the tattoo shop was toast. The brunt of the explosion seemed to have gone their way. I walked around and studied the situation. The epicenter of the blast was indeed the Lucky Supreme's bathroom, left rear wall, back corner. A trash can had been there. The front of the shock wave had torn through the tattoo shop, but a powerful percentage of the energy had torn through the mini mart. Almost nothing remained. Their part of the roof had mostly collapsed, and everything left by the looters was trash. I never knew much about the family who ran the place. They didn't speak English, and after twenty years I'd never bothered to learn a single word of Korean. It wasn't like they were rude. They were a family and they stayed close together. They'd been scared. Old Town had been a shitty place for them to land, and I never had any idea how they wound up with the mini mart in the first place. The tattoo shop was a strange place for them to deal with, just like it was for many neighbors. We were handy to have around if bad shit went down, and car theft directly out front became less likely. But allowing neighbors to remain anonymous was part of the deal, and they'd been especially good at it.

I went back and stood in front of the Lucky and tried to let some of my dreams, something of me, even if it was just my fury, shore up the place. It was one of my rare spiritual moments, but I was feeling something, and that almost never happened, so I went with it. I was about to whisper something cryptic, in Spanish maybe, when something moved inside.

A dark figure flashed past one of the empty windows, stooped over and moving fast. I looked both ways. A few random cars were driving past, headlights on, wipers wiping. Down the street a woman was walking rainy-day fast, her face hidden by an umbrella. I ducked under the police tape and danced silently over the random bricks and chunks of masonry to the jagged rectangular hole where the front door used to be.

Dane Bane was stuffing things into a second-generation black trash bag. He was a local junkie skate punk who harvested trust fund chicks cruising Old Town for coke and X. He came around the Lucky on a regular basis looking for handouts, and once I'd taken him to the hospital. I never liked him, but catching him picking through the remains of the Lucky brought the fury in me all the way back to a rolling boil.

"Hey, fucker," I said.

His head snapped up, eyes bright, his face sheened in sweat. He was high on something, but not the right thing. Probably coming up on Mexican tar time with nothing but speed. I wondered how many times he'd been in there, what he'd already taken.

"Darby!" he gushed. He licked his lips. "I heard you were dead."

I stepped inside, out of the doorway and into the relative darkness.

"C'mere," I said.

Dane Bane looked down at his trash bag and then back up to me. Slyness spread over his skinny face. His game was like an on/off switch. It was back on.

"I was getting some stuff," he said quickly. "Fucking people been in here, but they don't know what to look for. I got some machines the other night. Tubes. The good shit. Idiots were in here stealing Band-Aids and paper towels. I was going to hold it for you or Delia. For some money, of course. I have better things to do than pick through your trash, man."

"Thanks," I said. "I knew you'd do the right thing. Guy like you."

"Fuck yeah," he crowed. He peered out one of the windows, sketchy. "All the shit you guys done for me? But I still need some cash for all my effort."

"I have something for you," I said. I smiled. He nodded, smugly appreciative of my diminished social standing. I held my hand out for the bag. He took one more look around and sauntered over and held it out.

My first punch went into his hard gut just below the sternum and didn't seem to do very much. Dane Bane was one of those mutant termite junkies who somehow stayed solid on a diet of lies and day-old donuts. I didn't want to smash into his teeth with my naked hand, so I hammered him fast in the neck and the right temple in the same flurry and he went down. He looked at me with animal eyes; lost, trapped, dangerously empty.

"You go to the train station from here, Dane, and you walk far out down the tracks and hop a freight. And if you ever come back to this town I'll kill you."

He whimpered and crab-walked back into the deep trash in the corner. I kicked the bag at my feet and it ripped open. My flash. Some of Delia's. It was wet, burned, warped, and ruined.

I walked back out and ducked under the police tape. No one was watching, so I casually headed down the street and took a left toward my car. When the Lucky was out of view, I ducked in under the awning of a new coffee shop and lit a cigarette. My hands weren't even shaking. Somehow, I knew, that was a very bad thing.

Portland bars can be sympathetic to moods, as I've pointed out. But they never really cure anything. It's more like you could find a shitty place to blend if you were feeling shitty, et cetera. There were thankfully other kinds of places to use as mood alteration staging platforms, places to go when you want to feel anything like what you did, and after kicking Dane Bane's thieving ass in the wreckage of my tattoo shop I needed a vibe swap. I'll never know why, but that was my rock bottom. If I hit one more person in the near future, it was going to change me forever. It was time to start using whatever kind of brain I had left in my scarred head. And I was going to start with a stop at my favorite grocery store, the City Market.

I felt better almost as soon as I pulled into the cramped parking lot. I was going to make something good, something big, and I was going to eat the entire thing. I was going to make dessert, too. And I was going to eat that, too. All of it. And I was going to buy some decent wine, which I didn't even like, and I was going to drink every last drop. And I was going to buy flowers. Unusual ones, and I was going to draw them while I drank the wine. I got out and took a deep breath. It was still raining, but the rain made the air seem clean.

The inside of the City Market was just as I remembered, like I hadn't been gone for a day. No one looked at me like I'd been a bombing suspect, recently in the papers. No one looked at me at all. They were busy doing what I was itching to do: buying good ingredients. I nodded at the clerk, a frisky-looking young goth/hippie hybrid, picked up my hand basket, and mingled with the yuppies.

Meat first. I looked over the rabbit, then moved on to steak, then the pork. The pork tenderloin looked good, so I ordered one. The guy in the apron behind the meat counter offered me a roasted sample of the French garlic sausage, made in-house, and it was so good I got two packages. In order to round things out in the right direction, I picked up a hunk of tasso pork, a cured, spicy thing used for Cajun food in general. Meats in basket, I ambled over to the produce.

The green beans looked good, so I got a few big handfuls. The heirloom tomatoes were huge and brainlike, so I got a couple of those. They had blueberries, so I added them to the basket. Then I just stood there for a minute and considered. It took the entire minute, but an idea formed. I went down past the seafood to the freezers and got some frozen beef stock, then went back up to the breads, where I got four rosemary rolls, and then I ambled with meditative tranquility past the mustards and anchovies to cheese, where I waited behind an intense, extremely good-smelling power legal-type woman who was waiting on a fist-sized hunk of real Greek feta. Everyone was flashing smiles on and off and consulting lists and iPhones. It was a good vibe, almost like early holiday shopping, when everyone was still in a good mood.

The cheese gal I knew already, in the way you know some people you don't know a single thing about. She liked her job. She always seemed happy. She smiled at me with no recognition and didn't give my scar a second glance, just a cheery tree-hugger gal ready to deal out some dairy.

"What'll it be?" she asked pleasantly.

"I'm making pork medallions, sort of vaguely Cajun, and I'm looking for something sort of mild, on the grassy, nutty end."

"Fan of the goat?" One of her favorite lines.

"Who isn't?"

She nodded. "Try this." She took a quarter wheel of something out of the display case, shaved off a sliver and held it out. I took it and popped it in my mouth, arched my good eyebrow.

"Yumpery. How about a half pound, single chunk format is fine."

She got to work cutting and weighing and I wandered a little further down while I waited. Nothing really caught my eye, except for the Pilates-sculpted ass of another woman in a power suit, this one a blonde in black. I didn't look too closely, but I did look. The rest of the dairy section was right there, so I got a dozen duck eggs, whole milk, and Norwegian butter, then picked up my cheese with a nod and plucked a bottle of white wine out of a random display on my way to the register.

The line was three deep, which gave me time to look at all the chocolates. I took a big bar of something dark and added it to my basket. The flowers started at the end of the checkout and flowed all the way to the door, so when it was my time to set my basket down I picked out a selection of asters, giant stargazer lilies, and some unusual scarlet unknowns and brought them back. When she was done ringing me up, the clerk banded all the flower stems together and put them in my grocery bag with the heads picturesquely jutting from the top. She was momentarily dismayed when I paid with one of the nasty hundreds, but it was brief and didn't cramp my style. When I strode out into the fresh-smelling rain with lilies under my nose, I almost felt like busting loose with a Sinatra tune. Almost.

On the drive home, I hit scan on the radio and let it roll through the stations as I considered, with the fresh and uplifting vibe of the City Market still kissing my mood. First thing was to get the rice going. Then call Delia and get her to deal with Gomez, also see if she wanted to help me make dinner and draw flowers. And then try to find Suzanne after I took a nap. There was a ton of shit to do, but the very first thing on the list was to relax, eat, and be the good Darby Holland for a day, spend an afternoon like I used to before any of the last three months had ever happened. I was sure that version of myself was still inside me somewhere. It was time to let him back out into the air and light and wind.

I should have known it wasn't possible. As soon as I turned the corner on to my street, I knew something was wrong. I pulled to a stop in front of my house and looked up through the rain at my front porch. Then I almost bit off the tip of my tongue.

Suzanne was sitting in one of my chairs, wearing most of a tracksuit, her bare, corded arms tanned and tattoo-free, a beer in one hand, laughing beautifully. Dessel was sitting next to her, slapping his knee and lost in mirth, wiping beer foam out from under his nose.

It was Dessel's lucky day. Not only was he enjoying the company of a beautiful woman in the homey environs of my front porch, but after beating on Dane Bane and my subsequent feeling of cresting inner filth, followed by my lame transformation at the grocery store, I didn't feel like tossing my future down the toilet and breaking his beer bottle over his Poindexter haircut. In fact, I held on to my good mood as I walked up the steps.

"Hey stranger," Suzanne purred as I reached the top of the stairs. "Your note was priceless, so I thought I'd come by with a six-pack and try to hair-of-the-dog you back to life, but you look OK. Better than OK. Plus I found your other sock."

"That's our boy," Dessel said, raising his IPA in salutation. "Darby Holland, the only guy I know who smiles as much as I do." He turned his smile back at Suzanne. "S'why we're buds."

"Jacob was telling me about the time you guys used gypsy salami from the Russian market for shark bait. You two idiots should be glad I came by with some common sense."

I took a seat across from them and set my grocery bag down, then took the flowers out and handed them to Suzanne.

"Common sense has never been our strong point," Dessel continued. He took a beer out of the bag at Suzanne's feet and handed it to me. "Quick one before I hit the road? I was on my way to Andy and Bax to get those tent stakes for our trip to Idaho. Thought I'd stop by to see what you were doing and I run into this!" He gestured at Suzanne. "What the hell is it about you? You always get the good ones."

Suzanne laughed and slapped Dessel on the forearm. His high beam smile flickered for an instant at her touch. Maybe it was the size of her hand.

"I keep telling you, Jacob," I said, grinning myself, "if you spent less time at your mom's house playing video games and touching yourself, you'd be so buried in poon you wouldn't need me to pal around with. Which would be sad for everyone, of course." I took the beer and twisted the cap off, looked at Suzanne, who was smiling. "Jacob tell you about our new game?"

"Game?" Suzanne took a sip of her beer and looked back and forth between us.

"Our new game," Dessel said, perfectly in sync, our dynamic as a theatrical routine born in the moment. "It's great. Really, really great. Darby's the creative type, so I usually just follow in his wandering footsteps. See, he's doing this Easter Egg type thing where he leaves, like, clues. All over town. If I find them all, then I can prove once and for all that I'm smart enough to be his boss. Then he comes to work for me."

"I see," Suzanne said, amused. "And what is it you do, Jacob?"

Dessel stretched and draped an arm over the back of her chair. "I sell golf clubs, baby, and I am the best."

"Golf clubs?" Suzanne thought he might be joking. "Really?"

"Sure," Dessel said, breezy about it. "Sporting goods of all kinds. Even guns and exotic stuff. I'm a regional hotshot. Just ask Darby."

"It's true," I admitted, "but don't let him brag too much. Jacob is a rising star in a field of guys with severely limited career options, if you catch my drift."

"Hence the game?" Suzanne asked. "He needs a smartypants?"

"Oh yeah," Dessel said, pointing his beer at me. "I'm going to lock you down on this, Darby. Don't you forget it."

"Best of luck with that," I said, raising my beer. Suzanne raised hers, too.

"To the game," she said. The three of us drank.

"I better get," Dessel said, rising to his feet. He looked down at Suzanne. "Milady, it was a pleasure. I hope I'll be seeing more of you."

Suzanne rose to her feet as well. She was over a foot taller than Dessel, who seemed both astonished and delighted by it. He did a little jig and giggled. She smiled down at him and held out her hand. They shook, Dessel beaming boyishly.

"Awesome," he exclaimed sincerely, almost breathless. He gave her one last sigh of admiration and started toward the stairs. As he passed her, his eyes met mine and his face spasmed into a mask of wild hatred. And then he was gone, down the stairs and moving at a peppy gait, a spring in his step and a song in his heart, almost skipping. We watched him go.

"He seems nice," Suzanne said. I turned and looked up at her and she looked down at me, shy all of a sudden.

"Are you hungry?" I asked. "I'm making something good."

"Starving," she said. She rubbed her lean stomach with one hand and batted her eyelashes. "Can I help?"

"I need a helper in the worst possible way," I replied honestly. Suzanne picked up the flowers and my grocery bag and I got the rest of her beer and dug my keys out of my pocket. I unlocked the door and looked at her.

"Prepare yourself," I said.

"I'm ready for any kind of bachelor mess," she said. "You should have seen my place this morning."

"That's not really what I meant."

It always pleased me to see my place with someone else for the very first time. People generally expected something far different from the reality. I opened the door and motioned for Suzanne to enter. She paused in the doorway. I watched her slow grin spread from the side as she entered and paused again.

"You live here by . . . yourself?"

"With those two obnoxious cats."

"Ah."

Her eyes went from the two bristling, wide-eyed Chops and Buttons in the center of the small living room up to the walls and the four strange paintings I'd bought from a

Mongolian painter a few years before, an unlikely little man who had been in San Francisco for some reason and decided to skip his two-week visa and hitchhike around, paying his way by making art. They were all studies of American life that were just as odd as he had been: a skinny dog eating from some drifter woman's hand, a fire hydrant with some weeds growing around it, an old Tibetan-looking woman wearing a severe raincoat in an anonymous downtown, a streetlamp with pigeons roosting against a stormy sky. Her eyes lingered on the antique sofa I'd sanded and refinished and had one of Flaco's nephews reupholster. My old Navajo wall hanging. The bookshelves. The cats never moved while she took it all in.

"Don't touch those fucking cats," I cautioned.

"I wasn't going to."

I walked around her and gently pushed the cats aside with one boot. They broke formation and regrouped on the couch. Suzanne paused to peek into my office and then stopped again at the antique dining room table and ran her hand along it. She inspected her index finger and raised an eyebrow.

"You dust," she observed.

"The cats roll on the table when I'm not around. Same thing."

She moved on to the big antique AM radio and the walnut and glass curio cabinet next to it with all my sketch porcelain. She opened one of the glass doors and took out an old tin rocket I'd picked up at the Salvation Army, back before *Antiques Roadshow* had made that kind of score impossible. I'd drawn that little rocket dozens of times. It was one of my favorites. The cats liked it, too.

"OK," I said gently, "you can play with all my toys later. You said you wanted to help, so you get the rice going and I'll do the rest."

"What are we having?"

"Surprise."

We went into the kitchen and she set the bag and the flowers down on the counter.

"You like old stuff," she observed, nodding at the brass rack with my cast iron cookware hanging from it, more pre-*Roadshow* loot.

"We in the trade call them antiques," I replied. I turned the oven on. Even the stove was old, mostly because my landlord was a retired trust fund bum who spent most of his time in a whitey colony in Mexico. I opened the cupboard and took down two glasses and a vase. There was a small collection of booze bottles on the counter; Delia's vodka, my Jameson's, some kind of scotch, and a forever-to-remain-unopened bottle of extreme emergency sambuca.

"Whiskey?" I asked. Suzanne shook her head. She took the vase and added some water from the tap.

"I might puke," she replied. She put the flowers in the vase. "We should have never started drinking wine at that place. I still can't believe . . . I mean, the restroom. I don't know about you, but I'm pretty sure that's where we lost our underwear."

I poured myself a shot and downed it. "Mnn. Probably shouldn't go back until we change our hair." I patted my stomach.

"Darby," she said, shy again. "I was wondering. I mean, you can be honest. Is it OK that I just showed up like this? I mean there was your note, but after a night like that. If you were just being polite. What we did, it was, you know. Insane. I'm still sore. I never, ever really behave like . . ."

I closed the one step between us and looked up into her eyes. She was blushing, I was sure of it. I was, too. I reached out and touched her sternum, right between her small, hard tits with the flat of my hand. Her skin was warm. We stood like that for three heartbeats and then I reached around and cupped one incredibly firm ass cheek. She jumped slightly and her eyes widened. Then I rocked up on tiptoe and she knelt in the same motion and our lips met. Her tongue was hot and as hard as the rest of her. I pulled her in and she wrapped her arms around me and lifted. We stayed like that until the crush of her embrace made the bruise on my sternum ache and my sore ribs screamed, and then I arched my back and my breath exploded. She dropped me back on my feet and took a small, staggering step back.

"Now that," I breathed. But I couldn't think of anything else. She smelled like shampoo and something else, a whiff of sporty chick deodorant. Intoxicating.

"Was good," she finished for me. She took a deep breath and stepped back. "So, rice."

I snapped out of my trance. "Right. Two big cups should do it." I opened the cabinet and took out two pots with lids; a small one for her and the big copper bottom for me. I put mine on the stove and cranked the burner. Suzanne took the smaller pot over to the sink.

"Rice is in that mason jar," I said.

"Got it." She scooped out two coffee cups and started rinsing the rice to make it sticky. Good girl, I thought, turning back.

I dumped all my ingredients out on the counter, took the cutting board down, got my knife out of the drawer, and went to it. First I cut a quarter of a stick of butter, peeled the paper off, and tossed it into the pot. It immediately began to sizzle and smoke, so I picked up the pace. I quickly took the cellophane off the tasso and cubed it, then threw it in and shook the pot, then turned back and diced the green bell pepper and added that, shook the pot around again.

"Need help?" Suzanne asked, appearing at my side with the rice. She put it on the stove and fired the burner.

"Onion from the fridge," I replied. "Quickly! It's a race against time!" Tasso smoke began to fill the kitchen.

I cut the plastic off the tenderloin while she rummaged through the refrigerator, then started cutting it into one-inch-thick medallions.

"Red or white?" she asked.

"White."

She plunked an onion down and I skinned and diced it fast. Suzanne shook the pot to scatter the ingredients.

"Get those two little French garlic sausages and drop 'em in there," I said. She did, quickly.

"Incoming," I said behind her. As neat as a ballroom dancer, she stepped to the side and I instantly filled the gap and tossed in the onion. There was a flash of steam and I backed up. She stepped in instantly and shook the pot. I took the lid off the bottle of Jameson's.

"Green beans or pork next?" she asked.

"Fire first," I replied. "Stand back."

She stepped aside with a grin and I reached into the empty space and dumped a half a cup of whiskey into the pot. A four-foot column of flame erupted and died, and then I added four big handfuls of pork while she shook the pot around. Then we both leaned close to the rising steam and smelled it. My mouth watered.

"Oh my God," Suzanne moaned, eyes closed. I took a small, medicinal sip of Jameson's and handed her the bottle. She took a small sip while I started working through the mountain of green beans, snapping the tips off. When I was done I added them while she watched, and then I took the lid off the quart of frozen stock. The outside of the container was thawed enough so that when I upended it over the pot then entire thing fell out in one frozen mass. I put the lid on the pot and turned the heat down while she lidded the rice and turned that down, too. Suzanne folded her arms. I scratched the top of my head.

"What do you call this?" she asked. I shrugged and smiled at her.

"Our first dance with our clothes on?"

Suzanne laughed while I took another plate down and put the rosemary rolls and the cheese on it. I squeezed the olives in on the side, still in the container in case she didn't care for them.

"Snacks while that cooks," I said. "Grab those fancy beers you brought."

Suzanne followed me out to my dining room table. I sat down and watched her move as she set the beer down and pulled out her chair. The long, corded muscles in her forearm rippled as she gripped the back of the chair. When she sat, she ran her hands through her hair and briefly massaged the back of her neck. From that angle, lit by the rainy light from the window behind her, I could see the fine white fuzz that trailed down the back of her neck. She raised her head and opened the beers. Her fingernails were short and she wore no rings or bracelets. Everything was spare, except for her stature. She noticed me watching as she plunked a beer down in front of me.

"What?" she asked.

"You look like a women's fitness model. Like for yoga pants or something," I observed. "I'd feel confident climbing a mountain with you. You could give me a piggyback ride when I needed a smoke break."

"I climbed Ranier last year," she said. "We got snowed in at our base camp. Three days of freeze-dried food." She picked up a roll. I did, too.

"So," she went on, "you were telling me about golf last night, briefly, before we moved on to the wine bar's restroom."

I shrugged. She nodded slowly and tore her bread. Evidently she was prepared to wait until I continued.

"I've had an interesting, like, six weeks."

Suzanne picked up an olive and set it back down. She still hadn't eaten anything.

"I . . ." I trailed off and shook my head.

"Interesting dinner conversation," she said finally. There was a tiny hint of irritation in her voice. I sighed and put my roll down.

"Suzanne, I like you. Totally fucking smitten. I'm sure you can tell. But right now, today, tonight, I don't really want to talk about what you want to know. I'm going to be perfectly honest with you when I say that I want to be perfectly honest with you, if that makes any sense. But if there is going to be anything between us, then you have to cut me a window of slack, timewise. I've been up to some questionable shit, even by my own standards, which are what they are, but a case could be made that . . . it will seem more understandable once you know me better. Essentially, you caught me at a strange time, and it would be great, just really, really great, if you would let me prove what kind of guy I am most of the time, instead of the alarming guy I have to be part of the time. Is that totally lame?"

Suzanne didn't meet my eye. She studied the olives with a serious expression.

"Darby, I read the papers, if that's what you're worried about. I know that the tattoo shop that blew up in Old Town was yours. I put all that together this morning. The mug shot they used, and I can only guess why they had such a recent mug shot. Recent or not, you didn't have the scar on your face. Your eye . . . Last night when you were passed out I watched you for a while. You are a fucked-up man, Darby Holland. I've never seen so many scars, old and new. That X on your ass. All your tattoos. What I'm trying to say is that I find you motherfucking beautiful, and I know you're in some kind of trouble right now, and I can tell from looking at you that it isn't the first time, either. I want you to understand that I don't understand, if that makes any sense. But I really want to, because I, too, am smitten."

I nodded. I ate some bread without tasting it and had a hard time swallowing. She was still looking down.

"Well," I said, forcing some lightness into my voice, "at least we know where we stand."

"We do," she said, "and some day you will have to tell me the truth. All of it. But I do have one question that won't wait. It can't. Take your shirt off."

My heart didn't skip a beat. It was not the prelude to anything I was going to enjoy and I knew it. I took my shirt off and dropped it on the floor next to me, shook a cigarette out of my pack and lit it, then leaned back and tried to look casual. It wasn't working.

There was an old, vaguely crappy dragon tattoo on one side of my chest. Big. Across my abs, in an arc, it read it florid vato script, also big, "It was You!" and then, below that, just under my belly button, "Run." All of the writing was upside down, a comical but predictably accurate suggestion to myself in those all too common moments when I've just regained consciousness and there was some question as to how I lost it in the first place. Delia thought it was hysterical, but Suzanne . . . maybe not so much. In the center of the writing, just below "was," were three old stab wounds, years healed. They weren't even that bad, just the tip of a cab driver's knife, because I'd been wearing a leather jacket with a zipper instead of snap buttons. The old knife scar across my ribs on the right side was even older, but a little more gnarly. The even coat of bruising on my ribs in general, courtesy of Cheeks, was close to gone in some places, still somewhat ugly in others. Suzanne reached out and touched the heel-shaped purple mark Ralston had left on my sternum.

"I'm an athlete," Suzanne began. "I know injury. Most of what you have is around six weeks old, maybe more. Except for this. This is only a few days ago, maybe the day before yesterday. The day before I met you. I want to know how it happened, or I'm sorry, really sorry, but I don't think I should stay for dinner if you won't tell me. And I really want to stay."

I smoked and watched her for a moment. If I told her the truth, it would only be the tip of a very black iceberg and she would know it. I decided to anyway. But first I put my shirt back on.

"OK," I said. "I had bad business with this guy. Some of it was straight-up vengeance-related on my part, some not. I kicked his ass, but he started it. Sort of. Anyway, he kicked me. Cowboy boot. Long story short. Satisfied?"

She looked sad as she toyed with her bread. When she finally met my eyes there was real pain there.

"No," she said softly.

Suzanne got up. So did I. We looked at each other and something hard in my chest fell apart. She turned to leave and I reached out and lightly brushed the back of her arm. She stopped.

"Please," I said desperately. "The fucking guy blew up my business and a fucking Korean mini mart. The police tried to frame me for it, but the motherfuckers were just trying to get me to stir the pot so they could see what floated to the top. So I stirred it. And I did have a choice. I could have left town like a total pussy. I could have gotten a lawyer out of the phone book and done whatever he said, but I fucking didn't!" I was yelling now. Suzanne turned around.

"So you beat up some guy because he blew up your shop rather than call the cops?"

"I sure as fuck did."

Suzanne sat back down. Then she slumped. I sat down, too.

"Darby, do you think . . . do you think that with the right kind of person in your life, you might handle things like that a little differently?"

Without telling her about Dessel and Oleg and Cheddar Box, Delia and Nigel and poor Monique, insane Dmitri and all the rest, she couldn't have known that it was a question I couldn't answer, so I stayed as honest as I could.

"Maybe," I replied. Suzanne nodded, once, and then she smiled.

"Then I'll stay."

I waggled my eyebrows.

It didn't surprise me that Suzanne could eat as much as me. She was an Amazon with a hangover, and she also worked out to the point where one of the side effects, other than her magnificent, hard, spare and powerful body, was a continuous and impressive appetite. I eat like a jackal—fast and without refinement—and it can be off-putting. What surprised me was that Suzanne did, too. There was no way

I was going to get my fingers close to her mouth while she was feeding.

We finished off the bread and cheese in silence. After the awkward "Ralston's Boot Heel" moment, I had a crazy confessional impulse to keep going and ruin everything, so I didn't say anything at all. Suzanne seemed residually pensive, but she also may have been a tiny bit embarrassed at being the intrusive voice of reason. Whatever the case, she finished another beer, two rolls, and a quarter pound of cheese about a second before I did.

"Now I'm hungry," I said, breaking the silence.

"Lead me to it," she said. She gave me a smile with only a touch of push around the edges.

We went into the kitchen and she watched as I got down two mismatched china plates, one with blue jays and brambles and the other with Christmas holly and tiny yellow chickens. I turned the burners off and removed the lids. The rice was a sticky, steaming mass. The steam that billowed out of the stew pot instantly filled the kitchen. I added some salt and last-second basil and stirred. Smoky tasso, the rich stock and pork fat, a hint of bourbon. It made me want to listen to zydeco.

"That smells insano good," Suzanne purred. "Can we just stand here and eat at the stove?"

I shook my head. "I try that about once a week. Burn my mouth every single time."

"I do the same thing. Mornings, mostly."

I made rice mountains on the plates and then ladled out stew until both plates were close to overflowing. "Carry these out? I'll get the soup spoons and the hot sauce."

"Roger."

She carried the plates with a tongue-out, mincing caution that told me she had never been a waitress. I poured us two Jameson's and joined her at the table. Suzanne was almost guarding hers, one long arm draped out over the table around her plate, palm up, ready for the spoon I slapped into her hand. I sat down and dumped about a quarter of the Tabasco bottle in the center of my steaming plate in a red puddle. Suzanne was already chewing.

"Tabasco cools it down, temperaturewise," I said. I slid the bottle in her direction.

"Mff," she managed, then made a puddle of her own. I picked up my spoon and got down to business. The stew was just what I'd hoped it would be: the pork medallions were falling-apart tender, the tasso had stained the sauce a deep red, and the green beans had a little snap left. The French garlic sausages were fat and rosy and added something unexpectedly herbaceous. There was more than enough sauce to drench the rice all the way through. About halfway through my plate I slowed down and watched Suzanne, who eventually looked up midshovel.

"What?" she complained. "I did my advanced rock climbing class yesterday. Four hours of hard core Spider-woman, and then I met you, and I'm pretty sure we skipped dinner."

"I see," I said. "Save room for dessert. Crepes. I know it sounds wussy, but they're so easy to make and I fucking love the things."

"Goom."

We ate in companionable savagery until we were done. When she pushed her plate back and licked her lips, there wasn't a single grain of rice left in front of her. I finished mine while she watched and with a groan I sat back from an equally clean plate. I wanted to drink my shot of Jameson's, but it was sitting just out of reach. I wouldn't have minded a smoke for that matter, but they were next to the shot glass. I could have asked Suzanne for help, but I didn't have the energy.

"Can we lie down now?" Suzanne asked.

"Don't expect me to be on top," I cautioned.

She laughed softly and stood up, held out her hand. I took it and she pulled me to my feet like she was curling a sack of cement. Holding hands, we walked into my bedroom. Suzanne glanced at my two walnut bureaus, restored in my half-assed way, and then at my neatly made bed with its old-lady quilt. Chops and Buttons had moved their operation to the center of the bed and were giving us their calm assassin look.

"Scoot over," I said. I crashed into bed with my boots on and the cats scattered. Suzanne took her running shoes off and lay down next to me. She sighed pleasantly. She was too long to fit, so she laid at an angle with her head on my pillow and her feet sticking off the edge, about a foot past the floorboard. I could smell her hair.

"This is nice," I said. "I was planning on stuffing myself, taking a nap, and then working out a little."

"I'm glad," she replied without sarcasm. "That's exactly what I had planned."

"You fit right in, don't ya?"

"Keep telling yourself that."

"You keep telling yourself that."

She placed a long hand over the top of my smaller, meatier, scarred one.

The sun peeked through the clouds outside and for a moment the windows lit up, watery gold, with shadows of unfallen leaves. The house was afternoon quiet and I could see motes of dust in the air. I felt warm, inside and out, and the feel of her hand, hard and calloused, was the feel of something outside of the dream I knew I had been in all of my waking days.

I fell asleep.

22

When I woke up two hours later, Suzanne had taken over most of the bed, with the help of the cats. She was mostly in a pile in the center, with a few lengthy extremities flung wide. Chops was sprawled in the negative space behind one of her legs. Buttons had commandeered my pillow, so I was in the cramped remaining area that had the rough dimensions of an army cot.

Suzanne was something to look at, even in her sleep. I took my boots and socks off and thought about waking her up, but right then her fingers curled and her eyes moved underneath her eyelids. She was dreaming.

I closed the bedroom door and padded out into the kitchen. My house looked somehow better than normal with Suzanne sleeping in my bed. I felt lighter. Somehow, in between making dinner and her coming to some kind of terms with Ralston's boot heel, some of the filth had been sluiced from my soul. Then again, maybe it was the nap, but whatever the case, I felt better than I had since the Lucky had blown up. Maybe it was the beginning of a roll.

I made coffee and quietly washed the dishes while it was brewing. When it was done, I wiped my hands on my pants and poured some in my favorite mug, chipped old porcelain with a faded ring of tiny blue cornflowers, and then I went into my office.

Office isn't really the right word. It implied that some kind of work went on in there, which was seldom the case. Library was too snobbish, book storage room too utilitarian. Sanctuary was embarrassingly hippie, sanctorum too Marvel Comics. I'd reluctantly settled on office, a word with a sense of depression about it, and considered it temporary.

The floor-to-ceiling bookshelves covered all of the wall space, and even branched out over the door. There was a space under the window I'd left for my drafting table and a freestanding lamp. There was only one chair, a green overstuffed thing on springs that leaned pretty far back and stuck like that if you worked it just right. I used to have my collection of thrift-store microscopes interspersed among the books, but it irritated me after a while, so now there was a single six-foot shelf reserved for non-book items. Sixteen microscopes, all of which I'd taken apart, cleaned, and brought back into working condition. Scattered between them were my Italian marbles, several small fossils, two tiny meteorites in test tubes, a hummingbird nest I'd found on the sidewalk, and a piece of amber with a mosquito in it I'd scored at the Saturday Market. Gomez had offered me a mummified mouse he found under his house a few months before, and I wondered what had become of it.

Loving books is a good thing. A solid thing. Having a big collection of good ones is important, or at least it seemed that way on every single day until you moved, and then it seemed like one of the worst ideas you ever had. I let my eyes wander over the shelves and I could see patterns. Fourth shelf up, second case from the door. Two years ago. *Dancing Bear* by James Crumley, an all-time favorite. I'd been full after rereading it, but that had been in February, when Portland was reliably miserable, with the entire city was half drunk around the clock, hunkered down in the darkness under the continuous freezing rain. I never minded the weather, but the people usually got to me right around then. Next to it was *Idoru* by William Gibson. Change of pace, which evidently led me on to *One Hundred Poems from the Chinese*, with some of Li Po's greatest hits and introductions by Kenneth Rexroth. The book was the most dog-eared, fucked-up, worthless, abused thing I owned, all of the damage done by me. I thumbed through Rexroth's introduction to his introduction. I'd never liked any of the poets I'd ever met in person, and I'd generally found poetry aficionados to be awful, voyeuristic human beings, but that was probably because I'd had the bad fortune to meet the wrong ones. But an introduction to an introduction brought out the special, scornful smile I reserved for academia, and I felt that rude grin on my face for the first time in ages, even though I'd enjoyed both introductions a dozen times, hence the condition of the book.

It went on and on. I must have been a little depressed that winter, I realized. The order of books was personal version of a feel-good mix. Two years ago and it seemed more like twenty. People who experienced long years often wished they'd been short, and vice versa. That's what I was thinking when I pulled my most recent sketchbook off the next shelf up. I looked at it for a few heartbeats and then carried it over to the green chair in front of the window and sat down.

The sketchbook was on the small side, just bigger than a standard paperback. It wasn't big enough to work out tattoo ideas in, but it was rainy-day portable. I thumbed through the first few pages. Those were always the hardest ones in a sketchbook, because you always had a superstitious feeling that they set an unbreakable tone, like the opening chapters of a novel. There was also an unpleasant governing instinct to establish a less-than-psychotic continuity in case you lost it or someone found it after you died. As a result, there were some constipated flower sketches on the first three pages, and then the lines became blown out and blowsy, with almost no refinement as I tested the ether of my imagination for signs of a theme. It finally came up on page seventeen; a sketch of a spindly tree frog, mid-leap. From there it flowed; a bird wing, a busted umbrella, a plastic grocery bag curling on the wind. Unusual motion. I took a shuddering breath. I'd been yearning for the journal because it was one of my most intimate tools. I skipped to the first blank page and took my mechanical pencil off the lip of the drafting table.

Sketching is a hugely important part of art. It's a loose idea in hundreds of lines, some good and some not, and the eye finds and guides the emerging image. As the image you're looking for begins to form, you press harder and the line darkens. When you're done, you have a version of what you set out to draw, but something better, sometimes, because the madness of the curves dances in your mind's eye, and new facets and options are born. There was no better metaphor for how an artist's mind toys and tinkers in the medium of apparent chaos. This skill was easily my greatest, and perhaps only, advantage in life.

The best curves followed the most natural, easy motion. For a right-handed artist, it looks like a C. I always stretched that curve so it felt good under the pencil, and I stretched it in a way that triggered some deep programming inside of me. The curves that resonated the most for me were the curves of a woman's body. Those lines are lovely. Everything good began with them.

I drew, in one perfect stroke, the line of Suzanne's hip, and that almost stopped me. Miro could reliably pull off stunts like that, but not me. It captured more than the feel of firm. It spoke of hard, of contained energy, of kinetic glory. I wanted to tear out the piece of paper and eat it. But I didn't. I made a few more strokes and turned the book sideways. My hand hurt, but not very badly. I began to relax. My mind started to wander. I snapped a curve sharply, and low: a duck bill.

Delia thought I should buy the building and rebuild. Fight the monsters like Oleg one battle at a time. I liked part of that idea. I liked the thought of owning the Lucky outright, of being my own landlord, and I didn't even really mind the concept of being Gomez's landlord. He could handle most things himself, and anyone was a better land-lord than Dmitri, even me.

And I had money. As beaten as I was, physically, I was far from broke. But it probably wasn't enough. I'd liqui-dated what I considered to be a small fortune in uncovered T-bills awhile back, but it had taken about 40 percent of their value to turn them into cold cash. The cash itself was in a gun safe in my storage space, along with the crappy art I'd found the bills hiding in. Now I had Cheeks's and Ralston's wads, but even with everything put together, I'd still be short. Plus, I'd worked hard for that money in my own way. I felt like I'd earned it. I didn't particularly want to spend any of it on a building, even if that building was going to be mine. It just didn't seem right.

I began shaping the head of the duckling. A little tuft on the top gave it wind and extra character. Wide eyes with big pupils and non-avian eyebrows for a splash of startled concentration.

Dealing with Oleg wasn't impossible. There were ways to get rid of him. But Dessel was watching, and it was clear that he understood on some cop-intuition level that something was going to happen, soon, and that I was going to be involved. He was pretty much sitting right on top of me. I knew he hadn't gotten anything out of Suzanne except that we might be getting something going, which was good. He would get the impression that I was distracted, which was unfortunately true.

The part of Delia's plan that I didn't like at all was dealing with the Olegs of the new Old Town one by one. Eventually, one of them would take me down. Just finding Oleg in the first place had nearly killed me, and he was only the first in a long parade of coming developers.

But it had to be done soon. Dmitri was so shattered that he'd sell instantly at this point, and though Oleg couldn't have guessed that he was dealing with such a wrecked maniac, the Russian would move soon. So I had to do the following: find the money to buy the Lucky, buy it, get past the Mexican Conan and remove Oleg without killing him and thus bringing Dessel down on me, and—what else? Send a message to the other developers, and maybe hire some muscle of my own.

I drew several arcs for the duckling's brave chest. Then the front edge of the wings, wild and hungry for sky. He'd be skittering across the water, on the verge of taking his first true flight.

A plan took shape as I moved on to the webbed feet, toes splayed, pushing off the still water. Short. Some brutality, but not a totally senseless amount. I'd need some drugs, but any number of people could help with that. And I'd need to call in a favor with the Armenian, which was sure to be expensive. And I'd need to borrow Delia's human dildo boyfriend's band, Empire of Shit. I could trust those scumbags. And I needed to use some of Delia's secret rich-girl know-how to navigate my entrance into the now-unavoidable world of the legit. She'd like that, because she'd be able to rub my face in it. Forever.

"What are you drawing?" Suzanne was standing in the doorway, hip cocked, sleepy eyed, holding a steaming cup of coffee. I held up my sketchbook and she tilted her head.

"Cute," she said, admiring it. "Come back to bed."

23

Women have preferences in all things. Some women are glamorous, with stiletto heels and deep red lips, diamonds and one-color dresses. Sometimes the diamonds were fake and the clothes were knock offs, but it didn't matter. It was the look. On the other end were the women who dressed like college lesbians, who themselves dressed like thirteen-year-old boys. In between were the trillion variants, but a look in the end had absolutely nothing to do with sensuality. The same could be said of men, I suppose, but since I'd never fucked any of them, I couldn't say with any real conviction.

Naked, Suzanne was still a mystery. I followed her into the bedroom, distracted, mentally forming a to-do list, and somewhere in my trance she became naked. And she wound up lying on the bed. Looking at me. Her expression was neutral.

I sipped my coffee. To some degree, almost every muscle in her long body was visible, and she'd been blessed with tendons of a Shetland pony. No tattoos. A few faint scars. I licked my lips. She licked hers. Evidently she enjoyed my inspection.

I put my coffee down on the dresser and tore my clothes off, then stood there, erect, and gave her the once-over again, this time looking for a place to start. She stretched, but made no sign. My call.

My eyes traced the lines of her body. Some women were all about foreplay and some considered foreplay concluded by the time they were naked. Last night had only left me with the impression that she was a passionate, womanly woman. So I decided to do what any sensible man would do in that situation. It was time to eat pussy.

I seldom dreamed about sex, but if I were to have a nightmare about it, there would be a hairy muff and a Joni Mitchell song involved. In the late afternoon silence I licked my index finger and then pulled Suzanne's legs apart. From there, I used the cunnilingus skills I'd honed, remarkably, at the behest of my previous girlfriend. She'd been in the feminist, former English major, bisexual vegan camp. Essentially a tad bossy. She'd been a real stickler about it and, according to the whimsical justice dispensed by the Scales of Cosmic Irony, the governing force of my existence, right when she'd been satisfied that her unpleasantly graphic and often arduous tutorials were finally paying off, I dumped her for cheating on me with another woman.

So after I had Suzanne tied into a shuddering, convulsive, heaving knot, I considered smacking her on her upturned ass and telling her where she could send the thank you card, but I didn't. Sodomy two nights in a row was out of the question, so I pulled her around to the right angle and entered her in one smooth stroke. The resulting spasm and the aftershocks gave me the rhythm and I followed it, riding the peaks and lulls, lost in her animal. I don't know how long it went on and I have no idea how we wound up on the kitchen floor, but when I finally fell panting against the refrigerator door I was spent, done, empty of everything but soft bluish light. Something like electricity played over my molars.

Suzanne made a noise of some kind, part sigh and part something else, the low of an elk or the opening note of a European police siren. I opened my eyes. She was pulling herself up the cabinet in front of the sink. I groaned and climbed to my feet.

"I don't speak Spanish," I said. "I realized that earlier." She looked at me sharply, eyes glazed, without comprehension.

"*What?*"

"English. It's my only language. I can speak menu and insult in Mexican, but I dunno . . ."

She made it all the way upright and looked down into the sink.

"Jesus," she said quietly.

Conversation was always a little hard to get started right then. The suggestion of playful banter set a tone. Occasionally, the women I'd known could be distressingly serious after sex, and even veer straight to the dark side and blast you with something they normally wouldn't say and you didn't really need to know, and that generally gave way to some level of embarrassment later that could sometimes last for days. It struck me as I wobbled over to the counter and poured myself a small shot of Jameson's that I was being entirely too calculating in regard to Suzanne, and being the smart woman she was, she was bound to notice, if she hadn't already. Act natural, I thought, but the notion itself seemed contrived. I had no idea how to behave.

"I have no idea how to behave right now," I confessed. I downed the shot, reached out, and smacked her on the ass. She jumped a little. "I think I'm developing gnarly feelings for you and whatnot. Fucked in the head because of it. But please, don't start talking about anything dark and heavy, and don't start in on the whole drinking, smoking, maniac thing. I'm gonna sit down."

I went into the dining room and sat down at the table, lit a cigarette. It was true I was naked and I hadn't turned on the heater yet, but I was hot as hell and I was never truly naked. Not really. I rubbed the part of my abdomen where it said 'Run'. Might have sprained something right underneath it. I took a physical inventory as I smoked. My eye was a little puffy, but getting better every day. The ringing in my ears was back to what I considered almost normal. All new scars were checking in as pink and itchy, but OK. The goddamned boot heel was still a week away from beginning to fade. Ribs stiff, but no longer Advil-worthy. That happened all the time and fell into the who-cares category. My hand had just drawn a duckling. Still a month away from holding a tattoo machine, but since I didn't have one, that didn't matter. All told, not bad.

I was going to need to get Delia some of the nasty cash, and fast. I needed to call a meeting somewhere Dessel wouldn't notice and get Nigel going on my drug list. I'd put Delia on getting the Empire boys fitted for waiter clothes and pray they didn't fuck it up. Hide Big Mike in the background as reserve cavalry. Also call the Armenian and set up the meeting, once again under Dessel's radar. Plus, I'd have to get the Armenian a present of some kind, considering what I'd be asking. Strong-arming Dmitri was going to be easy considering how furious I was with him. My list formed to the post-orgasm genius glow that never, ever lasted. I sighed.

"Whatcha' thinkin'?" Suzanne sat down across from me. She was still naked, too, and she'd poured herself some Jameson's.

"Just letting my mind wander and then listening to it. S'how I think."

"Ah. As in don't ask."

I rolled my eyes and she raised her palm in the universal gesture for stop. I cleared my throat and smiled.

"If you must know, I was thinking about tying up some loose ends so I could take you on a trip of some kind. Maybe the coast for a few days, or even this mountain you seem so fond of. Room with a fireplace. Big bed. Bath salts. We could buy a hibachi and live off barbeque. I'm even thinking I could buy you some more flowers and get real corny about the whole thing."

Suzanne swirled her drink around, a smile just touching her eyes. She sipped, considering.

"But there are some conditions," I continued. She arched an eyebrow.

"Really." She put one hand under her chin and gave me her full attention.

"Totally. For one thing, you have to bring a dress of some kind. Something that shows off your legs. We'll be dining out, and I'm going to wear my court suit for it. So there's that. If you don't have one I'll buy you one, but I get to pick it out."

"OK." Her brown eyes were flecked with gold and green.

"Yep. Also hotels come with TVs and I have rules. Harsh, real ones. If we turn the TV on, we only watch the Food Network, sappy romantic comedies, or shit with robots. I'm deadly fuckin' serious."

"What about travel shows?"

"Maybe some," I replied, "but nothing overtly depressing. Rick Steves swimming around in a giant bathtub in Switzerland hits me the wrong way because I don't think they'd let me in, so you can see how I might be bummed by that, and that Anthony Bourdain guy can't open his pie hole without me wanting to stomp the black grease out of his head, so . . ."

"Charming," Suzanne breathed. "Dreamy. What else."

I cleared my throat and looked as uncomfortable as I could.

"This last part might have to wait. I'm not sure we're deep enough into things yet for me to . . . Ah. I'll tell you once we're on the road to wherever we're going. It'll be too late for you to say no by then."

"You better tell me now," she purred. "No way I'm going to wait."

"Eh . . . no."

"Now," she insisted, mock serious. She leaned in closer.

"Well . . ." I pulled back a little. "It's the clothes thing. Your clothes. Your whole athlete thing?" I gestured at her encompassingly. "It works on some level in a public setting. 'Look, that deadly rocked-out dude has a respectable Amazon with a bad-boy complex. Isn't that cute?' I can roll with that. Happens all the time. But privately, after a few

179

days I know it's going to get on my nerves. So when we're power lounging in the hotel, no clothes. You can wear the bathrobe and maybe even the slippers, but that's it. Is that OK?"

Suzanne drank her drink and smacked her lips.

"Darby Holland, you simpleminded fool, what in the world gave you the impression I would be wearing clothes?" She reached out under the table and her long hand wrapped around my dick. "You got a deal, mister. But I have rules, too. Laws. No clothes for you either, the coast, because you're too accident-prone for the mountain, and I'm going to pick out an outfit for you, too, little monster man. I'm going to dress you in loafers, chinos, and a pink yuppie polo shirt, and you'll look like the perfect little vacationing criminal. And we're going to go to some crappy tourist bistro"—she squeezed—"and pay way too much, and watch the rain through the windows and fondle each other under the table, just like this. And then you're going to fuck me in the women's bathroom."

My eyes narrowed.

"You dirty foreign hooker," I said.

Suzanne ran her pink tongue over her teeth. I wondered vainly what she saw when she looked that deeply into my eyes. I could have sat that way forever, but the world never had much time for me and that kind of moment. My new cell phone rang, startling us both. It was in front of me next to the ashtray. Delia.

"Shit," I said. I could hear the disbelief loud in my voice. Suzanne let go of me. It rang again.

"Just a sec," I said, picking it up. She mouthed the word "shower" and got up. I watched her walk away, then flipped the phone open as the bathroom door closed.

"Safeway east, security desk," I answered. "This better be a lawyer."

"I know for a fact that you can't go into Safeway, dummy." Delia smacked her gum. "Whatcha' doin'?"

I ran my hand over my short hair and picked up Suzanne's drink. Delia had threatened to kill my last girlfriend, and even though I'd almost thought she had a good idea, I wasn't looking forward to this.

"I . . . see, I, there was this woman last night, it was sort of—"

"You boned her and she's still at your house." Her tone was flat. I sighed.

"Sort of. I boned her in the bathroom of this wine place, and then again later at her place. But she came over earlier."

"I see. Slutty?"

"Not especially."

"Hmm. Did you do anything important? Non-chick-related, I mean."

"I did. I went to see the Lucky." I heard the shower turn on. "Dane Bane was in there picking through everything. I kicked his ass."

"Good. Did you rob him, too?"

"Delia, fucking get over it. I don't really rob people and you know it. I will appropriate money if I've been seriously fucked with as a kind of special compensation, but there's a difference."

"Whatever. So you did or didn't rob him?"

"I didn't rob him, but mostly because he probably didn't have anything, which is why he was robbing us."

It was her turn to sigh. "So what'd you decide?"

I toyed with the glass.

"I'm going to buy it and rebuild. I need your help."

Delia was silent for almost a full minute.

"Really?" she finally asked. She sounded far away.

"Yep. Really. It's time for you to whip out some of your real-world powers. I need an actual business account at a bank, with checks and shit like that, I need a money order or something like it ASAP for ten grand, and I need to call a meeting with Nigel and Big Mike, plus I need to hire Empire of Shit for a day, but the very first thing is I need you to go to some swanky store and get a present for the Armenian's daughter."

"The Armenian? Empire of Shit? A ten-thousand-dollar check? A real bank account with—"

"Yes," I snapped. "When can I get the money to you?"

"Right now," she replied, without pause. "I'm over at the Bonfire, ten blocks from your place. Bring the slutty bathroom chick."

"Delia," I cautioned, "that was my doing. You be nice, understand? You might actually like this one."

"We'll see," she said, bored now. "Hurry up already. This place is dead."

"OK. I have to take a shower and get some clothes on, so—"

She hung up.

The shower was still running, so I went into my office and dug the paper bag full of the nasty cash out of the closet, where I'd cleverly hidden it in plain sight. I quickly thumbed out twelve thousand, which took about two minutes, and put ten in an oversized envelope, folded it and put it in the bookcase by the door, then took the remaining two and slid them into the slot where my sketchbook had been. Then I wadded the bag back up and tossed it back in the closet. For some reason I was furtive as I made my way through the house to the bedroom. The water in the shower turned off.

"Clean towels in the cabinet," I called.

"Found 'em," she called back.

I took a clean black T-shirt and newer jeans out of the top dresser drawer, then socks and boxers out of the next drawer down. I paused with the boxers in my hand.

"You need underwear?" I couldn't remember if she'd been wearing any.

"Maybe," she called. "I think you ate mine. Are we going somewhere?"

I took out an extra pair. Checkered.

"The Bonfire. I have to meet a friend real quick. Just take a sec."

Suzanne came in, towel-drying her hair. She looked moist and sparkly and fresh. I held up the boxers.

"Cute," she said, accepting them. "Are you sure you want me to tag along? I can head home or . . ."

"A walk through the rain would be romanticky, but you can kick back here if you want to skip it. Lots of books, and my big-ass AM radio. Cats."

She smiled. "I'll come. I'm sort of hungry anyway."

She slipped into the boxers and folded the elastic waist over so they fit. I started getting dressed, too.

"Maybe we can stop at the store on the way back and get more crepe stuff. I was thinking chocolate blueberry earlier, but maybe some kind of banana? I dunno. It's good to have options unlimited."

"OK." Suzanne pulled her pants on and my heart sank a little. I pulled my jeans on and rolled the cuffs a few inches.

"So this friend of mine."

"Don't tell me. I'm in for some sort of surprise." She finished dressing and finger-combed her damp hair in the dresser mirror.

"Maybe. Sort of. I mean, yes." I got my third and last pair of boots out of the closet. Old Docs that had gone from black to gray, with a big splatter of fading green paint on the right toe. The cats had been chewing on the laces, but they hadn't gotten very far. I saw Suzanne look at them out of the corner of my eye. She sat down on the bed next to me and put her arm around my waist. She smelled like my soap.

"It's OK." She kissed my ear. "I'm a big girl."

I finished lacing up and stood. Suzanne stood, too, and smiled down into my upturned face. I winked.

"Let's rock-n-roll, baby. She's waiting."

After we got our jackets on and I loaded my pockets with smokes, keys, my crusty wallet, and a ball bearing, I ducked into my office while Suzanne waited in the front doorway, gauging the rain. I put the stuffed envelope in my jacket's inner pocket and stuffed the naked cash in the front pocket of my jeans. It was time, I thought, for the beginning of the end of something.

24

A romantic evening walk through the rain with Suzanne was once again the kind of thing I'd never experienced before. Portland was filled with a sort of goth/hippie hybrid type of woman who generally seized that moment to talk about graveyards or the merits of kale juice. I'd also found frequent company with the bisexual but mostly lesbian English major dropout chicks, and their sense of romance generally involved dissecting depressing Tom Waits songs and self-absorbed tirades on how they hated one thing or another, usually their mother or in a vague, hinting way, men, so me. But more often than not, they couldn't hold their booze and quickly wound up too bitter to make sense about anything.

Suzanne was unique in that she hummed some song, so quietly I couldn't make it out, and she walked like someone who really knew how to walk, with the easy Zen gait that only comes after your first million miles. She ignored me for the most part, but not in a bad way. She was happy outside, as rainproof as a swan in her Gore-Tex. It gave me breathing room to think about what I was going to tell the Armenian, but I found myself mostly quiet, internally. Suzanne's lilting voice and companionable presence was infectious. It even made me feel briefly young and stupid for never having experienced that kind of casual peace before.

The vibe was shattered with the intensity of a grenade blowing in a pickle jar as we rounded the corner of Stark. The Bonfire was right there. Delia's red Falcon was just beginning a block-long screaming slide as she braked at the tail end of a mad race to beat us.

Suzanne and I stopped as the smoking red Falcon came to a shuddering halt in the middle of the street and stalled. We were the only onlookers I could see from where we stood. The Falcon's starter ground, loud in the empty night, and the engine turned over after a few tries. Delia pulled into an empty space and killed it, then raced across the street into the Bonfire. She was wearing pink rubber pants, white combat boots, a black bra, and three layers of Hank Dildo's festive Empire of Shit jacket finery, all unbuttoned and several sizes too big. Suzanne and I looked at each other.

"Your pal?" she asked lightly.

"Best one I ever had," I replied. We started walking again. "You can pick your friends, but not your family? That's actually the most ass-backward bullshit I've ever heard. In the truest sense, that little gal is the only family I have."

Suzanne made no reply. The statement might have had a lonely ring to it, but I hadn't meant it that way. She did look a tiny bit sad as I opened the door for her, and I resolved to start cursing less, at the very least.

The Bonfire was mostly empty, with two red-faced power drinkers at the bar and one booth taken over by hipster zombies at the brittle end of a coke binge. Delia bounded out of the otherwise empty adjoining room, beaming. Her eyes ran up and down Suzanne and she winked at me, luridly. She stuck her tiny hand out for Suzanne to shake.

"Why hi there!" Delia began in a thick Louisiana accent. "I'm Lobelia May Bizby, songwriter, and I declare!" She turned her hundred watts on me. "Mr. Holland, this here is the jackpot in the leg department. Who'da thunk yew had it in yew!"

"What the unholy fuck," I growled.

"I'll get us drinks," Suzanne offered. She walked quickly to the bar and stood with her back to us. I grabbed Delia by her skinny arm.

"C'mon, Lobelia," I said. "Let's me and you chat."

I dragged her back into the adjoining room and pushed her into a booth. She folded her arms defiantly as I sat down across from her.

"So, Lobelia from Alabama or whatever the fuck you're—"

"Just shut up, fool," Delia spat. "I read your whole vibe in less than a second. Your game is gone. That fucking Amazon has already tamed your inner wolf, you fucking pussy. Right when you need it, too. The world is going to eat your scarred ass alive if you don't snap the fuck out of it, Darby. Game over. Done. And I'm going down with the ship, you fucking asshole? Fuck you."

She was furious. She leaned in fast and landed a solid right hook to my jaw, hard as hell. Delia could man fight. From there it was on. I surged over the table and head-butted her on the way in. I'd aimed for the bridge of her nose, but smacked into her sternum instead as she rose like a striking snake to knee me in the breadbasket. I twisted skin on her stomach as she squirmed and punched me in the side of the neck. Her next punch bounced off the top of my head and I let go and rammed my elbow into her stomach. She got me in a headlock and I elbowed her ribs. The air shot out of her and then I was on top. Her wild eyes flashed over my shoulder and I knew what she was seeing; Suzanne was coming.

I scrabbled into a sitting position and struck a casual pose. Delia did the same as she sucked in her breath, and then she let out a wild peel of insane laughter. I smiled at my imaginary joke as she straightened her hair.

"I miss something good?" Suzanne asked. She was carefully carrying a tray with three shots and three pints. I reached out to steady it as she set it down.

"Darby was list'nin' to my story o' all the pig wrasslin' I did on my holiday vacation. Blue ribbon winnah."

Delia and I were on the same side of the booth now. Suzanne settled across from us with a curious half smile. Delia and I were both panting.

"I do a little stand-up 'tween songs," Delia gushed. She elbowed me hard in my sore ribs and guffawed with a snort at the end. "Holland here's mah biggest fan."

Suzanne picked up her shot. Delia and I did, too. My knuckle was bleeding from where I'd scraped it on the edge of the table, so I raised my glass quickly.

"Suzanne," I said, dropping her name for Delia.

"Lobelia," Suzanne said, smiling and raising hers.

"Mean Daddy Darby Holland," Delia chimed.

188

We drank. I wiped my knuckle on my pants. There was an awkward silence.

"So," Suzanne began, "you and Darby go way back?"

"Oh yeah," I said before Delia could launch into something. "Me and this creature"—I punched Delia on the arm—"have some history. On prom night I pried a beer can out of her—"

"Holland is a hero to all manner of villainous miscreants, great and small," Delia interrupted. "Why, just today he told me about an incident, where, bless his soul, our own Darby went out of his way to—"

"We met in reform school," I interjected. "She was pregnant, of course, though how a white girl can give birth to black Chinese twins is—"

"Darby was there at the end of his gay porn career, which was unseemly for a twelve-year-old—"

"She does dogs these days. The things you can sell on the Internet . . ."

Silence again.

"Excuse me," Suzanne said, rising. "I'm going to get us a menu."

As soon as she left Delia pinched me viciously on the arm and twisted. I yanked my arm free and caught her wrist as she swung for a ringing slap.

"Calm the fuck down," I hissed.

"Make me," she snarled. "Pussy."

I rolled my eyes and let go of her. She crossed her arms again. I dug the envelope out and put it on the table in front of her.

"Ten grand," I said. "Get some kind of cashier's check."

She took it and stuffed it into her innermost jacket
pocket without looking. I took the wad of cash out and
slipped it to her under the table. She palmed it and it
disappeared.

"Two more. I need you to fix Dildo and the Empire
boys up with waiter outfits. They have to be ready the day
after tomorrow. Dye their hair back to some natural color
and hose the fuckers down. They need to be convincing.
Tell them if they do this, I'll pay for their 45, recording and
pressing, and you'll do the jacket art. If they say no, you'll
dump Hank and I'll beat the fuck out of all of them. Two
hours' work, they get a record. Got it?"

Delia nodded, once.

"All right. Take the rest and buy that present for the
Armenian's daughter. I need it tomorrow by noon,
wrapped, cheesy bow, the whole nine yards. Anything left
over is yours. Do you still love me?" It just came out.

Delia gave me a hard look. Her dark eyes glittered. "Yes."

My own face went as hard as railroad steel and my good
eye watered. "I love you, too."

And then we hugged. I could feel her heart hammering
against my chest.

"Don't get us killed," she whispered.

"I won't," I whispered back.

We let go of each other and Delia wiped her eyes.

"I better get going. That uniform place over by the
liquor store might still be open. Two birds with one stone,
considering how drunk they'll need to be at hair time. Tell
Suzanne . . ." She trailed off. I knew she wanted to finish
with "to fuck back off to the sane side of the world for

now," but she didn't. I got up and let her out. Delia went out the back door without another word.

When Suzanne got back I was deep in thought, rambling through variables and grim possibilities, casting dice into a dark cave filled with snakes. She sat down with a menu.

"Where's Lobelia?" she asked with her special smile, the warm, happy one that made me think of the smell of a heater on a cold morning, or the first glimpse of a distant, grassy hill.

Somehow, it was the saddest thing I'd ever seen.

Suzanne and I finished our drinks in silence. The quiet was because she perceived something bad had happened, that "Lobelia" had been a messenger with news relating to my new scars, destroyed business, the forestalled police hunt, and even the boot-heel bruise. She was right, of course. It didn't take any woman's intuition to lead her to that conclusion. My flimsy newborn inner peace was gone, the last vestiges of my confusion had vanished, and I could feel my soft parts mummifying right in front of her. I was brooding and I knew it. There was a low-grade hostility radiating from me and there was nothing I could do about it. I didn't even want to. I believed I could fuck Oleg on a train-wreck level and get away with it, and maybe even end up with the Lucky to boot. I was that good at being that kind of bad. I also knew, deep down, that something in Suzanne could make me happy in the kind of way that might make me wise. But I also understood that I couldn't fit both of those things inside of me.

Delia was right. It had all started when Oleg hired Ralston to blow up the Lucky and pave the way for the bright Starbucks and art loft future for the blight that was Old Town. I'd been factored in as a thing that had to go and I'd decided not to. Every single facet of the plan based on that decision was illegal, and the reason for that was, I knew, that at heart I was a criminal, too, a card-carrying member of the element society rightly tried to exterminate. It didn't matter in the least that the same society, with its mazes with no end and tests with no answers, had gradually forced me into that position, and the comfort or sense of achievement I got from being a creature refined by darkness, grown powerful and cunning enough to murder a pimp and potentially flush a power-crazed Russian mini-tycoon down the crapper without getting busted, was bullshit when it came to Suzanne. I could never tell her any of it. She'd believe I was insane by her standards, and if I took her through my life, step by step, to guide her to an understanding of what I'd become and why, all I'd be doing was talking her out of being in love. Fact.

"I have a job interview tomorrow," Suzanne said eventually. She'd been toying with her tumbler and watching me. I tried to perk up.

"Really? I have job-related shit tomorrow, too."

"Maybe I should head on home."

"Let's have one more," I said. I forced a smile I didn't feel at all. Maybe, just maybe, everything in the next few days would come off without a hitch, and it was possible I would be able to live with all the lies I would have to tell afterward, and all the lies that would come after those. Forever. She didn't buy the smile either way.

"Something's changed," she said. "Is that woman your girlfriend? Ex-girlfriend? Something like that?"

"She should be," I confessed. "I've been waiting to love her, and don't get me wrong, I love that little mutant like the rising sun. But not in that way."

Suzanne let that sink in.

"The bad news is this," I continued. "I told you that all kinds of awful shit has been going on in my world, and the reason I couldn't be specific is the same reason I still can't be. It's bad. And here's the truth. We all know raw shit goes down in the world around us. Most people read about it in the papers. Movies get made about bikers and gangsters and tons of other stuff. Right now, I live in that shit for real. You don't. The next few days? People are probably going to try to kill me. Real people. The police, like that pig you were jabbering with on my front porch? Jacob, I think he called himself? He wants to hang me out as a target. This is the second time he's tried. They're going to try to arrest me if using me as bait doesn't pan out. And me? I'm in my endgame, and if I make it, I not only get to live, but I might prosper and grow into something that, to you, might be more objectionable than what I already am. So I'm kinda wondering if I'm wasting your time."

Suzanne frowned in a way I hadn't seen a woman frown since I was a boy. Not sour or condescending. Disappointed, slightly impatient, wistful, and with a little tired disbelief.

"Darby," she began, shaking her head. "Look. Listen. Try to hear me. I already know you're up to your neck in quicksand. But let's be clear and get everything out on the table, right now, before you piss me off to the point where you totally blow it. And I'm moderately pissed off already, so let's start there."

Here it comes, I thought. The beginning of the end I was predicting, just a different prelude to the same conclusion I was expecting.

"Drinks!" Suzanne roared. The lazy bartender peeked around the corner. I held up two fingers and looked apologetic.

"To start with," she began, "I want you to understand exactly how much shit I've put up with from men in general. I'm fucking beautiful and I know it. I have a career. I have interesting things going on in my life. I'm a righteous score, if you pitiful jackasses could look past the fact that I'm six foot five. The percentage of men my height or taller, as in the ones who feel comfortable with me, is like 1 percent. A tiny group to choose from. All extreme shitheads so far. It makes me fucking sick. And you, *you*! With your scars and your ridiculous personality crisis, which you're rudely having right in fucking front of me, you think I don't know what's going on here? You think I'm stupid? Then fuck you. You fuck like an animal. You have so much passion for everything it makes you seem insane to other people, and now you even believe them. You don't fit in and you never will. Ever. Just like me. I could give half a shit in the end about all the crap you get up to in the course of a day. If you think it's that horrible, then be a real man and bottle it up. I'm applying for the girlfriend position, but I can tell you have some baggage in that department and it's tripping me up. I'm not going to bother with being your judge and jury. And you know why? Can you even guess? Because I'm a woman, not a girl. Which means I'm actually too fucking busy."

The bartender arrived with our drinks. He looked like he wanted to squeeze off something about being yelled at, but Suzanne gave him a withering glare and I blasted him with stone-cold killer when he looked at me for support, so he wisely stayed shut. It was probably our last round, though.

"So you," Suzanne concluded, stabbing her finger at me, "best get your shit together."

I shook my head. "I am. I will. Swear to God. But why the fuck does everyone keep telling me that?"

Suzanne snorted. "If that's what Lobelia, or whatever her real name is, told you that provoked this pitiful display, please tell her that I think I'll buy her lunch rather than step on her." She sat back, finished for the moment. I picked up my shot.

"If it's any consolation, everything you said made such perfect sense that now I'm truly, totally confused." It was the wrong thing to have said. I knew it instantly.

"Why?" Now she had gone from angry to pissed. I set my glass down and raised my hands in surrender.

"OK. You're hot. Smoking. You're interesting. Extremely. And I'm sorry if . . . no, wait. I'm not sorry about anything. If you can live with the fact that I'm in a shitty position and I have to do some shitty but highly creative stuff that I may unfortunately, possibly enjoy because of the admittedly questionable nature of my character, then we're right back to planning our trip to the coast, and I apologize for the rude interruption."

Suzanne stewed for a moment, which I used to down my drink. But she was right about herself. She was a woman, not a girl. She picked up her shot glass and looked at me over the rim.

"You might just do after all," she said evenly. Then she drank.

After that, we ate six blueberry chocolate crepes each. I invited her to stay the night. I was tired and it showed, so after we both brushed our teeth with my toothbrush, which I considered a situation that had to be remedied first thing in the morning, we went to bed, and rather than maul each other, we talked. She even let me smoke in bed.

"So where are you from?" I asked.

"San Diego," Suzanne replied, stifling a yawn. She was lying on her side, relaxed, watching me. "I moved here to work for a law firm, but after a year or so my journalism degree finally started paying off. Travel stuff, mostly." She'd told me something about that the other night. "What about you? You didn't tell me."

"I'm not really from anywhere," I confessed. "Moved around a lot as a kid. My favorite place was Houston."

"How come?" She seemed genuinely curious, but in a charming, whimsical way.

"I dug the rain, I guess. The food was good. Houston is mostly black, or at least I remember it that way, so the school food was geared toward them. No pizza or meat-loaf. They would have freaked out and rioted. Greens, corn bread. About a billion kinds of ham. Catfish, which is cheap as clay down there. Peach cobbler. Shit like that."

"Mnn." For some reason it made her smile.

"Frogs, too."

"They served frogs to schoolchildren?"

I looked at her like she was crazy. "No, dummy. There were lots of frogs in Houston. We didn't eat them, we played with 'em. I had a pet frog under my house named Wyatt. Every little boy's dream."

"What kind of little boy were you?" She reached out and started playing with my hair. I thought about it. The wind shifted outside and the rain pattered on the window.

"Mostly OK," I said eventually. "Big reader. I drew comics. Played basketball. Everything went to shit around ninth grade. I was on my own after that. It was hard and I somehow wound up having to take care of my older brother as soon as I had enough money to get a place. He ditched me after a while and things got worse before they got better. I had a mother and a little sister, but they stuck together and I just sort of lost them, I guess. More than twenty years ago, now. I went to Montana when I was sixteen and worked at a gas station in Billings. Had my first live-in girlfriend. Then I discovered the punk scene. It was small, but it led me to LA for a while, then Denver, which I sort of had to leave in a hurry. Then I moved here. Got a part-time job at a tattoo shop called Lucky Supreme, janitor and lookout for all the shady shit the owner was up to. I was tattooing on the third day. That was back in the good old days, when no one knew what they were doing."

"The good old days," she repeated softly. "You're still too young to have good old days."

"I know," I agreed. "But you know how it is. I've had my share of fun, and believe it or not I still do. But generally, if I'm trying hard enough, yesterday was the good old days. Just like today will be tomorrow."

Suzanne lightly smacked my forehead. "You're so full of it. But I guess I agree."

"Which leads us to tomorrow. You said you have a job interview?"

"Yeah." She resumed playing with my hair, but slower, and she watched me with different eyes. "Travel Asia. Based out of Bangkok. English language, glossy, outdoor to food. I'm interviewing for an editor slash contributing writer slot."

"Huh." I sat up a little. "Does that mean you have to, like, move to Asia?"

She didn't answer right away.

"Not anytime soon," she said after the unreadable pause. "I don't even know if I'll get it, and if I do there's still the question of what they're offering, paywise. I can't take a job for a trust fund kid, which is sometimes the case with these kinds of gigs. Right now, at this moment, I don't even want to think about it."

I relaxed again. Mostly.

"You said you had job-related shit, I think you called it?" Sleepy, seemingly uninterested.

I shifted uncomfortably. "Yeah. Meetings, mostly."

"I see."

"Yep." I put my cigarette out and put the ashtray in the bed stand drawer. "Official corporate business. Putting in a bid. Complicated banking crap. It's a long story."

Suzanne purred and stretched, but had no comment.

"I'm free tomorrow night," I said casually. "Maybe we can do something." It was terrible and I knew it, but I was anticipating Dessel picking up my trail tomorrow and spending the evening doing something innocuous with Suzanne would confuse the fuck out of him, make him think he was wasting man hours.

"What were you thinking?"

"Let's have dinner. Someplace nice. Test-drive a new dress for our trip. I have this whole fantasy thing going on. Nothing greasy, as amazing as that sounds. I just want to see you walk into a restaurant and know you're there looking for me. Me. Total corn."

She sighed, pleased. "We can do that. Black OK?"

"Oh yeah."

She smiled and closed her eyes. I watched for a few minutes as she fell asleep and dreamed about whatever tall women dream. After a little more of that, I got up quietly and padded out into the dining room.

Suzanne's purse was on the floor beside the chair she had been sitting in. It was small and looked like a Special Forces camera bag. I guiltily snapped it open and looked through it. Lip balm. Sunscreen. Keys, but none to a car, one to a PO box. Her wallet was a tiny black thing. I took it out and opened it, and there it was, the thing I had been looking for for two days.

Suzanne's last name was Barnes. Suzanne Evelyn Barnes. She was thirty-one. Yesterday had been her birthday. I put everything away and went back to bed with one less thing to worry about.

I woke up at ten a.m. to an empty bed. I'd slept for nine hours. I pulled at my face for a minute and something crinkled next to me. It was a note from Suzanne.

"You don't snore, but you did mutter a few times. Had to go get ready. I kissed you on the stomach, right below RUN, but you didn't wake up. See you tonight, 8:30, Brasserie Montmart. I'll make the reservation under Holland. Be good at your meetings. —S"

Not a bad way to start the day. I sat up. My ribs felt sore but sound. I felt reasonably solid again, and in the morning, right when I wake up, is when I'm usually at my most happy and paradoxically also dangerously easy to piss off. I rolled my head and snapped my teeth a few times, then hopped out of bed and dropped.

Push-ups first thing is a good idea for everyone who can do them. It warms you up right away, and that warmth seeps into your core and acts as a thermal armor, which was great for a rainy place like Portland. After the first ten I felt last night's cigarettes blow away. By twenty, something popped in the center of my back and my spine went from dog to cat. By thirty, my blood had all pumped through my liver and my kidneys and everything felt a little cleaner, if such a thing was possible, and by forty, I was hungry and thirsty and thinking about Suzanne's ass. As I muscled my way through fifty, I had a clear vision of punching Oleg in the throat. At sixty I started to feel the burn, so I stopped. Energy of the best kind for later.

The coffee was already made, which had never happened before except when Delia spent the night, and then only when I was injured, and she usually put Gummy Bears in it. I poured myself a cup and lit a cigarette, then walked over to the sink and looked out the window. Rain, which was no surprise. I flicked my ash into the drain and noted there was no coffee cup in the sink. Suzanne had either washed hers and put it away, or she'd just made coffee for me on her way out. Rare news, either way.

I carried my coffee to the dining room table and sat down, picked up my cell phone, and dialed. Delia answered on the first ring.

"Done," she said.

"All of it?"

"Yepper. I went by the bank and got all the forms for your business account and filled them out. You have to drop them off and show them your ID and pick out your check register. You already have your DBA, but the certificate got blown up, so they're sending a new one to your place. I got the Armenian's daughter a super-cool passionflower pendant at Gilt. Four bills, European, not bad. And I got the uniforms for Dildo and the rest of Empire secondhand. All four of them are the exact same size, 120 pounds and five foot seven. They agreed to your terms, I had to throw in a blow job for Dildo, and after they got liquored up they even agreed to the hair color of my choice, as long as it was temporary." She sounded exceptionally pleased with herself.

"Excellent. What about the big fat check?"

"A tiny bit sticky. That cash was totally disgusting, by the way. But I got four money orders and then rolled it into a cashier's check at my bank just now. So I made twelve hundred bucks this morning. I like the way you roll, dude. Always have."

"You did have to suck dick," I reminded her.

"I was going to anyway. Neener."

I shook my head. "All right then. Meet me at noon . . . fuck. Let's see. Dessel might be waiting for me right now. In fact, I'm sure he is. Tell you what. I'm going to drive over to Northwest Portland, say Burnside and 21st. There's always a shit-ton of people milling around there. I'll hop the eastbound Trimet bus just before noon. You get on in the Park blocks. Call Nigel and tell him to get on in Old Town, Mikey the first stop on the other side of the river. I'll get off at 82nd and walk over to the Armenian's from there. You guys scatter into cabs after that. Good?"

"We'll be waiting."

"Good. I'll call the Armenian now and then I'll call you in a couple hours when I'm about to board."

"I'll line 'em up."

It was going to be good to see the dudes again. Maybe I'd even bring snacks. Meeting on the bus was a good idea on many levels. It was higher than most of the other traffic, and the four of us together would create an instant no man's land, so we'd be alone, moving, and with a commanding view. I just hoped they didn't still have my photo on the permanent eighty-six list they kept on the wall in the driver break room. I sighed at the possibility and lit my second cigarette of the day.

The Armenian. Now there was a puzzle I had no interest in solving. He'd briefly dated the hot, grumpy French woman who owned the chocolate shop around the corner from my house about a decade ago, maybe longer. From then on I'd kept running into him, until one night Nigel and I had crashed some kind of weird Gypsy party at the Greek Cusina and I'd run into the Armenian again. Everyone there had treated him like Don Corleone, which made me consider the wisdom of getting pathetically wasted with him, but I'm an eternal advocate of throwing caution to the wind, and that night had been no exception.

From then on we were friends, of a sort. He was twenty years older than me, so there was that, but he was also an impossibly secretive guy, and much like Nigel, when you had too many secrets to keep track of, they fell out at random in the oddest way. The Armenian positively hemorrhaged secrets on an embarrassing level.

He had three kids, he said, though I'd met seven so far. He claimed he was from London, but then again he'd been in a semi-public uproar a few years ago when US customs had stopped him for being born in Iran. He had an automotive shop, but the one time I'd taken my BMW there, he'd rented me a newer Mercedes for three weeks and then returned my car unfixed, no questions please. And that was barely scratching the surface.

The three guys who worked for him were shadier than he was, if that was even possible. They were Chinese, and I could swear that the Armenian spoke to them in their own dialect. The most valuable data I had on the table at the moment actually came from them. One day, when I'd been at their shop to go out to lunch with the Armenian— which usually meant becoming a component part in one of his plans, the rewards of which varied from a pack of cigarettes to the use of a convertible for the weekend—I'd engaged the Chinese guys in casual conversation while they were inspecting the engine of a new Lexus. The transmission was "broken," and that was all that mattered.

When the Armenian and I got back from lunch, they had the transmission out and it was sitting in a big, sturdy box. I'd asked the Armenian about it.

"Ah Darby, yes." He began everything that way. "The transmission of this vehicle is very, very expensive. But to ship it is very cheap. Here, maybe four thousand to rebuild, minimum, three weeks time, minimum. Minimum! But I have friends at pier six. To mail this to Russia is nothing, and hey." He'd shrugged. "They work for pennies. Pennies! The Russians put a trash can into space, Darby. Those engineers are happy to work on a transmission. For them, it is a child's game."

On the drive over to northwest Portland, I couldn't tell if I was being followed or not. Any crime novel would give you the impression that a three-car, radio-coordinated tail was impossible to bust, and I wouldn't put it past Dessel, so I wasn't taking any chances. I called the Armenian from the road. He hated telephones unless he was trying to impress someone by keeping them waiting in his office, so the call would likely take the duration of the first stoplight.

"This is George." He called himself George. The name on his driver's license, which I'd caught a glimpse of once, said something unpronounceable, and it didn't begin with the letter G.

"I have that present for your daughter," I said. I hadn't spoken to him in almost three months, so he would have forgotten by now if he'd asked me for such a thing.

"My friend, thank you," he said smoothly, exceptionally warm. "Please come." He hung up.

More good news. The warmth meant he was up to something as usual, and would be up for a trade. Interesting. It was raining a little harder than when I'd left, which made for good cover once I was on foot, but I was going to get wet later, no doubt about it. I turned on the radio and listened to the rambling jazz station while I rambled myself, for all the world an aimless guy with no job, bored out of his mind.

Midway through cigarette number four and just past Old Town and headed east, I spotted Dessel and Pressman four cars back. They were good, which was obviously bad. The car was an instantly forgettable grayish Pontiac of indeterminate age. Both of them were wearing anonymous baseball caps, Pressman prescription glasses, Dessel looking down, but I could still see the line of Dessel's jaw. The thing that tipped me off was that they were pigs. The dashboard was cluttered with wrappers and empty cigarette packs, which meant they'd been in there all morning, which in turn meant they'd picked me up within a block of my house.

I ignored my rearview from then on, but I tried not to be conspicuous about it, which was harder than it sounds. Breaking the law right then actually seemed like a good idea, so I made a wide, meandering turn onto 19th without signaling. When I hit the first stop sign, I risked a peek in the rearview. They were already parked about halfway down the block. A red Miata with a blonde power yuppie woman behind the wheel came to a stop behind me. It may or may not have been the same woman getting into a red car at the Starbucks by my house. I'd had a stray nasty thought about her. Either way, it was time to hoof it.

I parked on 20th and Couch and got out, stretched, scratched the top of my head, lit a smoke. Then I started walking up to 21st.

When I'd first moved to Portland two decades ago, I'd loved the area when I found it. Old Victorian houses mixed in with Gothic apartment buildings, wig shops and hippie cafes, weirdo boutiques and even a lone skateboard shop. Gentrification had hit it slowly, but a certain percentage of the original element had held on and still rotted away in reasonable peace, so it had kept much of its character. A rainy day stroll through the area wasn't entirely out of keeping for a Portlander.

Foot traffic got thicker when I hit 21st, and I immediately found what I was looking for: umbrellas. Normally you didn't see too many umbrellas in a place where it rains all the time. They break, people lose them, they only keep your head dry if there's no wind, they poke other pedestrians and piss them off, et cetera. In short, they ultimately aren't worth the effort, plus there were awnings everywhere. People mostly gave up on them after their first winter. But not in touristy northwest Portland.

I merged right into the medium-thick crowd of umbrella-toting walkers and visibility instantly dropped to ten feet. After a dozen yards or so, I paused under the awning of a sushi place and looked at the menu in the window, then ambled on to the convenience store next to it and went inside.

There were a few soggy people in line with chips and toilet paper and one guy with a six-pack of beer. I walked to the back and studied the beer selection through the glass. From there, I could keep an eye on the sidewalk, and selecting beer in a serious microbrew town could take some lengthy consideration.

Pressman blew by on the sidewalk with his head down, not really looking around. The dumb-ass didn't even glance in my direction. I took out a six-pack of Full Sail and walked over into the generalized crap section of the store. Emergency raincoats, folded into tiny rectangles about the size of a pack of cigarettes, were ten dollars, which was wildly overpriced considering you could buy the exact same ones at the Dollar Store, but they came in multiple colors, including a glaring, warning buoy orange, which almost made up for it. I took an orange one and went up to the register. There was a hat display to stare at while you waited, all baseball caps with local slogans on them. I picked out a green-and-yellow one with a beaver. When I got to the front, the clerk rang me up without so much as a hello. As soon as he had scanned the hat I put it on and pulled the brim low.

"These come with hoods," he said, holding up the rain-coat packet.

"Lifelong beaver fan, what can I say. Bag for the beer?"

When we were done I tore the raincoat out and shook it open. There was no one waiting behind me, so the clerk just watched as I put it on and pulled the hood up.

"Those things never work twice," he cautioned. The raincoat smelled like a Band-Aid.

Disguised as a distressed motorist with a sports fetish and beer-drinking plans, I went outside and merged with a group of assorted fanny-pack gawkers drifting toward Burnside. I kept my eyes on the ground like I was more interested in keeping the rain off my face, and I didn't look up again until I'd reached Burnside. There, I had to pause as my protective cluster of pedestrians came to a collective halt. A few of them began angling their umbrellas this way and that to get a better look at each other. I knew there was a line a few blocks down to my left outside of a place called the Ringside, and I considered disappearing into the darkness of the old place as a fallback if detection appeared unavoidable. The walk sign went green and my group began to move. I stuck with them and politely worked my way closer to the newly emerging center. When we were across, I took a hard left toward downtown and picked up the pace.

At that point I was exposed. The rain was slacking off and foot traffic was light. The first bus stop was half a block down in front of a gas station, so I ducked down the side of the first business, which was some kind of yogurt place with completely empty wraparound covered seating. It was thankfully closed, but the tables and chairs were chained in place. I sat down a few tables in, gathered my billowing raincoat tight, and took my phone out. I could see a few blocks up Burnside through the glass, so I'd be able to spot the bus. Delia answered on the first ring.

"Where are you?" she asked.

"22nd and Burnside. Dessel and his posse are out there somewhere, but they're going to pick me up again any minute if I don't get the fuck gone. When's my bus coming?"

"I'm at Burnside and 6th and mine is at 12:11, so it should cross your stop in"—she checked the time on her cell phone—"less than two minutes."

"Nigel and Mikey?"

"Nigel's at the bridge a few blocks down from me, Mikey's at the first stop on the other side. They just checked in."

"OK." I kept my head down. "Keep talking to me. It makes for good cover." I cradled the phone under my chin and dug my cigarettes out and lit one.

"Well, chatwise, let's see," Delia began sweetly. "Hank has been so kind lately. He's off the glue, you know. I did some sweet graffiti on the living room walls the other day and he relapsed. All of them did. It was cute, but I swear, give four punk boys spray paint and they all wind up in their underwear. One more mystery, but I've seen it before so it's, like, universal. I'm having a really heavy period and my inner hippie is—"

"Delia!" I snapped. The bus was coming. "Get ready. I'll be in the back. Beavers cap."

"I love beavers! Did you—" I snapped my phone shut.

Burnside was a busy street. The bus paused to disgorge some people a few blocks up and was once again rumbling my way, but not very fast. Everyone was driving slow because of the slick streets and the high percentage of out-of-town drivers. My timing had to be perfect.

I waited until the bus was about five car lengths away from my stop. There was a restaurant delivery truck two cars in front of it, so right when it passed my yogurt place I stepped out and power walked alongside it, invisible to anyone across the street. When I got to the bus stop I tossed my cigarette and knelt to adjust my bootlaces, the bag with the beer on the wet pavement in front of me. From that low position, the passing cars hid me for the most part and there was no way the driver could miss me squatting at the stop in hazard orange. I flagged him anyway as he approached and he stopped. When the doors hissed open, I stepped in quickly with my bag. The bus lurched into motion.

"Just a sec," I told the driver, grabbing the open seat by the door. "Gotta set this bag down to get at my change."

He nodded without taking his eyes off the road. I pulled the raincoat off in one motion and stuffed it into the bag, slouched, and adjusted my beaver cap as I dug out a handful of quarters. Then I risked a peek outside. No one seemed to be scanning the sidewalks through the rain. No red Miata and no nearly invisible gray sedan. I glanced back at the rest of the bus. Two stoner kids listening to their headphones, but otherwise empty. I dumped the change in the terminal slot. The driver tore off my transfer and I took a seat in the second to last row. From there I ventured another peek out. Still clear. I slumped low, pulled the brim of my cap down, and pretended I was asleep.

Five stops later I heard the bus door hiss open and I didn't even need to look up.

"Two bucks and change?" Delia complained. A wave of her newest custom perfume wafted over me, all the way at the back of the bus. She had perfected the essence of birthday cake. "That cuts into the whack doodle budget my horny stepdad worked out for me."

The driver muttered something, and a moment later the seat rocked next to me. I sat up and returned Delia's huge smile with a little less wattage.

"This is so cool," she whispered. "I feel like a spy in a seventies porno movie. Can we strangle somebody?" She was wearing her huge, red-splattered motorcycle boots, pants that looked like they'd been made out of a motel shower curtain, three of Dildo's Empire jackets, and a Burger King kid's tee. Her hair was up in two rude little pigtails.

"Maybe later. You smell fuckin' great."

She wiggled her butt, lap dancing briefly. I got two beers out of my bag and passed her one. We popped the tops with our lighters together, the sound covered by simultaneous coughs.

"I'm almost positive they have no idea I'm on the bus," I said. I slumped low and awkwardly drained half my beer.

"Those two baked little dudes got itty bitty boners when I walked past, so they can't be five oh." She patted my knee. "Very clever, Darby."

I grunted and waited for the follow-up.

"Nigel," she said brightly.

The bus stopped and Nigel got on. He'd gone overboard on his disguise in the worst possible way. He was wearing a dark gray banker's suit with a blue tie and a black overcoat, and he was carrying a briefcase. His short hair was slicked back to the skull. The net effect was that he looked like a representative of the Devil, on his way to a virgin soul swapping. He scanned the bus with hard eyes and then dropped a handful of change into the slot. The driver meekly offered him a transfer and he took it without looking. Nigel slowed briefly to give the stoner kids a terrifying once-over, then continued on to where Delia and I were sitting. He sat down in front of us and casually turned around.

"Hi, Darby. Cool scar. Who brought the beer?" He winked at Delia.

I handed him one and he draped his arm over the back of his seat to keep it out of the driver's line of sight. Delia popped the cap with a dainty cover sneeze.

"So what's the plan?" Nigel asked. "You do have a plan, right? You lost the cops, didn't you?"

"The cops are lost as hell by now," I replied. "We'll get to the plan in a minute."

Nigel sipped his beer and nodded. He looked good, but I could tell things had been going on in his life. They always were. He looked a little tired and wired, and the knuckles on the hand holding the beer had been torn up recently. He noticed my noticing and shrugged.

The bus started over the Burnside Bridge then. I looked out the window, and beside me Delia turned and looked, too. I could feel her warmth as she leaned in, smell her bubble gum breath. The river below was slow and wide and the exact same gray as the sky. Across the river were grain silos and assorted railroad garbage. My right eye felt good. Visibility wasn't great, but about a quarter-mile away a big bubble of oil bloomed prismatically on the surface and slowly diffused into nothing.

"Oooh," Delia murmured. "Pretty."

I elbowed her off me and we snuck sips of beer until we hit the first stop on the other side, where Mikey got on. Even Nigel turned to look.

Big Mike looked like shit. His normally bald head had several days of multi-hued stubble on it, and so did his face. He was sporting a medium black eye, too. He was obviously depressed about something. It was in the slump of his wide shoulders, and the way he wasn't bothering to suck his gut in. His classic olive drab bomber jacket was wet and vaguely dirty, zipped up all the way to the neck with some of the collar turned up. His jeans were wet, too, like he'd been waiting a long time without bothering to stand inside the empty bus shelter. Even his boots were scuffed. He pepped up a little when he saw us, dumped his change and got a transfer, and headed in our direction with a brief pause to mad dog the two kids, who finally elected to move to the front of the bus as soon as he passed. He dropped into the seat next to Nigel and turned.

"Hey guys," he said. He sniffed at Delia with a weak smile and then looked at me. "Lame hat, man. The scar is very B-movie villain. Who brought beer?"

I popped the top of one with a cover sneeze and Mikey draped his arm next to Nigel's. I could tell I was going to have to talk to him later. A month without my idiot brand of psychotherapy had done him no good at all.

"So," Nigel began, "this plan. The Darby Holland Masterstroke. Let's have it." His eyes glittered with delight. Delia squirmed in anticipation. Mikey forced a smile and took his first sip of beer.

It felt good for all of us to be together again, and I knew they felt it, too. It felt great. But it also made me scrutinize my plan again in a new light. I realized part of what I was planning would sound utterly insane to most people. The three of them would be different, but I decided to hold the second half back for the time being. The whole thing, all at once, might be too much.

"It's pretty simple," I began. "I'm going to see our landlord Dmitri later. When I do, I'm going to beat the fuck out of him, although that's just a maybe, but I'm going to tell him to sell the building. A Russian real estate developer named Oleg something or other was behind the bombing, but naturally there's no proof. He wants to buy anything in Old Town with a price tag on it and he's really ingenious about changing the value. So Dmitri spins it like this. This Oleg character is already all over him. Dmitri calls and says you win, game over. Meet me in a public place with the papers and I'll sign, then retire somewhere far, far away. But Dmitri will want cash, say two fifty, to avoid whatever paranoid fuckers like him want to avoid."

"Good so far," Delia said.

"Lots of cash in the air. Confusion," Nigel mused. "We do good there."

"Exactly," I said. "So the meeting is at Gomez's brother's restaurant over on Alberta. Romero's Taqueria. The wait-staff will be replaced for the duration of the meeting by Empire of Shit, who already have their uniforms. First task goes to Nigel. We're going to rufie the fuck out of Oleg and his bodyguard. Big-time, near-coma-level shit. Delia takes whatever Dmitri signed while the drugs kick in, uses her computer and her art skills to white out Oleg's name and information and replace it with mine, Dmitri keeps the loot. I get the building for free. I need the money I have right now for a new roof and shit like that."

"What about Oleg and the bodyguard?" Mikey asked. "When they wake up they'll kill us or have us thrown in jail."

"No they won't," I said. "I can't kill Oleg and get away with it, but I have a plan. I'll keep that part to myself for now. That's where you come in, Mikey. I need you to go to the Bismarck Motel on 82nd and rent a room for a few days. Pay cash. That will be our base of operations. I was just there a few days ago and I had a chance to scope the place out. Get the room at the edge of the courtyard right by the parking lot and park your van in the spot closest to the door."

Big Mike looked uncomfortable, but he nodded.

"Try to keep in character. Drink lots of beer. Slum for a few days. Get some hoes and blend."

Nigel and Mikey looked at each other. Nigel cleared his throat.

"The ho thing might be a problem," he said casually. "See, this mouthy pimp Clarence? Limpy dude? He, ah, well . . . he was running his mouth all over Old Town and our street cred was going down, kept going on and on about how he beat your ass and we were all his butt vaginas, shit like that, plus if the cops caught wind of his bullshit . . . Delia said you were busy getting pussy and whatnot, and we all know you needed it. Pussy is good. So Mikey and I tracked him down and had a talk with him. He loves us now. Especially you. You ever run for mayor of Old Town, this guy Clarence? He's your PR guy. But me and Mikey are on the ho shit list big time right now."

Mikey snorted. "Did you really pour toilet water on him? That fucked with his head somehow."

Nigel clanked his beer against mine. "Points for style, boss."

My eyes watered and my throat felt tight. Delia patted my thigh again.

"We got your back, monster boy," she whispered.

"You guys," I said. "You guys. Damn. So this all happens tomorrow afternoon. With any luck we'll be up and running in six weeks or so. In the meantime, everyone get your vacation time in. Draw flash. We need about fifteen sheets each, plus I can make copies of the vintage crap I have in storage. Anyone needs money, hit me up tomorrow night.

We can meet at Dante's for drinks and you crazy mother-fuckers can meet my new chick."

"I'm goin' to Cabo," Mikey said. "Draw my flash poolside."

"Paris for me," Nigel said. He yawned. "Those tacky fag-gots need an infusion of game, plus I can tell people I was just chillin' there, working on art, blah blah blah. Score cool points."

"Maybe I'll take Dildo to San Francisco for a week," Delia mused. "Record shopping, motel porn . . . fuckin' dreamy."

"Good." I turned to Delia. "My shit?"

Delia dug around in her purse and came up with an envelope and a small wrapped box.

"Check and gift. Don't forget we still have to go by the bank at some point."

"Phone number for Gomez?"

"I'll call him first," she said. She took a pen out and started scrolling through the numbers. "He loves me."

"I can get the rufies this afternoon," Nigel said. "You know people actually do bong hits off 'em now? Even I wouldn't do that, but I know who does."

"Two nights in a motel and I can't bring my woman." Mikey shook his head. "She already freaked out about my eye, so this might actually be a good thing."

Delia handed me the number. "I love it when a plan comes together."

We were approaching 82nd, so I scanned the rainy streets again and zipped up, put my new things away.

"I'm off," I said. "You guys finish the beer and then leave one by one. Take cabs back to wherever you came from or catch the oncoming bus back." I looked at them one by one. "Thanks."

None of them said anything, so we sat in companionable silence until we rolled up on my stop. After I rang the bell, Delia scooted her legs over so I could get out. I looked back once as I got off. They seemed contemplative, but I saw hope there, too. The dim kind. Then it was out into the rain.

27

I wondered for the hundredth time what the Armenian would want in exchange for my request as I walked through the rain toward his garage. Negotiating with him was always an exercise fraught with traps, extortion, thinly veiled vice, and unabashed bullshit. I always lost, too. Every single time. The trick was to realize that any interaction with him would always work out in his favor. With that clearly in mind, the strategy was to minimize losses and incur maximum debt in my favor. There was no doubt that the Armenian would do what I asked, but the exotic price tag had to be considered with great scrutiny as it developed, literally, on a second-by-second basis.

This strategy had been partially successful in the past, but the rulebook was his. If, for instance, the Armenian called in the middle of the night with an emergency, and you had to walk ten miles through the rain, shoot several rabid attack dogs, pick a few complicated locks with nothing more than your fingernails, dress his battle wounds with your own shirt, and then carry him to a black market doctor and wait with him for a few days while he schemed to rip the doctor off, a plan he was sure to involve you in, well, if you did all that and he bought you a sandwich afterward, everything was even. Impressing the gravity of a

favor on him was impossible. Everything had to be negoti-
ated incrementally, act by act, motion by motion. And you
still lost.

So I would stall on whatever it was he wanted me to
do. It was a simple as that. The Armenian had many powers, but the gateway to the underworld was mine, and he
knew it. I was valuable to him, and for once I really needed
him to come through. So I went in prepared to raise the
stakes to the maximum. Do what I want or no more Darby
Holland, forever, with the remote possibility that I might
be vengeful. Or the almost unthinkable alternative: the forever debt. I hoped the stakes wouldn't rise anywhere near
that high.

I'd never walked through that particular stretch of 82nd
before, only driven, and then I was never paying attention.
It turned out it was mostly Asian. I thought about stopping
for pho, which was represented by very specific places spe-
cializing in just one kind. The soup market was evidently
pretty fierce. But there wasn't time, and I was getting wetter
by the minute. I kept my eyes out for any sign of Dessel,
but saw none. They probably had my car staked out and
were combing through the dozens of possible places where I
might be eating lunch or getting drunk on 23rd. But looking around, I spotted a place that solved another problem
I'd been worrying about. It was after one, and once I was
finished with the Armenian I still had Dmitri to deal with,
plus I had to check in on Mikey at the Bismarck. There
might not be enough time to go home and change before I
met Suzanne for dinner, and I'd unthinkingly dressed like
a hoodlum. The solution was Southeast Asia Suit and Tie.

There were four mannequins in the window with trim, theater-quality Italian knockoffs that were good for one night. I could never wear a Men's Warehouse affair without looking like a hit man or some other unsavory variety of impostor, but Asian gangster might be just the ticket.

The door chime sounded as I entered. There was a zitty kid sitting behind the register talking to two of his friends. They were all wearing tracksuits, and the air smelled like weed and menthol cigarettes. All three looked alarmed.

"Hey dudes," I said, smiling. The clerk went blank and the other two went scowly. I'd interrupted a drug deal.

"Problem," I continued. "I have a date tonight. Super tall chick, nice place, you get the scenario. I have cash and I need a suit, way fucking fast, too. And shoes. I'm basically a scumbag, just like you guys, so you'll get it when I say I don't want to walk in looking like I just got back from chatting with my parole officer. Swanky. Sharp. Like a professional gambler."

The clerk interpreted that for his two associates, who loosened up as he went along. They smiled at "scumbag," which probably had no easy translation, and laughed aloud at "parole" and "swanky," which evidently didn't, either. When he was done, the clerk slid off his stool and came over to me.

"What you weight? Take off coat. Shoe?"

"Ten and a half," I said, shrugging my coat off. He studied my shoulders.

"About so-so average," he observed. He squeezed my forearm. "Hard like muthafucka." He barked something at the other two and they sprang into action. One of them

222

came back with a shimmering gold imitation silk suit, the other with imitation leather shoes. I nodded my appreciation at both. I tried the coat on and it fit reasonably well. The label in the pants had the right waist size. I took the coat off and put it back on the hanger.

"Shirt and tie," I said, holding the suit up and looking at the back. It looked like it might stand up to one dry cleaning. The shoes had about five miles in them. The clerk took a white shirt off a rack and after a moment's consideration selected a skinny blue tie. He held them up and I nodded. "How much, the whole megillah?"

He added it up in his head. "One hundred ten, cash."

"Bag it."

It was a little high for a cheap suit, but I was cutting it close timewise, and I wasn't quite big enough to fit into my old one anyway. I gave him some of the roll in my pocket and he winced as he took the exact change with his fingertips. The other two guys waved as I left. I made it another two blocks and was closing in on the Armenian when my cell phone rang. I dug it out and looked at the number. Delia.

"Almost there," I answered.

"I'm in a cab. Nigel and Mikey are meeting the everything drug guy in about an hour and then going to the motel. I sweet-talked Gomez just now and he can't wait to talk to you."

"Good. I know this is going to be a pain in the ass, but can you pick me up at the Armenian's in about an hour?"

"I could," Delia replied, "but time is tight on my end, too. I have to take the Empire boys to get their waiter shoes at Payless, and then I still have to dye their hair and wash 'em."

"Fuck. OK. I guess a cab would be better, but I don't want the Armenian to know I'm taking one. I'm getting secretive already. It's like he has a two-block halo around him that changes your behavior when you enter it."

"Buck up," she said. "Tell him something mysterious, like you're on the way to the bar at the airport for a meeting. Then let it dangle."

"I'll call in a few hours when I'm done with the Armenian and Dmitri."

"Don't hit anyone."

I sighed. "Believe it or not, I'm all cranium for the duration."

"Whatever." She hung up.

The Armenian's garage had red flags all over it. It was situated between a lawn and garden supply place and a custom wheel outfit. The garage itself was on the small side, with two bays and a front office with a smaller, windowless office behind it, a storeroom behind all that. There were newer BMWs and Mercedes filling the small parking lot. Too many cars. Some Mexican guys were standing around out front, smoking. New faces were bad in this situation. They watched me through slitted eyes as I approached. When I paused with my hand on the front door and gave them a hard look of my own, they had no reaction. It was like staring at mean-ass statues. Off to a promising start.

There was no one in the front office, so I stood at the empty display case and rapped on it.

"George," I called. The back office door swung open, but there was no reply. I went in.

The Armenian was on the phone. He waved at me without looking and gestured at a chair. I sat down and put my bag on the floor next to me, took out my smokes, and shook one loose. My hair was wet enough to drip and my pants were soaked. I lit my smoke and settled back. The preamble was going to take a while.

When people talk for a long time on the phone in a foreign language right in front of you, they always mistakenly assume you can't follow along. Only rarely are they right if you're paying close attention, and I was. The Armenian was talking about me. He made several dismissive gestures with his free hand as he jabbered, which combined with his tone to translate as "what the fuck?" and "he's alive, but he's just another white criminal, they're like roaches or cats," and then "I know, but they're not really that bad, c'mon."

All people also tend to pepper their dialogue with English words, just as the Asians had earlier. The Armenian was seriously guilty there. I almost betrayed my attention by raising an eyebrow at the word "disco," followed by an insistent monologue. Then "strippers" caught my attention. A minute later "zero," twice.

In the next ten minutes he also dropped "Mexicans," "cash only," "Stark Street," and "balloons." Whoever he was talking to was evidently a friend of some kind, because then the conversation lightened up with short questions, long answers from the other end, followed by laughter. The Armenian absently touched his face where my new scar was more than a dozen times, especially in the beginning. A full forty-five minutes after I'd entered, he finally hung up. That would be considered rude by most people, but I knew better. The Armenian had been communicating a great deal already. He wanted me to understand that he knew I wanted something, but in the grand scheme of things I was small potatoes. He was on top of the world, wheeling and dealing with tremendous success, chatting about family after closing a huge deal, a magnanimous giant, benevolently tolerating my mosquito-esque presence. For whatever reason, the Armenian was desperate.

"Darby, my God!" he began. "Your face, these newspapers, your shop, what happened?" He didn't take his eyes off me for a second as he took a bottle of cognac out of his desk drawer. He was in scan and record mode. I shrugged and lit my seventh cigarette.

"Some douchebag blew it up to make room for rich people with better ideas. I was thinking about moving anyway. Old Town is dead these days, so no big whoop. Bought a new motorcycle with some of the insurance money and totaled it in the first ten minutes. Hence my face."

"Ten minutes," he repeated, amazed at the direction my lies had already taken. "My God. Did you even make it to the freeway?" He took his eyes off me for an instant to pour us two shots in paper cups, mine huge, his tiny. I'd just established that I had money, so half of whatever he'd been planning had just gone up in smoke. He had to pause recording for an instant to think.

"Nope." I took my shot. "Wiped out on the on-ramp. I was out for three fucking days in the ICU at Providence and the police freaked out. So, the papers. The idiots eventually tracked me down to the hospital and apologized a million times. I was just beginning to remember who I was. Three weeks of that. Anyway, small out-of-court settlement from them for the bad PR, don't tell anyone. And hey, is there really any such thing as bad publicity?"

"Good for you!" He raised his glass and we drank. Cognac is terrible stuff, but I made my tasty face.

"So what about you?" I asked. "How have you been?"

He looked down to his left and smiled faintly. I had formally opened negotiations. "Ah, Darby, I have been great. Just great." He looked up. "I've been meaning to talk to you, actually. Moving from Old Town is going to be good for you. When I heard about your place being destroyed I was so worried, Darby. I thought, 'What can I do to help this guy? What can I do!'" He slammed his hand down on the desk.

"You're too much, George," I said. "I'm fine."

"No, Darby," he scolded patronizingly. "A man with no business is too much like a child or a woman. I know you. It will kill you. But this I can do. I will do! I have a place on Stark Street, a nice building, two shop fronts, actually, much bigger than your old place. One is for you, for your new tattoo shop, and one is for I don't know yet." He poured me another cognac. "First, I was thinking a restaurant, but in this town? Then maybe a strip club, but I don't know those people. Art gallery, artist space, with booths? I don't know those people, either! So then I think, they're your neighbors! You decide! Help me run the place and I will give you a good rent!"

The building had a For Lease sign in the window for the last six years. The Armenian wanted triple the going price for anything else in town and the building was full of trash. He was having cash flow problems and he needed to get something up and running in there for premium dollars, faster than yesterday.

"I like it," I replied. He sipped his drink without taking his bright eyes off me, the cognac just wetting his upper lip. "A strip club is the way to go. I know about a billion strippers. We'd need a bouncer, someone huge and dangerous, and a bunch of crap. Tables, chairs, a bar, one of those poles. That kind of stuff. Probably a disco ball and a jukebox."

The Armenian's eyes lit up. "Exactly!"

"Yeah. No. I mean I don't want in, personally. If I had a shop next to a strip club I'd have security issues of my own, and I'm planning on moving to Costa Rica anyway."

"Costa Rica! It's full of Mexicans!" The Armenian was wildly alarmed. "No, Darby, no! You're giving up! One bomb and you give up? C'mon!"

I drank my drink while he watched. He was on the ropes. I could feel it. I pretended to think while he sat there on the verge of exploding.

"Tell you what," I began, speculating now. "For old times' sake, because we're friends, and also because I may need a place to work from time to time if Costa Rica's boring . . . OK. I suppose I can track down everything, now that I think about it. Pretty easy. The furniture? I know people. Strippers? They love me because I've never fucked any of them. Head bartender? No problem. Manager? Easy, too. I can get you up and running for next to nothing now that I don't have anything to do, but . . . I want twenty-five percent of the place. And that's a friends deal."

The Armenian cringed into a protective posture. "Darby, it makes me uncomfortable to talk this way. I don't even know what you're proposing."

"Strip clubs are a gold mine," I said. "All the strippers in this city? They actually pay to work at those places."

He was stunned. "*Really?*"

"Oh yeah. Totally fucking disgusting. If we didn't charge them? Every back-flipping, pole-climbing, fire-breathing bombshell in a hundred miles would be knocking down our door to get in on it. It's a simple idea, George."

He played pensive. "My children would hate me." Meaning he wanted no involvement whatsoever. The risk and the exposure, the entire burden, would all be mine.

"Kids," I said sympathetically. "I can see that. Just keep your name off the liquor license and stay away from the place. Blame the whole thing on me. But I'll be honest, that sounds more like a fifty-fifty partnership."

He squirmed again, and then played his only remaining card. "Speaking of children, you said you had a present for my daughter?" Meaning, what are you here for, let's get down to hard trading.

"Yeah. Day before the Lucky blew up, I traded this local photographer for some work. He shoots models, mostly. High end, tasteful stuff. Anyway, he was going to reshoot all my big pieces for my new portfolio, but with Costa Rica and all, I don't need him anymore. He still owes me a super classy photo shoot, and Delia thought your daughter might enjoy it. Something upscale, cosmopolitan, or maybe natural, like out in the gorge. Chicks love that stuff. But now, I dunno. Maybe we should just spin it into the PR campaign for the strip club."

"Hmm. I see." He chewed his thumbnail. "Maybe both. My daughter visits next week. She would love this. Maybe we can use her as a test, to see how good your photographer is. Then, maybe, I don't know. It has to be worth something to him to spend a day with beautiful women and get credit for it. Advertising his work for him for free? I don't know."

"So, fifty-fifty. Get the papers going and I'll have my guy look it over, we can be up in two months or less, and then . . ." I rubbed my fingertips together in the international sign for money.

"Lawyer, papers . . ." The Armenian seemed exasperated by it all. "That slows everything down. I don't know, Darby. I know you need to get something going, but . . ." He shrugged.

"What I really need to get going is my move to Costa Rica. My new girlfriend will go for it, but if I don't move fast, she's going to take this job in Japan or some shit and then I'll never see her again." I got up, in no hurry. "Let me know about the photographer thing."

"Wait, Darby, wait," he said gently, patronizing again. "I can't let you go like this. I'm concerned. To run off to Mexico with a woman. The insurance money cannot be that much. You will go broke and then what? I think you're still in shock. An explosion, an accident, a new woman? This is too much for the mind. The mind is fragile. I know you have no father to advise you. Come. Sit."

I took my phone out and dialed a cab, told them where I was. When they told me five minutes, I repeated it for George to hear. The countdown to the end of the market day had officially started.

"Maybe, George," I replied, snapping my phone closed. "You can see why palm trees and pussy sound good right now. But the future should be bright, you're right. Tell you what. I'll put the word out to the strippers and get someone going on the booze. Drop the keys by my place and I'll put someone on cleaning everything up. New paint and all that. Get the buzz started."

"I see." He didn't like that I was standing up, or that we were nearly done. Negotiations were supposed to take hours. Days, even.

"That part is easy. These clubs usually gross cash by the van load, so I want my part to stay cold."

"Ah yes. Van load." He brightened a little, but I could also tell he knew something was coming.

"How's the transmission business coming?" I asked. There was no point in feigning casual. He met my eyes, on scan and record again.

"An interesting question. Why do you ask?"

"I need to mail something to Russia, two-day air. It would fit right into one of those transmission boxes."

"I see. I see. What is it?"

"Just junk. Tattoo crap for my friend Constantine. He has a shop over there and I don't need most of the stuff I had in storage."

"Ahh." The Armenian sat up. "Some of these items might be . . . not illegal, but frowned on? Questions and questions? My transmissions get through easily because I mail them back and forth so often. I could do this for you, sure, but the shipping cost is high."

"When do you mail this stuff?"

"Three times a week. The day after tomorrow my Mexicans are taking seven boxes down to the pier. They'll be in Magadan on Friday."

"Great. Constantine can make arrangements from there." I took my greasy, bloody, smelly roll out. "What's that cost? With the fancy armored box."

"Around eleven hundred," he replied instantly. Probably more like seven. I peeled off fifteen.

"Little extra for the Mexicans. I don't want them opening the box and stealing my art supplies. They look sketchy, man."

"I will take care of it." He didn't flinch at the quality of the money.

"Great." There was a beep outside. My cab had arrived early. The Armenian stood. He knew whatever was in the box was going to be unusual, but dealing in the unusual was his game.

"My good friend, so wonderful to see you. We will have lunch next week. For now, can we settle, just for the moment, at sixty-forty, and you'll work your magic to find the furniture and the strippers?" He held his hand out. He wasn't going to pay for a chair, a shot glass, even a single napkin. And he'd never walk through the door, either.

"Say fifty-five-forty-five in my favor, I hire the Mexicans you have out there to clean it out on my dime, you provide the truck they need to haul stuff in and out. I stay cold cash all the way through, and the photo shoot is on."

"For now that is OK. For now." Meaning he needed an opening to bring my percentage down. "Let me think and we can work out the details. Good to see you, my man!"

The Armenian guided me out the side door into the first bay. There he snapped his fingers at the Mexicans and told them to put a clean transmission box in the trunk of the cab. They had to use some twine to secure it, so we watched them work. I patted the Armenian on the back when they were done and shook the rain off my suit bag.

"Exciting times," I said.

"I still cannot believe they pay to strip," he said, almost to himself. "It is darkness, brightening the future."

The cab driver was a standard Portland hipster. He was happy that he'd hadn't had to get out to help the super-efficient Mexicans. In fact, the huge box seemed to be the best thing that had happened to him all afternoon.

"So what's in there?" he asked immediately.

"Nothing yet," I replied. "We're having a benefit at Dante's in a few weeks for that punk band in Russia who got arrested for mouthing off. Everyone is going to put shit in it. You know, CDs, old guitars, hair gel, that kind of stuff. Then we're mailing it. Solidarity, yo."

"Right on, right on." He had no intention of attending the hypothetical event, but the idea tickled him. "Where to?"

"Punk dignitary headquarters is some shit hole down the road called the Bismarck."

"Ambulance central these days," he said, taking a left out of the parking lot.

"I wouldn't know," I replied. "I almost never get out this way."

I dug my phone out and dialed Mikey. He picked up on the third ring.

"I fucking love this place," he answered. "It's so craptacular I feel like I'm in a comic book."

"I'm on my way. Need anything?"

"Nah. I picked up a twelve-pack and a pizza on the way here. I got the room at the edge of the parking lot, just like you said. My van is right outside. The lot's empty except for a mattress. Nigel got those pills, too. Wanted me to tell you. He might come over later and bring me a cake. Might have been kidding about the cake, I don't know."

"Good. See you in a sec."

The driver turned up the radio when I snapped the phone closed and we listened to two Creedence songs, which I considered a pleasant omen. When we were across the street from the Bismarck I told him to pull around to the parking lot in back. He nodded and reached under his seat, pulled out a shrinkwrapped CD, and handed it back to me.

"For the box," he said. "My alt country band."

"Thanks," I said. "I'll put it in."

We pulled around the back and I paid and tipped him five bucks. Other than Mikey's van and the stray mattress, the lot was still empty.

"Need help with the box?" he asked.

"Nah. I'll drag it." I didn't want him to know the room number.

I got out and pulled the box out. Even empty, it still weighed more than thirty pounds. I lit a cigarette and watched the cab pull away, then tossed my suit bag on top of the box and pulled it over between Mikey's van and the motel. Then I went to the first door and knocked. Mikey opened it and glanced both ways.

"Leave the door open and help me real quick." He nodded and followed me around the corner. I nodded at the box. Mikey didn't like the looks of it.

"In the room with this, double time," I said. He reluctantly grabbed one of the handles and I took the other one. We got it into the room and I closed the door, then peeked through the blinds. No one had been watching.

"What do we need this for?" He sat down on the bed and picked up his beer. The TV was on. Perry Mason.

"I have to mail something big," I replied. "Long story." I took my phone out. There was most of a twelve-pack getting warm on top of the scarred dresser. I pulled one loose and popped the top.

"No ice," Mikey said. I shrugged and took a sip, then dug Gomez's number out and dialed. Delia had prepped him, but only a little.

"Hola," Gomez answered.

"Hola vato. Darby." I sat down on the box.

"Delia just told me you were alive! What the fuck, esse?"

I could tell he was glad to hear from me. Gomez was a hard dude, but it was in his voice.

"Long, long-ass story man. All kinds of shit going down. How's the bar?"

"Totally fucked, hombre. Dmitri's gone crazy, your place is sort of dangling off the side of mine, the power is down, no phone. My door is gone. All my shit is still in there, but I can't even get it out. I don't have no place to put it anyway."

"You working at your brother's?"

"Me and Flaco, yeah."

"Good. Your brother's place is what I'm calling about. I need to rent the whole thing out tomorrow. Private party, about three hours. I'm bringing the waiters. You and Flaco are the cooks. No one else and you get a grand to split between you, plus another five bills for your brother, and I'll give you a free month's rent when the Lucky and the Rocket reopen."

"*What?*"

"All this goes through, starting tomorrow I'm your new landlord. Rent stays the same, I fix the holes and shit like that while the Lucky is getting redone. The mini mart is our new parking lot. Deal?"

"Dmitri is selling?"

"Tomorrow. Want in as a buyer? We could split it."

"I'm fucking broke man! Fuck . . . OK. Tomorrow. I can do that. Fifteen and a free month, plus the new door and some other shit. Windows, the booths in back, my fucking—"

"I'll see you tomorrow at eleven a.m.," I interrupted. "You can give me the list after we all get back in there. Don't be late, and no one but you and Flaco."

"We're the kitchen anyways. Flaco is on the dish machine. Fucking pissed off, too. I got this."

"Right on, right on. One last thing, hombre. You remember you told me you found a mummified mouse under your front porch and you saved it for me? For my collection of weirdo sketch crap?"

"Yeah. I think it's in a baggie in my garage. Why?"

"Can you bring it?"

"Yeah, but . . ." He trailed off.

"Mañana."

"Sí."

And that was that.

"You should, like, sell cars if this doesn't work out," Mikey said, laying back. "Boy got game. Did you see a remote anywhere?"

I looked around while I dialed another cab. Hopefully it wouldn't be the same guy. "Nope. Maybe ask the desk."

"Guy's sleeping. When I asked about the ice he almost cried. I don't think they let him go home too much, poor little bastard."

We bullshitted about nothing until my cab arrived a few minutes later. While we did, I stripped and put my new suit on. It fit, with my belt. The shoes even looked sharp, though I could tell they were going to be hell on my feet. I transferred the contents of my pockets and adjusted my cuffs in the scratched-to-hell mirror. I looked like a loan shark or a midrange pool hustler.

"Not too shabby, boss," Mikey observed. "Where'd you get that thing? A Chinese grocery store?"

"Fuck you." I put the tie in my outside pocket. Neither of us knew how to tie one. Then I stowed the fat check and Suzanne's birthday pendant, which I had traded the Armenian for a fictional photo shoot without him even knowing it. "I'm on a roll, Mikey boy."

"Right on, man." Mikey saluted with his beer. My phone rang and I checked the number. My cab had arrived. The time on my phone when I closed it was just after six. Everything was ready except for Dmitri.

I got to "mitri's izza" at little after six thirty. By then I'd worked myself into a truly foul mood without even trying. The cab driver was silent the entire way. A brooding, scarred guy wearing the latest in Asian gangster fashion and headed from the Bismarck Motel to the epicenter of decay in Old Town wasn't his ideal when it came to gab.

"You know how to tie a tie?" I asked out of the blue. His nervous eyes flicked to the rearview.

"Nope."

"Fuck." We stopped and I paid with my disgusting money and slammed the door. I couldn't help it. I stormed up to the door of "mitri's izza" and kicked the metal lock with my heel as hard as I could. For some reason the door was unlocked, so the door flew open and banged against the wall.

"Dmitri!" I roared.

Dmitri peeked out from the kitchen, eyes wide. The lights were off and the place was cold and filthy. It smelled thickly of pee, stale cigarettes, lingering whore, and wet dog.

"Darby?" His voice was soft and trembling. I locked the door behind me.

"Why was the door unlocked? Get out here, now. If you're holding a gun I'm going to rip your hands off."

Dmitri slunk out with his hands up. He looked terrible. He was wearing the same gray parka and green pants, but it was all dirtier. His hair was so greasy it was actually lying down for a change, which was an unlikely improvement.

"The giant hooker was here," he whispered. "The very big one. She let herself out. I don't have any money, if that's what you came for."

"Sit the fuck down," I instructed. He did, instantly. "I'm here to make you money, not take any, so you're going to do every fucking thing I say, understand?"

"No," he whined. His lower lip quivered. His eyes teared up.

"The Russian guy, he's contacted you, right?"

Dmitri nodded. "Yes. The papers have been drawn up. I'm selling the Lucky and the bar for three hundred thousand. I'm sorry, Darby." He started crying.

"Shut up," I said. "You have to pay a ton on taxes, don't you?"

"Yes," he managed. "I inherited everything. In the end I'll be lucky—I mean fortunate, to walk away with these clothes and one more blow job." He broke down again. I sat across from him, careful not to touch the table.

"Listen to me, fool." He kept crying, so I reached out and slapped him once, hard. He went from despair back to stark terror before the ringing echo faded.

"This fucking Russian is paying cash or I'll kill him," I said. "Total fucking corpse, and you're going along with it. Understand?"

"How—why—is that—"

"Just shut up," I said. I took out my cigarettes and lit one. It was time to calm down.

"OK," I began. "Here's how this is going to go down. You"—I stabbed my cigarette at him—"are going to call them in a few minutes. You want two large, cash, fifties and hundreds, and then you'll sign and walk. If they want this place, too, and you know they do, you tell them the same deal next month after you're sure it worked out the first time, and then you'll be gone for good. You got that?"

"I can't sell both buildings," he pleaded. "The blown-up one is dead to me, but this place is all I have left! If I—"

"You're keeping this dump," I said. "You aren't going to sell it. Only the Lucky and the bar. Cash. Then you can fix this place up with a little help, which I'll arrange. Say yes, Dmitri."

"Y-yes," he stammered. "Why would you help me, Darby? You don't even like me."

I took my cell phone out and checked the time. Not good. I showed it to him. "You have their number?"

"Oh yes," he replied. "A very huge man gave it to me."

"Call it," I instructed. He took his phone out. His hands were shaking.

"What do I say?" He was pleading again.

"Two hundred thou, cash, tomorrow, same deal in one month for this place, then you blow town forever. They have that kind of cash lying around, I know, because it's how they paid the bomber. Public place, Romero's on Alberta, noon tomorrow. Make the call."

"So much to remember. Romero's on Alberta, noon tomorrow . . ." He finished dialing and put the phone to his greasy ear, on the verge of a heart attack.

Someone answered, a sharp, one word bark. Oleg himself.

"It is I, Dmitri," Dmitri said in a quavering voice. Another bark.

"No more waiting. No more games. I will sell tomorrow. At noon, in a public place for my safety. Romero's on Alberta. Two hundred thousand in cash. Cash. If I live I will sell my other building in one month the same way, the same price. I must get this over with or I die. My heart is old and poisoned. My bowels, my hands, my eyes—"

Bark.

"Yes, yes," Dmitri continued, eyes on me now, some new horror dawning on him. "But cash. Two hundred thousand. A bargain. If you do not try to kill me or rob me, the second will be the same. I can go to someplace small and safe. A beach, with—"

Barking.

Dmitri hung up. "I'm going to vomit."

"Hold it down. What did he say?"

"He seemed relieved," Dmitri said. "Even happy, in a greedy, awful way. I hate this man, Darby. I hate him twice as much as I've ever hated anything."

"Then you'll love what happens next," I said.

"We should drink together," Dmitri declared. "For the first time, as friends."

I dialed the number for a cab. That deep in Old Town it would only take a minute.

"Don't get all mushy on me," I said while the number rang. "Do you know how to tie a tie?"

"Of course I do! What kind of idiot do you think I am?" He scurried into the kitchen and came back with a mostly empty bottle of vodka and two wax paper cups. While he poured I put my blue tie under my collar and then looked at him, helpless.

"Here," he said. He reached out and pulled at the tie, then got to work on it. This close up, I noticed an impressive yellow crust in both his eyes. He sat back and looked, then made a final adjustment. Tying my tie seemed to have calmed him. "There."

I felt the knot and then raised my drink. He saluted me with a shy smile.

"Thank you, Darby Holland."

"Don't thank me just yet, old man," I replied. "This goes to shit and we both die." The vodka tasted dusty. Dmitri shook his head sadly when he downed his, and then said one of the most truthful things that ever came out of his mouth.

"If being any kind of hero falls all the way down to men like you, then we have already lost."

I didn't want to think about that as I got in the cab. But I knew what I felt about it, and I wasn't smiling.

My cab pulled up in front of Brasserie Montmare with five minutes to spare, and as I dug out my roll I realized I'd been fueled all day by one vision—my ridiculous fantasy of watching Suzanne walk in. Maybe the Armenian was right and my mind had cracked, and Delia was correct about my rampant pussification. Bullshitting Dessel into believing I was hopelessly distracted by a woman wasn't any kind of fiction at all.

I didn't care. I told the driver to keep the change, stepped out into the rain, and got into character. I swaggered a little as I walked in, just in case she'd beat me there, but I also wanted to set the tone in my head. The maître d' looked up from his podium and smiled. I adjusted my tie and shot my cuffs.

"Holland, table for two," I said in my best James Bond. He consulted his book and picked up two gilded menus.

"This way."

I strolled behind him, as sinister as possible. The place had an old European feel to it, with lots of wood, brass, and glass. Half the tables were full, and a jazz band was bubbling away on a stage somewhere around the corner. He led me to an empty two top and my heart soared.

"A drink while you wait?" he asked as I sat down.

"Martini," I replied. "Smoky."

He nodded and set the menus down, said something to the bartender as he passed. I looked the other diners over. Yuppies mostly, dressed with a universal touch of artsy. I took my present out and gently shook it. Clunky. I briefly prayed that there wasn't a beetle horrifically embedded in the design, or tiny albino skulls or anything like that, but mostly I kept my eyes on the door.

At five past eight, Suzanne came in. She looked like a million clean bucks. Her shoes were black stilettos, with heels so high she was mincing on her toes. Her black dress was sleeveless and came to the middle of her thighs. She had a white lace shawl draped over her shoulders and a tiny white patent leather clutch purse. Her short hair was glossy and curled, and she was even wearing a touch of makeup, which I didn't know she could do.

The maître d' took a step back as she approached him. Suzanne was two and a half heads taller than him, but she didn't slump even a fraction or deign to bow her head. She was positively regal when she addressed him. He giggled something and they started my way. She trailed far back, sashaying a little, just for me, I knew. Every head in the room turned and tracked her. The bartender paused midpour.

I stood up, music thundering in my head. The maître d' vanished. I looked up into that tall, tall woman's smile and I almost couldn't breathe.

"You just made a dream come true, baby," I said. I narrowed my eyes. "Let's do this more often."

She leaned down and gave me a kiss as long as she was tall. When we were done, I pulled her chair out and she sat. Conversation around us resumed.

"What's this?" she asked, picking up the box. I dropped into a casual slouch across from her.

"Birthday present. It . . . well, see, I hope you like it because I sort of traded in the longest possible series of events to get it, and I have to confess, at the end of it all, I have still not seen what's in that box."

"How did you know it was just my birthday?" She toyed with the box.

"Looked in your purse to find out your last name."

Suzanne laughed and started unwrapping her present. She opened the box and took the surprisingly unclunky pendant out. The passionflower looked like it was made of emerald glass and set in slightly tarnished, extremely delicate brass. The stamen rods were a deep yellow, tipped with scarlet. The color interpretation was satisfying, in a playful way. And it was old. She let out a tiny gasp.

"I love it," she breathed. "I'm not really the jewelry type, but this is fabulous! A passionflower." She put it on, in the center of her low cut dress, just between her small breasts, and then gave me a glittering smile. The waiter arrived and set my drink down.

"One of those," Suzanne said, pointing and smiling up. She looked at me and arched an eyebrow. "Oysters?"

"Oysters," I agreed.

"Kinda big ones," Suzanne said to the waiter. "Short of jumbo. Just big. Meaty. Whatever you're moving the most of on that end. An even dozen to start with."

"And some mussels," I added. "Clams, too, if you recommend them. And the crab cakes."

"And I love the snails here," Suzanne said.

"Snails, too. And calamari. Let's go all in."

The waiter kept nodding and nodding. "Which first?"

"Bring them out as they come up," Suzanne suggested. "We eat like hyenas, so we'll keep up."

"It's true," I said. "We have tapeworms, too. Real bad."

"He has rabies on top of it," Suzanne said proudly. Our waiter retreated, amused. Suzanne fixed her smile on me again.

"What?" I asked. She picked up my drink and took a sip, set it down in front of her next to the pendant box.

"I was just wondering where in the world you got that suit. It's perfect."

That night in bed, with Suzanne sleeping next to me in her now customary and unselfconscious sprawl, I thought about what Dmitri had said about gutter heroes and how in his blurry, broken head it spelled generalized doom. It was odd to think of him saying anything so broadly sensible, that a wretched man might have an insightful opinion about humanity in general.

I didn't want to smoke in bed, so I got up and went all the way out into the living room and lay down on the couch. I used to sleep on it with my clothes on half the time, but I somehow doubted I would ever do that again. It wasn't like I'd been cured of anything. Things had changed. More signs of dangerous pussification.

Old houses are never totally quiet. I listened to the wind and the rain through the thin walls. Something creaked and settled in the sturdy old Douglas fir frame. The refrigerator motor turned on. I lit a cigarette and the lighter sounded loud, even the hiss of the gas, the crackle of the first puff.

Suzanne and I had eaten almost every appetizer they had, and then we'd split a porterhouse steak and a pecan-encrusted halibut with all the sides that came with it, followed by cheesecake, and finished it off with a bottle of white wine before taking a cab home.

It had been expensive, of course. When I paid with the blood money she had looked away, only for the second it had taken for me to slip the bills into the folder, but I'd noticed. Quiet houses were a breeding ground for memories like that. They got together, those memories, and those horny memories had kids. The offspring of Dmitri's analysis of the human condition and Suzanne's averted gaze was an ugly little guy with beady eyes, blotchy newborn skin, and an itchy, spastic palsy. I was terrible hero material, embarrassingly bad.

Consoling thoughts are hard to find for colicky newborns. Some people liked Johnny Cash songs. Some people actually understood them. That was a good one. I sighed and waited for another one, but nothing came to mind, so I thought about Suzanne.

The lovemaking when we got home had been just that—lovemaking. I'd tried not to tear her apart and she had let me try not to, while at the same time showing restraint herself. Everything took a long time and it felt weird, too. Passion, the fiery kind, was a very fine thing. Unfortunately, it was probably the part she was falling in love with, and also the thing that would eventually drive us apart.

Maybe that was the real reason why I couldn't sleep. Not self-doubt or some kind of idiot spiritual crisis. In the face of what I was about to do, what I'd done to get there, and what I would do if I made it, it seemed like some introspection was called for, even if it led to the same dead end it always did. Was I simply underpowered when it came to common human behavior, so much so that I was incapable of solving life's problems with a measure of cleanliness? Night questions.

Things were sticking to me in a way they never had before. I didn't know why, and that fact alone troubled me. The image of Cheeks's bloody face came bright and clear to me, how he'd looked almost peaceful after I stepped on his neck, like all the red was watercolor from an experiment. I got up and went into the kitchen. I didn't feel like beer. Whiskey might work, but it could also lead all the way down into an unexplored corner of hell. I opted for a glass of water, but when I looked at the glass a flash of white-hot fury tore through me. I dumped it into the sink and poured two fingers of Delia's vodka, grabbed my coat and smokes as I passed the table, and went out onto the porch.

It was cold, so I put my jacket on and sat down in my favorite chair. It had been a month and a half since I had last sat there. I leaned back, took a sip of vodka, dug my phone out, and dialed.

"This better not be bad news," Delia said quietly.

"It is," I replied. I shook a smoke loose. "I'm turning into some kind of horrible vaudeville burnout. When they finally retire me, assuming I live that long, I'll write my memoirs in some French insane asylum and the guards will use the pages for toilet paper."

Delia sighed. "Hang on."

I listened while she rustled around. There was a click and some walking. An old door opened and closed.

"There." Her voice was louder. "I'm out on Dildo's front porch. You're on yours, too, aren't you?"

"Yep."

"That woman you're so smitten with is asleep in your bed, isn't she?"

"Yep."

"Figured. The Dildo is asleep, too. All of them are. The shower after the hair operation knocked the stuffing out of them."

"Jesus."

"Tell me about it. So what the fuck is up with you? Pre-show jitters? This isn't the whole pussy thing again, is it?"

I almost hung up, but I didn't.

"No," I began. "I think I'm getting sick of the character questions, though. But no. Existential crisis, minor. I was mostly wondering if all the shit I'm always up to is going to make me more . . . questionable."

"You dummy, of course it is." Delia sounded genuinely disgusted. She took a sip of something and coughed. "Look, douchebag. Check out the world around you. Look at your own history. When I first started working for you, years ago now, you were with that one chick, what's her name. And the spoiled little middle-class twat thought just enough of you to show you your station in life by ripping you off in the worst possible way. That was right when we became BFFs. Poor baby needed me to pet his muzzle and scratch his tummy-wummy. Then you had a long period of assorted petty theft and backstabbing, non-women-related, up until your nearly fatal encounter with big money, this time courtesy of a guy you did nothing worse than give a job to. I don't need to remind you how fucked in the head all those people were. And now this Russian dude. Now tell me, friend. Who did you rip off? You can't whine about it if they started it. Who did you stab in the back? Huh?"

"Well . . . I can't say I've behaved in a way the Dalai Lama would—"

"That guy is another culture's fiction. He'd be dead in Old Town."

"Maybe he wouldn't go to Old—"

"Darby! Snap out of it! Every time shit like this goes down, we could just walk away. We could start a boutique-style, limp-wristed, soulless dental clinic tattoo shop, get our toenails done at the mall and take up polo. People do it. Life could be bland for us. But we won't go for it. Know why?"

"No."

"Me fuckin' neither, but I'm glad we don't. I know you feel it, Darby. Life, the definition of it as it applies to a person, is in the realness of things. The wildness. Taste, sound, light, and I want it rich and loud and blinding, and so do you. I'll wear a diaper and a fucking helmet with blinders on when I finally go crazy. But for now, we fly . . . and baby, that wind?" Her voice had become soft. She whispered what came next. "Promise me something, Holland. Promise me you won't ever give up even a tiny bit of your soul for something as pitiful as easy sleep. Promise me that tonight, right now, or my soul will stagger. Swear to me. Swear to me." I could barely hear her.

"I swear." We listened to each other breathe for a minute. She finally took another sip of something and cleared her throat. Her lighter clicked and she inhaled.

"The Dildo is psyched about San Fran. He wants to bring the whole band and do an acoustic tour of Bay Area laundromats."

"Lots of quarters."

"Dildo's thoughts precisely. I told him no. Romance and records only. Long midnight walks looking for bars we never heard of. You have plans for after whatever happens tomorrow?"

"Weekend in jail." I scratched my chin. "After that, pure chaos. I have to get all those contractors we had out after the city inspector fiasco to come back. Get started on this idiot strip club scam with the Armenian."

"Strip club?"

"Over on Stark. One of his abandoned buildings. We'll see how it shakes out."

"Huh. What about your new chick?"

"I don't know," I said honestly. I took another sip of vodka. "She might have this new job in Asia. The interview was today. I didn't ask and she didn't bring it up."

"Asia. Maybe we can start a satellite shop somewhere out there, get Mikey away from white women."

"Maybe."

"You two, the ah, the fuckin' OK?"

"Tonight was weird. We're finding our way into the communicative zone."

"Yeah. I skip that part in general. College for me was two types of guys. The trying to be sensitive type and the jacking off with a chick on his dick type. I never developed a tolerance for either. I'm pretty much in charge anymore when it comes down to it."

"Sounds bossy."

"Maybe, but you try going four fucking years without an orgasm."

"I don't think so. I need women, which has always been most of my problem with them."

"How do you mean?" Delia loved to talk about sex. She knew I didn't, so it was a rare opportunity for her to get some much-needed ribbing ammo.

"Actually, the Armenian of all people put it best. This is right up your alley. He called it 'The Watching Man.'"

"Sounds like the wrong kind of pervert."

"His point exactly. We were driving around somewhere years ago, I forget where or why, but he spots this dude wearing a Blazers jacket. The hat, the shorts, whole nine yards. Anyway, the Armenian points him out and says 'masturbator!' in a scathing-ass way."

"What?"

"Swear to God. He was freaked out, disgusted. It was one of those rare moments when his religious side came out. He goes on to tell me that men who watch sports are the same men who watch porn. Voyeurs, I think he was getting at. Watch, instead of play, and in his mind the only reason to watch porn is to whack off because you're too lazy to pick your shit up and go get a real woman, risk the possibility of love and hate, that kind of thing. So there's a clear link between wearing team sports crap and jacking off. A dude with a Lakers shirt is essentially advertising that he's a furious masturbator."

Delia laughed for a solid minute. In the end I was laughing, too. Abruptly, she stopped.

"Wait a minute," she said. "You don't even have a TV. Does that mean—"

"It does, but not for esoteric Eastern European Gypsy Catholic Whatever reasons like the Armenian. For me it makes the sex better. The hunt for a beautiful woman, all that. My feathers shine more brightly. I'm more devoted."

"Ahhhh. Now I see why you've put up with so many awful bitches. You poor fucking idiot."

"Yeah."

Quiet.

"Maybe I should stop, too."

"The first twenty years or so are the hardest. Constant fucking can be a nightmare. But then you hit forty and once or twice a day is fine."

"I can't believe we're talking about this." Delia yawned. "Long day tomorrow. We should sleep our uneasy sleep. Feel better?"

"I do."

"I don't. I was going to diddle around before bed and now I'm on the fence about it. Asshole."

"It's probably different for women," I said.

"Whatever. I forgot already. What's your timetable tomorrow?"

"Wake up early. Get rid of Suzanne, which makes me sad to say. Then get Nigel and cab over to Romero's. You guys should be there at ten sharp. Back entrance. Have Dildo park the Empire van right by the back door facing out."

"OK."

"OK."

More breathing.

"I'm going to sit here for a while," she said finally.

"Me too."

She blew me a kiss and hung up. I sat and watched the rain fall through the halo of the streetlight. Just when I was about to get up to go inside, the red Miata rolled past one block down, slow, almost coasting. I listened for any sound of the engine for a moment, then went in and curled up on my corner of the warm bed.

Suzanne had already made coffee when I woke up. I sat up in alarm and looked at the clock, then relaxed. It was just after eight. She peeked in and winked.

"Coffee?"

"I'm coming," I said. I pulled my jeans on and padded out into the kitchen, rubbing the top of my head. She handed me the cup she'd been pouring.

"Eight a.m. and you already look worried," she observed. She was wearing one of my flannel shirts and a pair of my socks. It was still cold inside. "You OK?"

I nodded and sipped. "Yeah. Just a whoppin' ton of shit to do today."

"Me too," she replied shortly. It looked like she had been getting ready to make pancakes. Flour was measured out in a bowl. She fussed with the coffee machine for a second and then walked back into the bedroom. I followed.

"Pancakes?" I asked. I put my coffee down and wrapped my arms around her. She was facing away from me, holding her pants.

"What the hell are we doing? You wake up and give me the distant treatment first thing? No morning stuff? No—this is bullshit." She started getting her pants on, ignoring my embrace.

"Nope." I picked her up and carried her over to the bed, tossed her as far as I could. It wasn't far, admittedly, but it was OK. Before she could react I pounced on her and bit her neck. She squirmed and I flattened on her.

"You make those pancakes, in your underwear, or no dick tonight. I will cut you off, woman. Wait and see. I have Yoda-level dick control."

She pushed at me and writhed. She was strong, maybe stronger than me and ready to test it, but I caught her wrists and fast as a cobra I bit her neck again. She grabbed my dick through my pants and it was on.

This time, I was communicating pure animal and she bounced every bit of it back. We tore the bed apart, worked our way through the kitchen and into the bathroom, where she tore down my shower curtain, revealing at last who kept doing it. When she climaxed for the third time I exploded, and for one blind moment I was a thing thrown into a hurricane on the violent tip of a cresting wave, the spinning hallucination of an unknowable aberration, lost in deep space and unconcerned.

When I could breathe again, I helped Suzanne out of the bathtub and kissed her once, long and hard.

"I still have time to make breakfast," she panted. "If you want it."

"I do."

It was nine by then, but I felt curiously light and free. Most of the time after sex, even passionate sex, I felt vaguely bummed out, because the aftermath was never quite as good as the act itself. Falling in love made that different.

Suzanne went back into the kitchen and got back to work on the pancakes, buck naked. I wanted a cigarette in the worst possible way, so I got a new cup of coffee and went out to the dining room table and dug them out of my coat pocket. Pants could wait.

I smoked for a minute, and then I remembered the Miata. They were out there again. I knew it. I went back into the bedroom and dressed for the day. Baggy black jeans, black T-shirt, my scuffed boots, laced tight for no-nonsense high-speed activity, and a black wool button-up with a padded insulation liner.

I took more shit than usual, too. My crusty wallet went in a front pocket, also my last ball bearing, an extra lighter, an even thousand of the cadaver cash, and an unusual multi-tool Nigel had given me a few years ago for my birthday. I rounded things out with a rolled bandanna and the fat check from Delia, which I planned on carrying around for the next few days. When I came out of the bedroom Suzanne smiled. Two pancakes were already done.

"You look like the ghetto version of a ninja," she observed.

"That's exactly what I am today," I replied. "Got the secret handshake down and everything."

"Eat up." She handed me the plate. I sidled up next to her and ate standing. She plated one for herself and loaded up on butter and syrup while her second one was cooking.

"Today I have to leave by the back door," I said around a mouthful of food. She nodded. She evidently wasn't going to ask me why.

"Where are the cats?" I managed. She swallowed.

"Let 'em out."

I finished eating and put my plate in the sink, wiped my hands on my pants.

"You free around seven?" I asked.

"Maybe. Why?"

"Well, if everything goes well today, I was thinking maybe we should hit that Ethiopian place over on Hawthorn. Food is so damn good, and I know they'll love you. I have championship eater status there. Sort of a friend of the family at this point."

"Hmm." Suzanne shoveled up her second pancake and started loading it. "I have rock climbing from one to four, then nap time, and then I teach my swim class. Eight OK?"

"Eight is great. Lock the front door when you leave and go out the back. The key to the back door is in the flower pot."

She nodded, chewing. "Leave the cats out?"

"Shitheads won't come back 'till dark." I kissed the middle of her sternum. Then I got my smokes and my cell phone off the table and went out the back.

It was raining, which was no surprise. My tomato garden was a leafless tangle of dead stalks and bare, sagging frames. Embarrassing. The weeds weren't too bad. I carefully looked around, but there were no neighbors out. There was a decent chance Dessel would have the front and the back staked out, which meant a car was somewhere in front of the house behind mine on the next street over. He'd already busted me once that way, but that wasn't the way I'd be going.

There were four houses between me and the first busy street, going through backyards. I could see the roofline of the cafes and crap shops from where I stood. The cafes and restaurants all had covered back patios for smokers. My target was the dive bar, dead center.

I tore off and hit my fence at a good clip for only having twenty feet of muddy runway. The fence was a rickety wooden thing about head high, but it held as I made a clean vault. I almost landed in a rain-filled wheelbarrow but just cleared it. I didn't pause to look around, just charged the next fence, chain-link, waist high. I barely touched it as I went over. A dog barked somewhere in the house, but I kept going. It was a tidy backyard. The next fence was taller and wooden again, much newer and about head high. There was an upturned five gallon bucket against it that I could use as a launch pad, so I did and rolled over the top, barely getting my pants wet.

The dog was on me instantly, biting my wrist and snarling, impossibly fast. I lightly pushed his head away and he rolled as I sprang up. The poor thing probably weighed thirty pounds and must have been scared as hell when I landed right next to him. It looked like it was part pug and part Pekinese, old and fat and half-blind.

"Watch for cats," I cautioned, and then I was off again. The last fence was a climber, a twelve-foot chain-link with slats to keep the drunks from the dive bar on the other side from scaling it. I caught the laugh of some breakfast drinkers on the far side.

There was nothing to launch from, so I hit the fence at full speed and dug my boot toe in and transferred as much of my momentum upward as I could. The entire fence rocked and exploded rainwater outward and I stretched. My bad hand caught the top and I rammed the fingers of my good hand through the slats. My boots caught just enough and I got both hands on top. One pull-up and I was going over fast. I caught a fraction of a second glimpse of table and chairs, and then I was falling.

I landed on the edge of a table, which partially broke my fall. The chair broke a little more of it, and then I was lying on my back, staring up at a rain-spattered plastic awning. I sat up and rubbed the back of my head. The patio was empty except for two goth chicks, paused in astonishment halfway through eggs and Bloody Marys.

"Hi," I said.

"Hey, dude," one of them replied. The other one snorted and shook her head.

I got up and righted the table and the chair, sat down.

"Are you, like, OK?" the same chick asked, incredulous.

"Oh yeah. Fine." I tried to look casual. "How are you two this morning?"

They burst into laughter. A waitress bustled out, a mousy woman carrying a coffee pot.

"I didn't see you come in," she said, pleasantly enough. "Coffee?"

The goth chicks laughed.

"Yep. Their next round of Bloody Marys are on me. I guess I'll have one, too. Spicy as fuck."

"Breakfast menu?" She cocked her hip.

"Nah. Just ate."

"Coming up." She took a coffee cup off the counter by the door and set it on my table. I dug my smokes out.

"Can I get more limes with mine?" one of the goths asked. Her friend nodded, mouth full of toast.

The waitress went back in. I took a sip of coffee and lit a cigarette, then took a survey. Everything was fine. The back of my head hurt a little and my tailbone smarted, but it was already going away. Even my sore hand still felt the same level of sore.

"So, uh, what the hell, man?" The silent one was finally talking. I poked my cigarette at the fence and points beyond.

"I met this chick in Vegas. She's from here, so we kinda sorta met on the plane. Got all mixed up with her, which was fine until we got back. Turns out her family is the worshipping kind. Her, too, though she never really brought it up until we got back. Anyway, I live right over there, two houses down. Fuckin' weirdoes are parked in front of my house in a bus."

"No shit?" They seemed to enjoy that.

"Oh yeah. It'll be better for everyone if they think I'm sleeping in."

I took my cell phone out and they went back to their breakfast conversation. Nigel answered on the first ring.

"Problem one is I bought all kinds of drugs from those fucking criminal fucks. Speedy coke kept me up all night. Problem two is they cut it with laxatives, so I have wicked fuckin' hellacious diarrhea." Nigel could complain with great conviction once you got to know him.

"Those are problems. Where are you?"

"Don't ask. Where are you?"

"Same answer. Meet me in twenty minutes at, oh, that cheesy bar over on 11th by the hardware store? You know the one."

"I'm at the motel with Mikey. I'm on the toilet. He's all fucked up, too. Wanna talk to him? Here."

"Hi, Darby," Mikey said. Evidently he was standing right next to Nigel, waiting his turn. "We are indeed all fucked up, but Nigel held his shit together, so to speak, a little better than I did until about an hour ago. But he's not half as drunk as I am. We got some anti-diarrhea stuff, but so far no dice. Here."

"Darby?" Nigel spat. "Get me the fuck out of this place. Just come get me. I can make it, but hurry." He hung up. I dialed a cab immediately and told them where I was, and they said three to five minutes. Then I finally had a sip of coffee. Not exactly the start I was looking for. The waitress came out onto the patio with our drinks and I thumbed out a twenty and a ten and waved off the change. After a mighty, vitamin-packed slorp, I dialed Delia.

"We are all systems go for launch," she reported. I could tell she was angry. "You should see these fucking idiots. Hey!" Sudden screaming. "Put that down! Now! Sit down, goddamn it!" Back to normal. "These dudes have a band called Empire of Shit for a reason. Not one of them is qualified to do a single reasonable, rational—Hey! Get in the van! Now! That's the last fucking ti—" She hung up.

I shook my head. I had another sip of coffee and another sip of Bloody Mary, then stood and dusted off my pants.

"Later," I said. The goth gals didn't even break their conversation as I walked past, which I thought was rude, considering my theatrical entrance and the round of drinks. The inside of the bar was dim, mostly lit by pinball machines and the beer lamp over the pool table. My cab was waiting out front, so I went straight through the place and out the door, across the sidewalk, ducked against the rain, and right into the back seat almost without stopping.

"82nd and Foster," I said. The driver nodded and pulled away from the curb. I sank low in the seat and pretended to be digging through my pocket for something. When I sat up a few blocks later there were no cars behind us.

"I'm just picking up a friend and then we're going to lunch over on Alberta."

"What's on Foster? House? Apartment?"

"Nah. Some shitty motel called the Bismarck."

The driver nodded with a wise guy grin. "Hope he didn't get any action on the side, you see what I mean. The Bismarck is like a discount grocery store. Everything there is set to expire tomorrow."

"Huh." I wondered about Monique and where she was. Cheeks had thought she was almost done. Maybe she made it with some of that money to someplace she knew, but I doubted it. If she knew good people, they would have been there for her a long time ago. Then again, maybe she was in Denver, somewhere in the snow, and some kind of helpful old pervert had taken her in.

I thought about that and kept an eye on the traffic until we got to the Bismarck. Nigel was standing under the awning by the front office, wrapped in his presidential trench coat. He'd lost his tie and the briefcase. Somehow he'd managed to shave and get some gel into his hair. Definitely grumpy, but he'd apparently achieved some kind of chemical equilibrium. He got in as soon as the cab pulled up and immediately started in with the bitching.

"Diarrhea stuff kicked in just in the nick of time," he began, without so much as a hello. "Mikey drank about twenty beers and the big bastard actually fell asleep. Did you bring me coffee? No? Prick. I have plans later, so let's not waste my whole fucking day. The hoes at the Bismarck are disgusting on a level that reminds me of—"

"Driver," I said sharply. "Let's hit a Starbucks drive-thru and otherwise haul ass. Dudeboy here is going to motor his mouth like this for the entire ride, I can tell." The driver nodded and did a high-speed swerve toward an upcoming coffee stand. Nigel wheeled on me.

"I shit my guts out all night and this is what—" I stopped him with a raised fist.

"Nigel, I like you. You know that. But right now I need to think, and that means you have to quiet down."

He pouted, of course.

"Can we smoke in here?" he asked. The driver glanced in the rearview.

"No."

"Fuck," Nigel muttered.

The cab pulled into the drive-thru and the driver ordered a large latte. I got a medium black coffee with four sug-ars. Nigel refused to talk, but he was a cappuccino man, I knew, so I ordered him one. When the drinks came the driver handed ours back. Nigel took his without a word, and we made it all the way to Romero's in silence.

Gomez's brother's restaurant was a medium-size place with an L-shaped parking lot that wrapped around the back. The big windows were festively painted with crappy pictures of sombreros and jalapeños. I'd forgotten about those windows, which took up two walls, one of which faced the street. The lights were on inside and one or two people were moving around. Gomez's Ford Taurus was in the parking lot and I could see the bug-encrusted, dented nose of the Empire of Shit van poking out just around the corner. The closed sign was up and there was a sign on the door that read PRIVATE PARTY.

"Here?" the driver asked, glancing back.

"This is my party," I replied. I looked up and down the street as we pulled into the parking lot. Traffic was light. If anyone had been tailing us, there was every chance I would have noticed. I paid the driver and gave him a decent but not conspicuous tip, then patted Nigel's bony knee.

"Get your game face on, boy," I said. Nigel cursed under his breath.

We went through the drizzle fast and I knocked on the glass. Gomez appeared out of the gloom and opened it.

"Hola, vato," I said. We bumped fists, which was high affection.

"Man, dude, your cheek . . ." His deep brown eyes were hard. He studied my scar without a hint of shyness, then finally shrugged.

"Lose the party sign," I said. "Where is everyone?"

"In back with Flaco. Man, homie, your waiters? They ever need work, tell them to stay the fuck away from me."

Gomez nodded to Nigel and locked the door behind us. It was just before eleven a.m. As we approached the kitchen, I could hear laughter and the clatter of pots. Nigel was still silent behind me as we pushed through the kitchen doors into what I knew was going to be the first genuine crisis of the day.

Empire of Shit, fully decked out in pristine waiter regalia, were lined up like French show dogs for inspection. They looked crisp, clean, rested, and professional in an utterly bland way. The transformation was astounding. Flaco had five pots of something going on the massive twelve burner stove and was monkeying around by the dish machine, himself decked out in checkered pants and a chef coat. He looked highly amused.

Most shocking of all was Delia. She was wearing a prim, professional-looking vanilla power suit and her hair, now raven-wing black, was neatly combed to the side. Her makeup was tastefully light, perfect for a therapist or an airline executive. She'd cleaned off the kitchen operations desk in the corner and set up her laptop and a complicated-looking printer. She was watching the miserable Empire of Shit dudes with a gnarly prison guard grimace. She was also holding a huge meat cleaver.

"I'll be damned," I said, mostly to myself. Nigel came alongside me and grunted.

"These idiots are lined up like this because if I look away for one fucking second they turn into howler monkeys." Delia slapped the flat of the cleaver against her palm.

"You look fabulous," I said. Her eyes flicked to me and Flaco made a tittering coo of delight.

"Darby, that kind of talk is so absolutely unacceptable that it actually stymies my imagination when it comes to a graphic death threat rebuttal. A singular event."

I turned to Nigel, who was studying Empire of Shit with a restaurateur's eye. He'd owned one-sixteenth of a gay bar at one point and his mother had a share in a Denny's in Phoenix, after all. I tapped him on the shoulder.

"Get 'em, Nige. Pretend like it's their first day at your dream bistro."

Nigel nodded, the terrible coke episode forgotten. He was in his element now. He vectored up to Empire of Shit, who still had little or no idea what was going on, other than impersonating waiters at a Mexican food place was leading to a record with cover art. They studied Nigel with subtle alarm.

"Present hands!" Nigel snapped. They did so as one, instantly. Nigel carefully inspected them from head to toe. He had suggestions for each of them.

"Suck in that gut, boy," he barked at the first Empire kid. He must have weighed all of a hundred and twenty pounds, but he came to attention. Nigel glowered at him and moved on to number two.

"Tuck that shirt in." The kid did so with all possible haste. Nigel moved on to Dildo.

"Hank. Your hair." Hank looked particularly henpecked, but he smoothed his hair and shot for a neutral expression. The last guy got "belt" and "eye booger." When he was done, Nigel took a few steps back and addressed them.

"Empire of Shit. I am Nigel. Other than Hank Dildo, I don't know your names. I don't need to. Now, Darby has offered you some kind of deal. I want you to understand that dudeboy is a sociopath. So am I. You fuck up, you play around, you screw this up, I will rape each and every one of you. Is that clear?"

"Yes," they said as one.

"What we have here is an easy to understand situation. We of the Lucky Supreme camp? We are high-order scumbags. You four are anarchists. Ideologically, we are cousins. But make no mistake. You are inferior. We are stronger, smarter, faster, and we make more money. We are superior in every way. For the next few hours, you too will be higher scum. If it helps, we're going to fuck up a greedy-ass rich real estate guy, all the shit you can't stand rolled into one. Are we clear?"

"Yes!" This time with a great deal of enthusiasm.

"Excellent. Now, no matter how much glue you sniff, no matter how drunk you get, no matter how awful your next acid trip is, even if an untold fortune in pussy is one story of conquest away, you will never, ever, ever speak of this day to anyone, even to the people here right now, even among yourselves, at any time. To do so will invite my personal wrath and Delia's as well, and it will also attract Darby's attention, which is a thing to be avoided in the extreme, as you will see shortly. Is that clear?"

"Yes." A little scattered this time.

"Good. Now, we serve from the left and clear from the right. Dildo. You're the bartender. Go out there and familiarize yourself with the setup by getting me four shots of vodka. If you return with a stain or a bruise or even a hair out of place, I will—" Nigel droned on. I went over and sat down next to Delia, who was loosening up now that Nigel had taken control of the lobby, as they say.

"Great job on their hair," I commented quietly. "The uniforms, too."

"Don't get me started."

We both lit cigarettes and watched Nigel pace and lecture. Hank had gone for the drinks. Flaco was watching the proceedings with the same expression he pointed at his TV. I turned back to Delia and leaned in a little. She smelled like lilies.

"So, this getup. You have to tell me."

"It's what you called my civilian infiltrator of secret real-world power costume, or whatever. I have to register the sale of the building later at the county clerk's office and go to the bank again, plus I have to file some permits. The kind of shit you don't want to hear about."

"Sorry."

"It's not a big deal. I feel kinda like a spy when I dress up like this anymore. Believe it or not, I have errands of my own which occasionally require this getup. Squeezing your shit in isn't all that big a deal."

"Groovy."

"Yeah," she said quietly, not taking her eyes off Nigel. "I'm shifting some investments around. My portfolio. Plus I'm having some of my designs transferred to fabric for a textile show in Taos next month. Those people take you more seriously when you dress like they do."

I knew Delia had all kinds of art projects on the side, but that was the first I'd heard of a textile show in New Mexico. She read my mind, as she often did.

"I've been busy."

"I see."

"Pills?"

"Check."

"Mikey?"

"Passed out."

"What the hell is wrong with Nigel?"

"Speedy coke. Diarrhea."

"You?"

"Fell off a fence."

"Chick?"

"Pancakes. Boned her."

"Good?"

"Yep."

"Dmitri?"

"Should be here any minute."

"Inner fury?"

"Contained."

"Well." She sighed. "I guess that about covers it. Sign these." She handed me a small stack of papers on a clipboard. On each page was a helpful little tag with SIGN HERE. She handed me a pen and I got to it. Hank Dildo appeared about halfway through, carrying a tray with drinks. He was pulling it off.

"Sir. Ma'am." He even bowed a little.

Delia and I took our drinks. Hank smiled and nodded pleasantly, then went to serve Nigel and Flaco.

"I'm never going to hear the end of this," Delia whispered.

"Are you paying for the trip to Frisco?"

"Good point."

Gomez poked his head into the kitchen. He looked grim.

"Darby. Dmitri. Worse than usual."

"Aw shit," I said, rising. "Bring him here. All right, people! It's showtime! Waiters! Take your stations out front. Hank, you hang back for a sec. Everyone do what Gomez says."

Nigel took a plastic bag of pills out of his pocket and began privately lecturing Hank Dildo on rufies. The other three Empire boys walked out with decorum, already in character. As soon as the door closed behind them it opened again and Gomez hurled Dmitri through.

"Jesus," Delia said in a low voice.

Dmitri had been in a fight of some kind. He had a black eye and his lips were swollen. He staggered drunkenly on the momentum of Gomez's toss and almost fell. There was a wide piss stain on the front of his pants and the shoulder of his greasy parka was torn. His rheumy eyes focused on me and he wailed. One of his front teeth was gone.

"The whore," he managed. "She robbed me! I am broken! Broken!" He sobbed and ran his trembling hands through his pile of hair. I could smell him from where I stood; the refined essence of rotting bum. I closed the distance between us and slapped him, then grabbed his filthy lapels to keep him from falling.

"Flaco! Nigel!" I snapped. "I need pants and a shirt of some kind in less than five minutes! Move it! I noticed some kind of sweaters and hippie junk from the Tibet place two doors down. Go!"

I steadied Dmitri and dug a hundred out, slapped it into Flaco's hand as he raced past. The two of them disappeared through the back door into the parking lot. Delia appeared at my side.

"Stand back," I said.

I dragged Dmitri over to the sink and tore his jacket off. The smell that rolled off him almost made me gag, so I backed away. The polyester shirt he was wearing stuck to him in places like a scab.

"Strip," I instructed. He weakly pried at one of his shoes, as if he had all afternoon.

"Dmitri, if you aren't naked in thirty seconds . . ." I let that hang. He sped up and less than a minute later he was naked; a skinny, mottled, hairy thing that reminded me of a freshly plucked and scaled vulture from famine country. He covered his withered genitals and whimpered.

"Get in the sink," I instructed.

"No!" he whined, horrified. I raised my open hand and he turned and started clambering. It was awful to watch, but I wasn't going to touch him if I could help it. He managed to get his upper body on the flat of stainless steel where the dishes were loaded, and then levered his legs up. One scoot back and he dropped into the industrial basin and banged his head on the dish machine door.

"Oh my God," he moaned, delirious.

I took the spray wand and tested the temperature. Warm enough. I pointed it at his head and squeezed the trigger. Dmitri screamed.

I grabbed him by the neck and widened the pattern, beginning with a general, all-over hose down. He thrashed with surprising strength until I turned the wand on his face again, and then his spirit broke and he went limp. Delia appeared at my side with a bottle of moisturizing hand soap from the employee restroom. She'd taken the lid off. I dumped it on Dmitri and watched the suds form. Delia backed away to a safe distance.

"Scrub, Dmitri! Scrub like a motherfucker!"

He began scrubbing himself weakly, mostly his chest and his armpits.

"Hair and face."

He smelled his hands for some reason, and then got to work on his hair. I dumped the rest of the hand soap on his head. Then Dmitri began to hum. He was that wasted.

"Face. Ears."

He followed my instructions and we went on to dick and ass, then feet. He was smiling as he lathered between his toes. I turned to Delia and cracked a grin. She was smiling, too, arms crossed.

"OK, Dmitri, open wide."

Dmitri closed his eyes and tilted his head back, his mouth wide. I shot water into it and he rinsed and spat, then opened up again. We repeated the process a few times, and then I gave him an all-over rinse one more time for good measure.

"Towel," I said, holding my hand out. Delia was one step ahead on me. She whacked a roll of paper towels into my hand and I let go of the trigger on the spray wand.

"There," I said. Dmitri wiped his nose and blinked at me. I started unraveling the roll of paper towels and feeding him the end.

"I never imagined this day would come," Delia said behind me.

"Me neither," I agreed.

"I did," Dmitri said.

Flaco burst through the back door, took one look at Dmitri sitting naked in the sink, and dropped the bag he was carrying. Delia picked it up and looked inside. She took out a pair of leather clogs with turquoise flowers stitched on the top and looked up at me uncertainly.

"They only had hippie," Flaco said defensively as Delia took out an oversized hemp peasant shirt with bellbottom sleeves and beaded tassels. She stuffed everything back into the bag without bothering to examine the pants and handed it to me. I scowled at Flaco.

"Where's Nigel?"

"Van." I could tell from the set of his shoulders that I wouldn't get anything else out of him. I kicked Dmitri's old clothes under the sink and handed him the bag.

"Get dressed. Fast."

Dmitri clambered out of the sink and started putting the clothes on. He'd tied the drawstring on what looked like karate pants and was stepping into the clogs when the kitchen door opened. It was Dildo.

"Car here. Huge-ass Mexican and a guy in a suit."

"Get 'em seated," I said, squaring my shoulders. He vanished back into the restaurant. I turned back to Dmitri, who was struggling into the shirt. I couldn't tell what he looked like when he smoothed it out and pushed his hair back. Maybe a New Age Guatemalan musician.

"You remember what to do?" I asked him.

"Sign the papers," he said. "Get the cash and sign the papers."

"Out with you then. No drinking."

He looked a little hurt as he went through the door into the dining area. Delia and I looked at each other.

"It will be a miracle if any of us walk out of here alive," she commented.

"I know."

Looking through the windows in the kitchen doors was out. They might see us. Looking through the slot under the heat lamp for outgoing plates was out for the same reason. I knelt and peeked through the tiny slot between the kitchen double doors. Delia scooted in just underneath me. It wasn't the best point of view, but it was good enough.

Cheddar Box came in first, alone. Gomez intercepted him with a menu and they chatted, too far away for us to make out what they were saying. Cheddar Box pointed at where Dmitri was sitting, a few tables away from us. Hopefully we'd be able to hear everything. Gomez led Cheddar Box over to Dmitri, who waved in greeting.

"Big guy," Dmitri began. "Where's your boss?"

"Stand up," Cheddar Box growled.

"No." Dmitri sounded a little angry. Below me, Delia stiffened. My scalp tightened.

"Fine." Cheddar Box took something out of his suit coat, a black oblong box. He tapped a button on it, watched something on it for a moment, and then held it out and slowly ran it over Dmitri. He consulted the box again and then did the same thing to the table.

"Wire," Delia breathed.

Evidently satisfied, Cheddar Box walked back to the door, said something to Gomez, who was innocently wiping down menus, and motioned through the glass for Oleg. Then he turned his back to the door and stood to one side. First major problem. Cheddar Box looked like he was going to stand guard at the door, which meant he wasn't going to sit down, which meant no rufies for the Mexican Conan. It was possible that Dildo would have the presence of mind to come up with something, but given what I knew about him, a serious dread came over me. My only comfort was that Delia was seeing the same thing as I was, and she wasn't on the edge of panic.

"Wait," Delia whispered, feeling my tension. "I told Dildo this might happen."

Oleg came in carrying a duffel bag in one hand and a briefcase in the other. Cheddar Box held the door for him and then resumed his guard post. Oleg was wearing a dark, generic suit and a tan overcoat. His hair was slicked back and his red, jowly face was set in what I'm sure he thought of as his most impressive grimace. He scowled across the room at Dmitri, who withered visibly. A waiter crossed our field of vision for an instant. I realized I was holding my breath.

Oleg marched with great authority to Dmitri's table and sat. There were no formalities of any kind. He put the briefcase on the table, opened it and took out a thick stack of paper, dropped it in front of Dmitri, and slapped a pen from his coat on top of them. Then he sat back, all without a single word.

Dmitri was crushed. Maybe he'd thought he would be treated with a little more dignity during the robbery, I don't know. He reached out with a shaking hand and picked up the pen, then turned the papers around to face him. Their waiter appeared with a pleasant smile, hands clasped in front of him. It was Eye Booger.

"Can I start you gentlemen with beverages?" He was calm, poised, attentive.

"Vodka," Dmitri warbled. Oleg nodded sharply.

Dmitri started signing, page after page. The waiter walked casually to the bar and Hank Dildo went into action. A second waiter appeared out of the darkness to our right and angled toward Cheddar Box, menu in hand.

Cheddar Box waved him away after a brief conversation. Then, as if a miracle had occurred, he changed his mind and said something. The waiter nodded and calmly walked over to Hank, said something, and then hung out by the bar. Hank worked efficiently below eye level for a moment more and then set two tumblers of vodka on the bar. The waiter stayed where he was, and then Hank set what looked like a pint glass of 7UP next to the tumblers.

The waiter took the 7UP and walked over to Cheddar Box, who accepted it with a distracted nod. He drank the entire thing in two sips and handed the empty glass back. The waiter said something pleasant and went back to the bar, set the glass down, and put the two vodkas on a tray. Just as he was about to turn, Dildo brushed the one on the right.

"I think," Delia breathed, "we . . ." she trailed off. I was too excited to say anything.

The waiter expertly carried the tray over, his poise far different from lovely Suzanne's balancing act, and set the right drink in front of Oleg, the left in front of Dmitri.

Both men drained their glasses instantly.

From there we just waited. My back was cramping a little, so I crept away from the door and went back to the desk where Delia had set up her computer. I lit a cigarette and was surprised that my hands weren't shaking. Flaco crept over to me and I passed him my smokes. He took one out and lit it.

"It's working," I said quietly. "They both drank."

"How long for the rufies?"

"I don't know. Fast, I guess. Go out to the van and ask Nigel."

Flaco nodded and crept away. Delia tensed up and backed away from the door, then turned and tiptoed over to me.

"Cheddar Box just drank another 7UP. He's going to have to pee soon. Dmitri and the Russian dude are on round two." Her voice was quiet, but I could hear the excitement.

"What about the waiters?"

"They seem fine," she whispered. "It's amazing."

"Thank God we hired performers."

I finished off my vodka from earlier and Delia did the same. I wished we'd had the presence of mind to get another round in reserve before the show started, but it was only a matter of time before we had access to the bar again, one way or another.

Flaco crept back in and knelt beside us.

"Nigel says it should happen right away. Five minutes or less. I think he is not napping. He is doing the cocaine." Flaco touched the side of his nose and sniffed.

A waiter came in carrying a decoy bus tub of clean glasses from the bar. He set it down by the dish machine and came over to us.

"The Russian guy is already acting strange. The hufuckingnormous dude has rubbed his face a couple times and looks like he wants to sit down."

"Get back out there," I said. "Signal Hank to be prepared to dose them with another round."

"I think he already did." He shrugged.

"Oh God," Delia said to herself. I wheeled on Flaco and motioned with my hand.

"Nigel!" I hissed. "Now!"

Flaco disappeared out the back door and the waiter spun and went back out front. Delia rubbed her hands together.

"I think there might be a big flaw," I said quietly. "I told Nigel to get enough for five or six people in case they had reinforcements. I have no idea what he gave Dildo."

"You idiots," Delia hissed. "All of you. Every single one of you."

"Those shitheads out there are doing great," I said defensively. Just then Dmitri screamed, high and long and loud.

Delia and I jumped up as the kitchen door exploded inward. Cheddar Box staggered through and roared. Hank Dildo was on his back and two of the waiters had him around the legs, one wrapped around each. Eye Booger flew through the kitchen doors in a high-speed dive and slammed square into the center of Cheddar's wide lower back, just below Dildo. The entire operation went down and Cheddar Box flailed once, then sagged, panting. Then he was out.

Empire of Shit were on their feet fast as wolves, circling, almost snarling, but Cheddar Box didn't move. Gomez appeared in the doorway.

"Russian guy is down," he reported.

Empire of Shit let out a shout and started dancing and capering around the kitchen. Delia hugged my side. I was so proud of everyone, especially the anarchists.

"Phase two," I called out. "Gomez! A round of drinks for everyone. Boys! Help me drag that Russian piece of shit in here. Flaco! Find something gnarly to tie the big dude up with. Good work, people, but this isn't over yet."

The back door clanged open and Nigel strode in. He glanced at Cheddar Box and then at me, smiling.

"It worked," he said. He glanced over at Hank. "How much did it take?"

Hank shrugged. "All of it, pretty much."

Nigel laughed and then stopped. His eyes narrowed. "Are you serious?"

"Yeah. Like, maybe six each."

Nigel shook his head, the smile gone. "Guy I got 'em from said the average person goes down with half a rufie. I told you that, Dildo."

Hank Dildo shrugged again.

"I got stuff to do," Delia said. She hustled out and came back with the papers, fed them into her scanner. The

Empire boys dragged Oleg in and headed back to the bar. Nigel followed them.

I checked Cheddar Box's breathing. Even. Then I checked Oleg's. He was about half the size of the Mexican Conan, and it showed. His breathing was slow and uneven. Shallow. He was also pale and a little sweaty. I decided to go through his pockets.

Oleg had seventeen hundred in cash in his wallet, which I pocketed. Four credit cards. Empire of Shit could use those. A driver's license and assorted business cards. He also had a pack of Camel straights, mine now; an expensive-looking silver lighter, which I tossed to Flaco; some keys, which I put in Cheddar Box's outside suit pocket; and last, a pocket knife. I held it up in the light. It looked old and precious, maybe an heirloom of some kind. I tossed it in the trash can by the dish machine. Then I went out through the kitchen doors and sat down in Oleg's chair across from Dmitri. I closed Oleg's briefcase.

"What the hell is going on?" Dmitri asked. I realized he had been frozen in a cringe for the last few minutes.

"Relax," I said. "I had to take care of this my way. Here's how this works. I'm buying the Lucky. Me. Nigel! The duffel bag!"

Nigel looked up from the bar, where he'd been guarding the bag and nursing a drink. He picked the bag up and carried it over to me, set it on the table on top of the briefcase. I unzipped it as he walked back to the bar.

"Here's your cash," I said, picking out a banded brick of five thousand and holding it up. "But of course there's a catch. Three of them."

Hank appeared with two tumblers. Our drinks had finally arrived. Vodka was the theme. I took mine and set Dmitri's in front of him.

"First, this five thousand is for the new building manager. I'm hiring one for both of us."

"I never said—" he spluttered.

"Shut up," I warned. "No more of your shit. The city or some other scumbag will eat you alive in less than a year and turn on me for dessert. We need to stand together or we both go down, and you're too weak. You can't do anything right, Dmitri. So I'm going to save you. And I want you to understand, old man. I want you to understand that I don't even like you. I'm saving you for entirely personal reasons."

Dmitri started crying. I watched and sipped my drink. It occurred to me that Dmitri was going to leave with a duffel bag full of cash. I didn't even know where he would go or how he planned on getting there.

"Dmitri, after you sign the papers, you have to go somewhere other than Old Town for a few days. Do you have a place to lie low?"

"No," he choked. I rolled my eyes.

"Does the Bismarck Motel sound good to you? Hookers? It's cheap."

"I'll get robbed," he whimpered. He looked at me cautiously, his lower lip quivering. "Can you keep this money for now?"

It took a little of the majesty out of the moment, for some reason, but I agreed.

"When can I go home?" he whined.

"I don't know," I replied. "You can't ever go back to sleeping on the floor in the back of the pizza place. You'll get busted." I'd see if the new manager could set him up in one of the abandoned apartments upstairs.

Dmitri nodded and drank.

"Where are your keys?" I asked.

"My jacket, I think. Maybe I didn't lock the door. My pants—"

I motioned for one of the Empire boys and told him to go through the pockets in the clothes under the dish machine. He came back a moment later with a single key and three dollars.

"I tossed all that shit. This was it. Those two dudes are still way the fuck knocked out."

I gave Dmitri the three dollars and then took an even thousand out of the duffel bag and gave that to him, too. It was a week of living large at a place like the Bismarck.

"Maybe Nigel can take you shopping in a few days," I suggested. Dmitri looked instantly terrified.

"No," he said emphatically. "No. These clothes are fine."

"Well, I'm sure as hell not doing it," I said. If I stayed out of jail, I probably would and I knew it. I needed new boots anyway.

Delia came out of the kitchen with a stack of warm paper and set it down in front of me. All the Oleg crap and Dmitri's original signatures had been replaced with Darby Holland LLC and blank slots with SIGN HERE tabs. I pushed it over to Dmitri.

"Go over to the bar and start signing again, same as before," I said. He got up and Delia followed.

"Everyone," I called out. "Over here. It's time to blow this place."

Gomez, Flaco, Nigel, and Empire of Shit quickly clustered around the table, holding their drinks.

"OK. Nigel, you're in charge of getting rid of Oleg's ride. I'd say long-term parking at the airport is good, but we're in north Portland, so just down the street in front of a sketchy crack pad is fine."

"Check."

"Keys are in the big dude's pocket. Just take the one to the car and leave the rest on him."

"On it." Nigel disappeared through the kitchen doors.

"Gomez, Flaco, just hang back for now. As soon as we're gone, take Dmitri over to the Bismarck Motel and get him a room." I gave Gomez fifteen hundred out of the money I had just taken out of Oleg's wallet. "For you guys and your brother. Cool?"

Gomez nodded and so did Flaco. They were going to hold me to the rent, too.

"And Gomez, you got my little thing? For my collection?"

Gomez looked briefly confused, then took a baggie out of his pocket and handed it to me. I stuffed it into my jacket.

"OK. Empire. We have to get those dudes into your van and take them to the Bismarck Motel." I held up my hand in case they protested and took out Oleg's credit cards. "These should sweeten the pot. One for each of you. Charge until they stop."

Hank snatched them out of my hand with the blinding speed of a snapping turtle and passed them out. They collectively marveled at the massive change in their fortunes. I smiled at the trail of pure insanity they would leave if Dessel was ever interested enough to follow it.

"Let's do it."

I led the four of them back into the kitchen and instructed Hank to wedge the back door open and then open the back doors of the van. While he was doing that, the rest of us sized up the situation. Cheddar Box was going to be the real obstacle, so I decided to deal with Oleg first.

"This is how this goes down," I said. "We have to make this fast, in case someone pulls into the parking lot. You two, grab his arms. I'll get his legs. Hank, you and what's-his-name here get his belt on either side. We charge the van and just sort of toss him."

It worked better than I thought it would. With five people, Oleg wasn't all that heavy. The hurl worked perfectly and everyone backed quickly into the restaurant except for Hank, who scrambled in and rolled Oleg to one side to make wide room for Conan.

Hank then joined us in our group contemplation of Cheddar Box and gave me a quick thumbs-up. "Still breathing. Bonked his head pretty good."

"Good," I replied. "So I guess we do the same thing with this guy, but let's watch the head. No toss this time. Hank, you and this dude"—I pointed—"take the legs, one each, you two the arms. Lift like motherfuckers and when you get a little more than knee high, I'll get under and lift with my back. I'm bigger than you guys, but not by much, and I also won't be able to see. We get most of him in the back and then I'll sort of roll free and we drag him the rest of the way. Don't let him squash me."

Empire of Shit got to it and it didn't look promising. They strained until they were red in the face and their veins were standing out. Cheddar Box was a cow-sized sack of dead weight. As soon as they got him high enough I crabbed under, settled my bent shoulders under Cheddar's waist, and tried to rise.

Pushing with every ounce of strength in my legs, we got him a little higher and I felt them slacking off a little to get their breath.

"Gheeh!" I managed. They heaved as one and I took a staggering step forward.

In that fashion, we made it all the way to the van. Hank and the guy on the arm opposite him clambered swiftly inside without losing too much lift and did their job from there, walking backward. When the bumper hit my head I made one Herculean push up and forward and gained us a few inches before I rolled free. The two on his legs jumped in the van and the four of them dragged Cheddar Box in the rest of the way. I slammed the doors as soon as his size-twenty feet cleared.

It was done. I rubbed my hands together. Cheddar Box and Oleg were rufied and in my possession.

I went back in and closed the kitchen door, then went out to the front. Gomez and Flaco were drinking at the bar waiting for Dmitri, who was just finishing up. I walked over and stood next to Delia as he signed the last two pages.

"There we go," Delia said, tidying the stack. She looked at me with an unreadable expression. She forged my signature all the time and this was evidently no exception. I reached out and gently brushed the bridge of her pug nose.

"Gotta run," I said. "Take the cash for the moment?"

"Sure. Tell Hank and the boys I'll meet them at the Alibi for drinks at five." She smiled. "Inside joke."

"Make a scene," I said. She cocked her head, quizzical, a close warmness around her eyes.

"Always."

I waved to everyone and walked back through the restaurant, into the kitchen, and out the back door. The rain was mild and it was cool, just hovering at the edge of another cold snap. I lit a cigarette and got in the van on the passenger side. Hank was at the wheel. He gave me a rather tight smile. The other three were passing around a joint in the back, squatting nervously around Cheddar Box, fearful of what would happen if he suddenly woke up in the close space.

"Out to 82nd and Foster, the Bismarck Motel. I'll show you where to park."

By the time we got to the motel, my elation with having scored a comatose Russian gangster and a snoring Mexican killing machine had crumbled all the way down into savage paranoia, and I had taken the already nervous Empire of Shit down with me.

"What the fuck now!" Hank snapped. We were in the median turn lane in front of the Bismarck with the erratic blinker on. The Bismarck looked extra shitty, all things considered. The rest of the Empire boys were in a state of sweaty agitation, chain smoking and totally silent. The van sounded like it would stall at any moment.

"Pull around back," I instructed. Hank cursed under his breath as I dialed Mikey again. He hadn't picked up so far.

"Aw," Mikey finally answered. Then he puked.

"Mikey!" I screamed. "Move your fucking van! Now!"

"Jesu—" He hung up. Hank gunned it into the parking lot, cutting off a station wagon. The driver laid on the horn.

"No more screaming!" Hank Dildo screamed. Behind me came a chorus of "Holy fuck" and "What the—" I dropped my cigarette on the trash-cluttered floor and ground it out.

"There," I said, pointing.

Mikey's van was already backing out. It was far newer than the Empire ride and I cursed myself for not having borrowed it in the first place, but I'd wanted to hold Mikey and his resources in reserve. He'd come close to blowing his limited role as it was.

Hank gunned it into the vacant slot and the engine died. He glared at me.

"Shut it," I said. "You guys are in way too fucking deep to start freaking out."

"Let's just do this," he said through his teeth.

We waited until Mikey had parked. He got out of his van and slowly made his way over, eyes down. He was wearing the same clothes as the day before and radiated sour and pissed off. He got to my window and raised his face. I rolled the window down.

"Go open the room door," I said. I couldn't keep the tension out of my voice.

"I can't leave the door open or the . . ." He trailed off when he caught sight of Oleg and Cheddar Box. "What the fuck?"

"They're alive," I said. "Now open the fucking door and help us get them in there."

Mikey's face hardened and he shook his head. He walked back around the corner and came back a minute later with his jacket on.

"Let's go," he said shortly.

Empire of Shit wanted their part over with as quickly as possible. They kicked open the back doors of the van and dragged Oleg out with no consideration for his well-being, stepping on him and clanging his head around. The Russian and Cheddar Box were side by side, so they stepped on the Mexican Conan a few times, too. Hank got him in a fire-man's carry with their help, and with strength born from desperation staggered toward the corner. I pointed at Eye Booger.

"Keep watch." He nodded and peered around the cor-ner, gave Hank the thumbs-up. Mikey looked at Cheddar Box and then at me.

"Dude is bigger than I am," he said grimly. Mikey was about six foot two and hovered around two fifty. He was right.

"Think you can carry him?"

"Instead of just standing around here waiting to get arrested? Guess I'll fucking try. Jesus Christ."

With the remaining two Empire guys' help, we pushed and dragged Cheddar until his ankles were dangling out of the back of the van. Mikey grabbed them and yanked backward with his entire body. The back of Cheddar's suit caught on something and there was a long tearing sound. Mikey heaved Cheddar over his shoulder and made a strangling sound. Hank appeared out of nowhere and scooped Cheddar's giant legs onto his skinny shoulders, taking a chunk of the weight.

"Move," Mikey managed.

With Hank in the lead they staggered to the corner and Eye Booger waved them on. They rounded the corner and I got out and gently closed the van doors.

"We'll wait here," Eye Booger said, joining us. We were all panting for different reasons. An instant later Hank rounded the corner.

"Bye," he snapped at me. Empire of Shit were all in the van in seconds. The starter ground a few times and the engine caught, then the rusted, dented piece of shit shot out a plume of black smoke and they were gone.

I lit a cigarette and stood in the rain for a minute, just breathing. The parking lot seemed like one of the quietest places I'd ever been right then. The air smelled and felt like more snow, the thin, wet Oregon kind, was on the way. The sky was a solid, flat gray. A lone crow was picking though some trash over by the dumpster. Reluctantly, I went around the corner and knocked on the door of the room at the end.

Mikey opened it with a gust of electric heater air and let me past without a word. He locked the door behind us as I peered through the closed blinds. Nothing.

Oleg and Cheddar were on the bed, flat on their backs, very neatly arranged for such a high-speed operation.

Mikey sat down by Oleg's feet and gave me a long, bad look.

"What happened to these guys and why am I in a motel room with them?" He was more than angry. He was also scared, disappointed, hungover, and tired in the soul.

I sat down on the only chair in the room. Mikey had gotten another couple of six-packs at some point and they were sitting on the dresser next to me. I opened one and sipped. Warm. I pointed at Oleg.

"The suit there is the guy who hired the bomber that got us. Russian real estate developer. Big guy next to him is a bodyguard. We just rufied the fuck out of 'em and I'm mailing the Russian guy back where he came from in a transmission box. Big guy goes free."

Mikey turned and looked them over, then slowly turned back.

"That . . ." He looked down at his big hands. When he spoke again his voice was very quiet. "That's totally insane, Darby."

There was nothing I could say to that. Mikey rubbed his stubbly head. He still wouldn't meet my eye.

"I, uh, I guess I'll help," he continued, softly, "but . . . I'm sorry, man. I quit."

I sighed. It made me feel shitty on some level, but I knew it was coming, somehow. Life was a complex thing and circumstance was the screamer in the choir. Everyone believed they chose between the paths they took. It seemed like there was always more than one option. But unfortunately, all of those paths led into the unknown. Just like Mikey, I had been a little boy once. Through the dense haze of the chaos of the years, I could still feel the sun on his face. But in the end, we all walked a secret and lonesome road that lay beneath all of our dreams and superstitions, and circumstance kept us on it. Every single one of us was in the process of becoming more of what we already were. And for all of his love of things wild and hard—the passions Delia reveled in even when she slept, the animal racing mad inside of me, the secret world of a man who called himself Nigel—for all of Mike's admiration and the covetousness of those things for himself, fate had not dealt him any cards from that deck. Made more truly by time and circumstance, Mikey was a pussy.

"I can dig it," I said. Mikey finally met my eye, smiled weakly.

"So what now?"

"I get the Russian in the box, take it where I'm taking it. I'll need your van for about an hour. The big guy should be out for a day or so, but you stay with him for now. When I get back, you go home. Pay the room up for another day or two before you go. He can find his way out of here when he wakes up."

Mikey nodded and went back to staring at his hands.

Together, we put Oleg in the transmission box. I used the blade on my multi-tool to cut an air hole in either end, just below the handles where no one would see them. Oleg didn't quite fit, so we had to lever him onto his side and bend his knees. Before I put the lid on, I took the plastic bag Gomez had given me out of my pocket and shook the contents into my hand.

The mummified mouse was gray and desiccated, contorted with whatever forces made it that way. Its lips were peeled back and its tiny teeth were showing. I knelt and put it into Oleg's breast pocket, gently patted the pocket flat.

Something cracked in Mikey when I did that. He seemed physically smaller as I put the lid on.

"Help me with this," I said quietly.

Together, we carried the box out and put it in the back of Mikey's van. He silently handed me the keys and then slowly walked back to the motel room. I got in and lit a cigarette. The engine started on the first try.

The Mexicans had a white Mitsubishi box truck pulled up to the garage at the Armenian's when I got there. I pulled into the lot and backed into a space between a Lexus and a Mercedes. When I got out, one of them wandered over to me carrying a clipboard, squinting in the light rain.

"Boss not around," he said. "You got your parts?"

"Box is in back."

He nodded. "What's the weight?"

"I guess somewhere around two hundred, give or take." I gave him an expression of bland indifference.

"Vatos!" he yelled. I opened the back doors and they slid the box out easily and carried it into the garage. There were five or six transmission boxes stacked in there already, along with some random smaller ones. An entire shipment was waiting. They set Oleg down on top of an identical transmission box and one of them began taping the lid while the other two got back to packing parts. The guy with the clipboard came back over to me.

"You supposed to sign?"

"Nah."

"Goes out at six a.m." With that, he went back in and started helping the other two guys with what looked like a manifold. It was done.

I got back in the van. I don't know what I was expecting to feel right them, but looking into that garage through the windshield, the very first thing that came to mind after a solid minute of blankness was curiously uplifting.

I was hungry.

My phone rang on the drive back to the motel. I hadn't gotten so much as a ticket so far, and now that I was in the final sprint into the clear zone, a little good behavior would be soothing, so I pulled into a gas station before answering. It was Delia.

"Package is away," I answered. "Sort of."

"I just got to the Alibi," she said. I could hear chaos in the background and it made me smile. "Hank and the boys were already wasted when I got here. They spray painted their waiter outfits gold as soon as they got home. It's a miracle they even made it."

"Mikey quit."

Delia sighed. "That was a long time coming. It was nice of you to hold him out of the main action, but I think it also depressed him a little. I like Mikey, always have, always will, but maybe he needs a smoother ride."

"Yeah. Heard from Nigel?"

"The Prince of Hell is on his way here. I think he wants to buy the boys a couple rounds. Display some humanity, that kind of thing."

"Good idea."

"So the deed is filed. Congrats. Bank went good. You still have to stop by there in the next week or so, but no rush.

And I met with my Taos hippie connection and cemented the deal, so me and Hank changed our Frisco plans. We're going to New Mexico."

"Right on."

Neither of us said anything. I listened to Empire of Shit howling in the background. There was no trace of tension left in them.

"What now?" she asked finally.

"I dunno," I replied. "Drop off this van. Send Mikey home for the last time. Then I guess I'll go get my car and pick up my tail again, take Suzanne out to dinner. Ethiopian."

"Jarra's?"

"Yep."

"You dog. Whippin' out the big guns."

"I am. Then a romantic stroll for enquiring minds to puzzle over, after that back to my place. I'd say I have a fifty-fifty chance of doing a little time in county in the next day or so."

"Seems likely. How you think your new squeeze is going to react to that?"

"Bad, if she finds out. But you can never tell."

"Huh. When all the smoke clears, you should adopt a policy of moderate honesty. In a couple of weeks, maybe. If she can't handle the bad then she shouldn't get the good."

"I know."

"Every time with you, man. I'm just saying. A chick who runs screaming at the first sign of trouble is definitely not for you. And a chick like that almost always rips you off on the way out the door. It's part of your personal pattern with women. As soon as the walking kind of woman walks, all your shit goes up for grabs."

"Bitches," I growled.

"You pick 'em, not me. Maybe this one is different. But being honest is the best way to find out before you get in too deep and she has the keys to your house."

"You don't like Suzanne, do you?"

"Why would I? My Darby, my brave, crazy, lovely Darby, has a woman he has to hide a part of himself from. So no, I don't. It's nothing personal. She seemed nice when I met her."

"You're just as fucked in the head as I am, Delia."

"That's just it," she snapped. "We're not fucked in the head at all. We just won." She hung up.

I sat there and smoked for a minute. I'd been thinking too much, which was an unusual thought to have. To stave off any more of it, I turned on the radio and surfed the airwaves for some Doobie Brothers. No dice, so I settled on mariachi music. They might have been singing about lost love or suicide, train wrecks or chlorine spills, but since I'd never know, the stuff always sounded a little cheerful to me. When I finally pulled into the parking lot of the Bismarck, I cranked it and cut the engine. When he got in to drive home, the deafening blast of Juarez would be his going away present.

Mikey opened the door as soon as I knocked. He was wearing his jacket and holding his backpack. I handed him his keys and pushed past him.

"Room's paid up for two more days," he said. "I had to show 'em my driver's license when I checked in, but they didn't write anything down. Still . . ." He glanced at Cheddar Box.

"He's not going to die, Mike," I said. He didn't seem relieved.

"It's just you sometimes . . . Fuck it."

I patted his wide shoulder and he jumped a little.

"We worked together a long time, Mikey. I'd go down before I hung you out to dry."

He finally looked up. That made sense to him.

"I guess I know that."

"I still want some flash for the new shop," I said. He smiled weakly, but it was still a smile.

"Sell you some, half off."

I nodded and we shook hands. Mikey was going to hate me for the secrets I'd put into his head, but not just yet. A minute after the door closed behind him, I heard the distant blast of the Mexican music I'd been listening for. For whatever reason, he didn't turn it off. The van idled for a moment and then the music slowly dopplered away.

I sat down next to Cheddar Box and lit a cigarette. He seemed to be resting easily. After a minute, I leaned over and patted him down. It took longer than I thought. Getting his wallet out was especially difficult.

Cheddar Box was loaded with an incredible variety of shit. His wallet was remarkably thin, with five hundred-dollar bills, an ATM card, and a driver's license. His name was Santiago Espinoza. Forty-seven years old. He lived in the hood. Other than the black scanning device he had pointed at Dmitri, he had a small gun that looked expensive (but I didn't really know), a pocket knife that looked like a surgical implement, an iPhone, Tic Tacs, dental floss, ear plugs, a condom, fingernail clippers, and a guitar pick. The last item was the most interesting. Santiago Espinoza was a musician.

I put everything back, then looked around the room for a piece of paper and a pen. I found a ballpoint on the dresser but no paper, so I dug around in my pockets and came up with the receipt from the coffee stand that morning. On the back I wrote in block letters "Please do not kill me until we have a chance to talk." I didn't want to sign my name for any number of reasons, so instead I signed it "Another fan of Julia." I put it in the same pocket as his iPhone.

Mikey had left the room key on the dresser, so I put my cigarette out, picked it up, and went out, locking the door behind me. Then I ambled down to the office. The temperature had dropped another few degrees and the rain had almost stopped. I could see my breath.

The clerk was a zitty little guy with his sneakers up on the desk, watching TV and grazing his way through a box of Oreos. He glanced up without much interest when I came in.

"Twenty an hour," he said. "Sixty for the whole day, but no going in and out with hoes or slinging dope. Cash is king."

"I'm looking for an old hippie with a missing front tooth. Probably came in with a hard Mexican dude."

The kid looked back at the TV. I dug a stained twenty out of my pocket and held it up. He leaned out and snatched it.

300

"Room eleven. Keep it down."

As I walked over to Dmitri's room, I wondered what loud thing the clerk imagined I might be planning. It turned out Dmitri was staying right next to Ralston's old room. I knocked.

"Come in," Dmitri called.

I opened the door on a pleasant surprise. Dmitri was reclined on the bed, propped up with pillows, eating tamales with a plastic fork and just getting started on a bottle of cheap white wine.

"My friend!" he cried as I closed the door behind me, "I cannot go clothes shopping today. It feels like snow and *Baywatch* is on. Can you find me a peaceful hooker for later?"

"Maybe." I sat down on the chair by the dresser. "The room OK?"

"Oh yes." He ate like I did. It made me wonder when the last time anything solid had hit his stomach.

"Dmitri, I need a favor."

"Of course you do," he said. "Everyone everywhere always needs a favor, and today I'm feeling . . . what do you want?"

"That huge guy from the restaurant? Guy who scanned you?"

Dmitri's eyes narrowed. He stopped chewing.

"He's sleeping one off in the last room down. I just need to know when he leaves."

"No," Dmitri said flatly. "If I see him from here, then yes, I'll call you. But that man is extremely dangerous, and I am not. So I won't go knocking, and now I won't even leave this room until I'm sure he's gone. So now I need the favor instead of you. Since you've trapped me here, I need my hooker worse than ever. She can go look from time to time, but I might also need to send her out for supplies. The news says snow is coming. I might need soup, or sterno. I don't have any socks right now. This wine won't last until dark."

I called a cab and told them where I was. I was on the verge of slapping him again.

"If I see any lookers on the way out I'll send them your way," I said, rising. I zipped up my coat. Dmitri nodded and started eating again.

"Get me an older one. One that might want to settle in for the afternoon. It's cold out there, so it shouldn't be hard. Even you could do it. I wonder—" He paused with his fork halfway to his mouth. "I wonder what ever happened to Monique. She disappeared a little while ago."

"I heard she came into some money. Split town." It was true, but I still felt bad saying it.

"She was from Alabama, you know. She had an aunt who used to send her letters sometimes. I still have them at my pizza restaurant. For some reason she couldn't take them home to wherever she lived."

I thought about that while the inside of my jacket warmed up. I thought about how she must have wanted to save those letters pretty bad to hide them with Dmitri. I also thought about how she hadn't taken those precious pages with her, so maybe she really had gone home.

"See ya," I said. Dmitri was already absorbed in the TV again. He didn't even notice when I closed the door.

The clerk was watching TV, too, as I walked past. I lit a cigarette under the awning in front of the motel and watched the rainy street. Traffic was medium-thick and slow. A high-speed hooker motored past, a scrawny teen in a mini and a LA Lakers coat, all meth and desperation and ruined hair spray. I kept smoking. A few minutes later, two guys a short step above hobo went into room four with a six-pack and a pizza. Just before my cab got there, Dmitri's dream whore staggered around the corner and ducked under the awning next to me.

"Bum a smoke?" she rasped.

She was somewhere between twenty and seventy, with frizzy, bright purple hair, clown-level makeup, a threadbare oversize men's tweed jacket over a spinach-green halter top, super high cutoff jeans, and ragged fishnets. Her shoes were by far her favorite item: carefully cleaned pink plastic gardening togs.

"Here you go," I said, shaking one loose. The dirty nails matched her hair. She fired the smoke with a wooden match.

"Rain reminds me of parts of Colorado," she croaked.

"That where you're from?" I asked, watching the street again.

"Aw hell no."

We smoked.

"You lookin'?" she asked finally. I peered over at her. "I ain't exactly no model from a magazine, but you get what you're payin' for, see what I mean." She squinted at me. "What th' hell happened up on yer face? You were my man, I'd cream that up. Hold you down and cold cream it. That's what I'd do."

"Is that right."

303

"Yep." She smiled and clacked her dentures. "Ain't a tooth in my head, mister. Tween that an cold cream, I gots me some magic."

I had to smile back. My cab finally pulled up across the street and the blinker turned on.

"Old hippie dude in room eleven," I said. "He told me if I saw something especially sweet to send it on back. You fit the bill."

"My luck's a-changin'," she said, tottering off. "'Bout fuckin' time."

"So you have championship eater status here?" Suzanne asked. Jarra's Ethiopian was on the slow side that night. It was a husband and wife operation. She cooked solo and he ran the front. Their kids hung out with a scattering of toys by the cash register.

"I do," I said proudly. "Don't even try to gain these people's admiration tonight. It took me years. Thousands of dollars."

Suzanne eyed the kitchen. "After my rock class I swam for two hours. I could eat two of whatever they bring."

"Overly bold," I cautioned. "And you have to save room for dessert. Either we make peach cobbler back at my place or we make peach cobbler with blueberries back at my place. Your choice."

"Hmm." She smiled at me and put her hand out. I took it.

I'd had the cab drop me off five blocks from my car. I didn't want anyone who might have been waiting to ask the driver and find out where I'd come from. I'd walked over with my head down against the weather, which had grown blustery and ominous as the sun set. My car had a ticket on it, which I'd thrown in the street to see if it might elicit a reaction. It didn't. Still, I felt something, even if I couldn't spot it. Maybe it was my imagination, but it seemed unlikely that Dessel and his cronies would follow me there and not bother to pick me up again. I'd done my best to confuse them in the last twenty-four hours, but nothing I'd done was terribly out of character, either. It helped to be the erratic sort.

Suzanne and I chatted and held each other's eyes and hands. The place slowly filled up around us and finally the food came.

"Sorry for the delay," the owner said, sitting our plates down. "My wife was making the bread. Darby, for your usual, the spicy lentils and greens, and for your very beautiful companion, the chicken."

The lentils were in a red slurry that covered half the big plate, steaming and radioactively spiced with unknown agents, bracketed with a kidney-shaped pile of minced collared greens, curried potatoes, lemon salad, and cottage cheese as a burn salve. Suzanne's was much the same, with half of a chicken rising from the center.

"Miss, I must tell you," the owner continued, beaming with great charisma, "Darby is very much an eater of great concentration, so please, if you become lonely, feel free to walk around and study our paintings and photographs. Enjoy so very much."

Suzanne tore off a piece of sponge bread that was used in lieu of a fork and leveled her gaze at me. I did the same.

"Ready?" she asked, poised. I knew I was supposed to say "set," but I cheated and dove in.

About three quarters of the way through we both slowed down. There was no sense in racing. She was beating me and we both knew it. There was still no talking until we were both done. Suzanne finished two mouthfuls in the lead, dropped her destroyed paper napkin on the pile of clean chicken bones, and pushed her plate back, dazed. When I finally did the same the owner appeared. He'd evidently been watching. He bowed and put a mint next to Suzanne's water glass.

"It is all we have in the way of a ribbon," he said somberly.

"I'm ready for the main course," Suzanne said, smiling up at him. Then she turned to me. "Unless you want to smoke a cigarette first."

We sat around for a few minutes, letting our abdomens adjust. Suzanne sipped her wine. I nursed my beer. I knew she wanted to ask about my day. I hadn't volunteered any information so far and before dinner she had talked about hers in great detail.

"You're not going to tell me anything about what you did today, are you?" She swirled the last of the wine at the bottom of her glass and then gave me another one of those looks that only women can give—slightly sad, expectant but already disappointed, and suffused with disbelief.

"If I did, you would publicly freak out. Even saying that is too much."

She leaned forward suddenly.

"I already told you I don't like being kept in the dark," she said firmly. "There has to be something you can share."

"I don't like keeping you in the dark. I thought we already went over this."

"At least tell me something," she insisted, exasperated. "You have to have done at least one thing worth mentioning."

I thought about it. She was right. Delia was right. There were no easy answers. I resolved to follow my gut, but it was barely whispering for a change.

"Well," I began, "all right. I bought my old tattoo shop and the bar next to it. Not the bar itself. Just the roof and the walls and the floor. Also, I was either tricked into or tricked someone into a situation involving my owning part of a strip club yesterday, so I sort of cemented that deal. That might not pan out, but if it does I'll end up with around 20 percent. Hard to say. Helped my old landlord out, even though a case could be made that I did it for purely selfish reasons. Shit like that."

"You bought a building?"

"A blown-up one, but yes."

"Wow." She laughed, eyes wide. "That's, that's big news!"

"People do it every day. I have a bank account and everything."

"Well." She laughed again and then studied my face, still amazed. "Good! Great! Why aren't we celebrating?"

"I guess we are. I was sort of holding back for a few days until everything settles down."

"Huh." Suzanne had something else to ask, I could tell. Her mood had swung all the way back into the positive zone, but something was still eating her.

"This morning when you left? I was in the kitchen eating pancakes naked? I thought you were going to walk down the side of the house and I wanted to watch you because you looked so hot. I saw you tear across the yard and go over the fence. Then the next fence. Then I lost sight of you for a second and you tore right up the side of the *next* fence and over that one, too. Then I couldn't see any more because your neighbor's house got in the way. I dropped my pancake in the sink." She sat back, highly amused, her eyes mapping my every expression. "Darby, exactly what the hell were you doing." It wasn't a question.

I had to admit, that must have been funny.

"Well. There's a division of the police I have an ongoing thing with. They glommed onto me over this little thing I had with some employee who stole some art from me a while back. Anyway, these guys specialize in interstate crime. And what can I say? They fucking love me."

I tried to frame my thoughts in a way she would understand that wasn't insultingly bare of facts. It took a minute, but Suzanne was patient.

"I make the perfect bait," I said eventually. "Because of my job and the people I come into contact with, all the way down to who I am and what I believe in. I don't know. I tend to take less shit than the average person." I touched my face. "I have the scars to prove it, and those are just the ones on the outside. So when, metaphorically, some yard bully slaps me in the face with his dick, I metaphorically shank him in the eye if I can. And a lot of the time I can. It just takes me a little bit, mostly because I have a roundabout way of doing things. The system, and I hate that term by the way, but the system is usually in favor of the dick swinger, very seldom the anomalous rebel shanker. And once you're branded as that kind of troublemaker, the brand never comes off. So for the last little while I've been climbing out of the stomach of the latest predator who made the mistake of eating me, and the RONC would have preferred it if I had quietly curled up and allowed myself to be digested so they could get a big, juicy, high-profile conviction. Since I didn't, and they suspected I wouldn't, they've been trying to pin some kind of bucking-the-natural-order violation on me. I'm sure they have a fancy name for it. Disgusting, isn't it?"

"So the police were outside the house this morning because of all this?"

"Yep. Dollars to donuts they're outside this restaurant right now."

"Well, holy shit," Suzanne declared, sitting back.

"I know. Exciting, isn't it."

"So." She was thinking, her eyes distant. "So this is what you've been working on?"

"Yep. And I won. Except for the strip club, and I even have a plan to get out of that."

Suzanne was silent, the wheels in her head spinning.

"What are you thinking?" I asked. She refocused on me and an all-over smile spread across her face, the sun rising over an ocean of flowers.

"I'm thinking that while the peach cobbler is cooking it would be a good time to practice my blow job skills. And I really do need the practice."

"Check, please!"

At exactly eight a.m. my cell phone rang. I sat up quickly, confused, the remnants of a dream about tree houses quickly fading. The phone was on the nightstand next to me, so I snagged it and answered before it woke Suzanne.

"Holland," I whispered.

"Good morning, Darby!" The Armenian sounded extremely chipper, which was never a good thing. He'd been thinking about our deal all night, so he was hours of mad scheming ahead of me. "The transmissions are in the air! The air! I mentioned the photo shoot to my daughter and she is very excited. Very happy. So let's schedule that for next week. It would be best, I was thinking, if you could arrange for the flowers. I also want to set up a meeting about our project! The investors! Very hush-hush of course, but now that we are on the road to partnership, I will leave the specifics up to you." Meaning, get on setting up an expensive night out for him and his friends.

"Sounds good," I said, rising. I was so relieved that Oleg was on his way to Russia that I could have kissed the Armenian. I walked into the kitchen. "How about stargazer lilies? Or wild roses? Maybe a giant collection of assorted whatever-looks-good, sort of play it on what she wants to wear."

"Whatever the photographer can afford," the Armenian said magnanimously. "If he pulls this off, who knows? He may be able to go professional. I love to help the artist! I love it!"

"I'll let him know," I said. "Meetingwise, my schedule should shake out in a day or two."

"Take your time," he said generously. "I'll wait for your call. These people, the investors. They are very big people." Meaning, spare no expense.

"That's great news," I lied. "Simply fabulous. Way to get it done."

"What. I. Do." He emphasized every word.

"OK, then. Let me make some calls, see what chef has been in the news."

"You go, Darby! Call me later and have a great day, a wonderful day!"

I put my phone on the counter. Waking up to that kind of interaction, as much of a relief as it was, made me want to go lie down and try everything again. I went back to the bedroom door. Suzanne, I knew by then, was a habitual naked sleeper who gradually shed the garments she had gone to bed in throughout the night. She also had a limited ability to keep the blankets on her, and she preferred my pillow over hers, even if we switched around four a.m. She was the worst bed hog imaginable. I walked over and pulled the comforter over her body. In the short time I'd been up, an arm as long as my leg had drifted right through the center of where I'd been sleeping, along with one knee.

After I got the coffee going, I lit a cigarette and sat down at the dining room table. For the first time in the longest while, I wasn't plotting or scheming or floundering in a river of vengeful rage. I felt happy, and that, of course, made me feel slightly paranoid.

When I peered through the blinds, nothing obvious leapt out at me. The block wasn't cordoned off. Cheddar Box wasn't standing on the porch pointing a gun at my door. A helicopter hadn't crashed in the street out front. Instead, some watery morning sunlight had made it all the way down the miracle distance to the surface of things, and the world was drippy and tinged with gold, dabbed with emerald winter grass. The street was a hard to soft silver. Pretty.

The brown Ford on the corner didn't belong to any of the neighbors, but plenty of people got drunk at the bars down the street and left their cars scattered around the neighborhood overnight. I'd leave it at that.

It was cold in the house, so I turned on the heater, snuck back into the bedroom and put on my last clean pair of jeans, then went back out and poured some coffee and sat down at the dining room table for a leisurely second smoke. I could have found out the date, and the day of the week for that matter, by stealing the neighbor's paper, but it was too nice a morning to start sneaking around first thing, so I turned on my big antique AM radio instead. It popped and hissed as something inside it slowly heated up, and then, with some fiddling of the dial, I got classical.

The cats hadn't paid any attention to me so far, but the crackle and ozone smell drew them out of the office, which they considered their formal bedroom. My bed was their daybed. The couch was naps only.

I petted Chops for a minute and decided he was getting fat. Buttons came shambling over for some love while the getting was good and I decided he had whorish qualities.

I was bored.

Sketching was out. I didn't have the creative juice at the moment. I realized that I had to get my nascent and fragile nugget of inner peace outside and build on it before the dark thoughts came and the paranoia grew, so I decided to pester Suzanne. Waking a woman is a skill. I'd learned that I could never get along too well with a woman who woke up irritated and had to be left alone until she built up enough steam to feign politeness. But one thing was for sure—bringing them coffee was usually a good idea. I poured her some and padded into the bedroom. The entire bed was hers now. The comforter was mostly on the floor.

"Coffee," I said softly.

"I've been waiting for coffee in bed for a thousand years," she mumbled into her arm. She rolled over and blinked. "Who are you and where did you get those pants?"

"I'm bored, so I thought I'd wake you up," I said. I handed her the coffee and she sat up on one elbow and sipped.

"Bad as your cats," she commented. "How long have you been awake? Hours?"

"'Bout twenty minutes."

"Well." She smiled and beckoned languidly. "C'mere."

I sat down and she stretched and ended up with a foot in my lap. It was almost as long as my forearm. She yawned impressively.

"I have absolutely nothing to do today," she said.

"Me fuckin' neither."

"It's Friday. We could hit the coast for the weekend, do the BBQ hotel thing. I'm up for it if you are."

I thought about it for half a second.

"I'll make breakfast before we hit the road," I said. "Bacon? Eggs? Leftover peach cobbler!"

She nodded with a grin and I bounced off the bed and went into the kitchen. There was still half a pan of cobbler left, so I turned on the oven and put it in. A picnic lunch on the way out there would be a fine thing. Fried chicken maybe, with potato salad and artsy beer.

"Can you use your fancy phone and track us down a hotel with all the stuff we need?" I called, pouring myself more coffee.

"Already on it," she called back. She padded out of the bedroom in her underwear, playing her finger over the screen of her iPhone. "Check this out." She held it up.

Jacuzzi. Fireplace. Balcony. Bistro next door.

"Right on."

"I'll see if they have complimentary sparking wine and check on the robe situation." She was calling them when my phone rang. I didn't recognize the number, but there was a good chance it was good news.

"Hello?"

"Darby?" It was Dmitri. "You told me to call. I sent Jenny to look in that room on the end. That guy is gone. And I need more of my money."

"Are you sure? About the guy?"

"Yeah."

"Well, fuck. Thanks." I hung up.

Santiago Espinoza, aka Cheddar Box, was awake and probably pissed as hell. Hiding Dmitri in the same motel only seemed like random good luck. Not only had it given me disposable surveillance, but once he was gone Dmitri would be safe enough, since Cheddar Box would be unlikely to return.

I thought about it. Cheddar would know as soon as he used his phone that Oleg was missing. There was my note, so he'd know I'd had something to do with it. It was time for confrontation, and for that I needed to flash a bat sig-nal, indicating my goodwill, and then give him a few days to calm down.

I went back into the bedroom and finished getting dressed. Suzanne finished with our reservations and lay back down, watching me.

"I'm going to go get us some supplies," I said. "Cobbler's in the oven."

"Over the fences again?"

"I'm driving. Going right out the front door." I finished lacing up my boots. "For some reason I don't think they're out there anymore."

"Why?"

"I dunno. If my suspicions are correct, their attention is otherwise occupied. They know I'm here, so if they wanted me I'd be downtown already. Right now they have bigger fish to fry."

Suzanne smiled. "Sounds like you have it all figured out."

"I fucking hope so," I said. I scooped up my wallet and keys. My ball bearing was sitting there and we both looked at it. I put it into my pocket and her eyes crinkled.

"I was thinking chicken. Potato salad. Beer. Maybe some of those big deli pickles. A lunch-type thing at one of the scenic pull-offs."

"Don't pick out a hibachi without me," she said. I leaned over her and kissed her right boob.

"Back in a flash. Don't let the cats out."

I got my phone and my cigarettes as I passed the dining room table. My jacket was still on the back of the chair, so

I swept it up and put it on. The fat check and Dmitri's five thousand were in the pockets, so I really hoped I wasn't about to endure a shakedown. I could always say I was on the way to the bank, but no one ever bought that.

It was still nice outside, but there was an edge to the cold left over from yesterday, and the clouds that covered most of the sky were of the heavy, frigid kind. I lit a smoke and studied the street. There was nothing going on other than the brown Ford, which looked empty. I decided to end any speculation and went down the stairs and walked over to it. The inside was full of hipster trash, very different from what I'd seen of cop trash. Some laundry, mostly tube socks and T-shirts with band propaganda, a few squashed Mountain Dew cans, a curling iron with no cord, and a can of hair spray were all dead giveaways. The headless hula girl on the dash said something about the worldview of the missing hipster pilot, but I didn't have any time to speculate.

Satisfied, I went back to my car and started it up. I missed my Doobie Brothers CDs, but it had been time to switch to iPod technology for a few years. I cracked the window and headed for Old Town.

There was the perfect deli about halfway there, so I made a brief stop and got everything we needed, including the pickles and some figs and plums for dessert. Most importantly, I picked up a box of cheddar cheese crackers. As I put the two bags of supplies on the back seat, I reminded myself to remind myself to remember to check the oil, and then I was off again, with the building excitement of a road trip/lazy hotel/police evasion/vacation.

Either the power had been cut, or the last of the neon had finally died, but "mitri's izza" was black inside when I pulled up in front. The sun had disappeared behind the clouds again and a cold, gusting, sleety rain had kicked up. I wondered if Suzanne had checked the forecast as I dug the crackers out of the back. Whoever had stolen my CDs had left the collection of half-dried-up pens and shredded napkins bearing important notes I kept stuffed between the seats, so I rooted around and found a Sharpie that worked and wrote on the back of the box:

"Let's talk. Monday 6 p.m., the motel you woke up in. Out front."

I took the box and got out, dashed to the door, and let myself in with Dmitri's key. The wall of stench almost changed my mind as the door yawned open. I stepped in and let the door close behind me, breathing shallowly as my eyes adjusted from the gloom outside. The fight that had cost Dmitri a tooth had evidently been a bad one. Several tables had been knocked over and a chair was broken. My decrepit former slumlord still had some bite. I righted the nearest table and pulled it to about ten feet from the door, directly in front of it, then put the box of crackers in the dead center with the Sharpie writing facing away from the door. I adjusted it just right and then stepped back and studied it. If Cheddar Box looked in, he'd recognize it as a signal, and any enterprising convict could get past Dmitri's dollar-store locks with nothing more than a flexible boning knife in order to find out what it said on back.

Something fired out of a cannon smashed into the back of my head and the world went white. I staggered and went down, twisting so I fell on my side instead of my face. My vision skittered for an instant and then my eyes focused. There was a siren going off somewhere and I could taste blood in my mouth.

Santiago Espinoza was dressed in a black suit. He was holding the box, reading the back. He dropped it on the floor and kicked it into the darkness.

"Not my brand," he rumbled. He flexed his gloved hands and grimaced as he came at me, in no hurry to finish the job.

I'd been prepared to negotiate, but I didn't feel like he'd listen. I was on my feet fast enough to make him smile.

"Tough."

I took two fast steps in and dropped seriously low, my entire upper body whipping in a gravity-assisted curve, and delivered my best punch, a straight arm left from the shoulder, flat-out pile driver, square into his dick.

Cheddar's teeth clacked together and he stooped as I rose inside his reach and drove a leg-powered uppercut into his jaw. It was like hitting a frozen horse, but his head snapped back and his arms went wide. Then I was on him, still climbing up. I left the ground and wrapped one arm around the back of his bull neck as I went higher, then balled up on his huge head and bit down on his face, getting a huge mouthful of cheek. Cheddar roared and fell backward. I landed on top of him, but I didn't let go. I sank my teeth in a little deeper. Spit ran out of my mouth down into his ear. I growled.

"Stop," he rumbled softly. "You weren't about to die. I just want to know where Oleg is. There's no need for this."

My ears were still ringing, but I heard him. Somehow my forehead had bounced off the ground when we landed, so my brain had been sloshed around pretty good for the day. We were at an impasse. I had a few more tricks up my sleeve, but bringing him all the way down again with anything like a mouthful of face to bargain with would be pure luck. Biting what I had in my mouth off would buy me an unknown window of time to find something to kill him with, but I didn't like the odds.

"How about I agree to hear you out," Cheddar Box continued. "I still have to know about Oleg, but I give you my word. You get your teeth off my face and tell me where Oleg is, then we both walk away and settle this another day, if we do at all. Maybe we don't even bother. The cop situation being what it is right now, I need a body to get rid of as much as you do."

I let go and sprang back in the same motion. Cheddar Box lay there for a moment. I backed away a few more steps and he wiped his face with his sleeve.

"You cheat," he said, sitting up.

"I keep telling people."

Cheddar slowly rose to his feet and dusted himself off. Then he checked his teeth with his pinkie. "Oleg?"

"Should be in Russia before midnight."

"Huh." That baffled him. "He'd be desperate to go back. About ten warrants waiting, all minor shit, not enough to extradite, but from what I gather there's also a price on his head. Why the hell did he do that?"

"No choice. Rufied. Air express in a transmission box."

"Good one," he said, smiling ruefully and rubbing his cheek. "Guess that means I'm out of a job." He took a deep breath and let it out slowly. "Can't say I'll miss that asshole." He was depressed again, I could tell.

"Santiago," I began. He looked at me sharply. I raised my hands. "I looked at your driver's license. So, here's what I wanted to talk to you about. Oleg didn't get the deed to the building. I did. I also sort of inherited the management of the shit hole we're standing in. Plus, in order to get it all done, I wound up with a percentage of a strip club. I have contractors galore to deal with, this place, three floors of apartments above us, and more Olegs might come sniffing around now that he's left a vacuum. I'm in over my head here."

"What the hell are you telling me for?" He seemed genuinely mystified.

"All my shit is aboveboard. Holland LLC. Your parole officer will like it. Think *Décor* Magazine. You could chase a James Beard Award if you turned this place into the fusion joint that would fit in with the new Old Town game. Plus, tons of pussy."

"You're offering me a *job*?" he asked, incredulous.

I slowly reached into my pocket and took out the fat check and Dmitri's stack of cash. I took two steps closer to him and held them out. He cautiously took them.

"Signing bonus, plus some cash to get this place cleaned out. First priority is getting one of the old apartments upstairs fit for human habitation. Eventually they all have to be brought up to snuff, but one of them has to be done up right away. Dmitri."

"He'll go for this?"

"That five grand is his. He's on board."

Santiago Espinoza looked out at the rain-swept street and his eyes grew distant.

"What'd be my monthly for all of this?"

"Say 10 percent off the strip club, plus manager salary and a bar shift. I'd pick a Friday. Pretty OK there. This place? Apartment manager, I'd say not much, but you're looking at a free place, maybe a grand a month on top of that. "Mitri's izza"? I'd gut it completely, put in a froufrou diner-type thing."

"Like that place in Queens."

"Sure. Fried chicken and waffles with Portuguese sausage and white truffle gravy. Painted Hills tartar with pickled fennel bulb and local goat cheese on an English muffin, toss on a sprig of kale and a side of poached beet French fries. Kick the shit out of happy hour with straight-up Creole. Brunch is always a gold mine."

"No one does braised beef cheeks right in this fucking town," he said, almost to himself.

"As for the Lucky and the Rooster Rocket, nothing until the next Oleg pops up, but by the time they do it will probably be too late. The Korean place, I'm not sitting on enough to fix that, so I was thinking a parking lot for our businesses, pay by the week on the side for locals. I'll give you 10 percent of that, too."

"Twenty-five if I have to keep an eye on it."

"Fifteen and you park there free. Save you that much in change."

Santiago Espinoza looked me right in the eye for a long moment. I could see years of things I'd never really understand in there. He'd had a long life, filled with the long kind of years, just as I had. Then he gave me a slow once-over, up and down. Finally, he smiled a tiny, cautious smile.

"I'd shake on it," Santiago said evenly, "but I don't want to get that close to you. But you got a deal."

"I'll be back on Monday," I said. "Let's meet up here."

"After six would be best," Santiago said, looking around. "I'll have to have people in and out all day. I hope the snow holds off."

I took Dmitri's key and clicked it down on the table. "Six thirty, then."

"Where you going?"

"Weekend at the coast. My new chick has been pretty understanding about everything, but some quality time would go a long way right about now. Plus, it'd be good for me to drop off the cop radar for a few days."

"The cops," he rumbled, nodding. "Now we're on the same team, what's our story?"

"If no one asks, then nothing. Neither of us knows what happened to Oleg. If he's alive when he gets there, from what you say he'll either be arrested or killed. Either way, it wasn't me, and the final episode of the Oleg Tenpenny Opera is way out of town."

Santiago nodded. "The cops were all over his office earlier this morning, so they know he's gone. I couldn't even go in. Too bad, considering there's one point two in cash in the safe. Way gone now."

"Maybe that'll be enough to satisfy them," I offered. "All they really wanted was a high-profile arrest. A ton of dirty cash goes a long way in that direction."

"Also keeps Oleg from wanting to come back. Lost everything now, and they probably issued a warrant to boot."

"Imagine that," I said, wonderingly. "Sort of everything he had planned for me."

Santiago chuckled. "He was that kind of sweet."

"Monday." I turned.

"And Darby?"

I turned back.

"When you're out there at the coast, you see any good menus . . ." He surprised me with a wink. "Steal 'em."

The drive home was uneventful, and the ringing in my ears died down a little. I considered driving past Oleg's office to check out the police swarm, but all I really wanted was to get Suzanne and hit the road. Plus, I needed some aspirin. Both sides of my head hurt and Santiago's horse jaw had done nothing for my knuckles.

The street was quiet when I parked in front of my place. I left the groceries in back and went up the wet stairs two at a time. At the top I turned back and looked everything over again. Unless they were waiting inside, the cops really were too busy to be keeping an eye on me right then.

I had to shoo the cats back as I went in. The whole house smelled like bacon and coffee, good smells. Morning smells. Suzanne was dressed and washing dishes, singing softly. She looked all the way through the house and squinted.

"Darby." She turned the water off and flicked her hands. "What happened to your forehead?"

"I fell on my new employee at his orientation. It worked out great, though." I put my keys down on the dining room table. "I wasn't gone long, was I?"

"No." She kissed me on top of the head and gave me the look of a judgment pass.

"Let's eat!"

On the way to the coast we stopped three times. First, to drop an envelope with five grand in wrinkled Cheeks cash through Jane's mail slot. I didn't include a note. The state of the bills said it all. The next stop was at a scenic viewpoint to eat an early lunch and listen to the static-lashed radio with a view of the winter storm rolling up a deep, pine-filled valley, and then finally at an everything style department store in the trashy town, where everyone who lived in the resort town we were going to secretly shopped.

We picked out a spirited red hibachi that looked like it might hold up for a week at best, four bags of coals and lighter fluid, a pair of size eleven men's fuzzy slippers for Suzanne, but none for me as I am disdainful of them myself, two real raincoats, a pair of jeans and three T-shirts for me, since all my clothes were dirty and still at home, ten pounds of assorted steaks and pomegranate juice to marinate them in, four tomatoes, salad, potatoes, butter, peaches, Italian sandwich materials, and a crappy Teflon pan. Anything else we could get at the more spendy little place down the street from the hotel.

Delia checked in on the cats for me. Hank was evidently pretty excited about Taos, where he hoped to join an Indian tribe. Nigel was busy planning his French campaign. Suzanne and I spent Friday night talking and cooking on the patio, with the rain pounding away just out of reach. We laughed a lot, and it was one of the best weekends I'd had in a long, long time.

Sunday morning Delia called. She was at my house to let the cats out and had found a Sunday *Oregonian*, mysteriously delivered to me. She read me the headline and most of the article.

Oleg Turganov had been arrested in Kiev on several warrants and was being held in an undisclosed medical facility awaiting trial. He was in guarded shape, after being found hiding in an abandoned construction site. He'd been seriously injured, though the nature of the injuries was unclear, and he was also described as incoherent. Three warrants had also been filed in Oregon, with more to come as the details of his business dealings in the City of Roses came to light.

There was a note attached, which confused Delia, but made perfect sense to me.

"Idaho here we come. Midweek OK? —D"

"Who was that?" Suzanne asked when I shut the phone. I laid back and smiled up at the ceiling.

"Good news. Some guy wants to take me to Idaho. Fishing trip."